THE FORGOTTEN THRONE

ELIZABETH KNIGHT

CREATIVE WONDER PUBLISHING

Knight, Elizabeth

The Forgotten Throne

Editing: Swish Editing & Design

Cover artist: Malice and Mayhem Book Covers

Formatting: Creative Wonder Publishing

You never know how strong you are...
until being strong is the *only* choice you have

CONTENTS

ONE

THE FORGOTTEN LAND

Sheca, the forgotten land of the mercenaries, was now our only hope of protection from the Lost King. We might have lost the battle in Royal City, but we were not beaten in the slightest. The time had come for me, the Dragon Queen, to reclaim what had been lost to us for far too long. Deep down in my gut, I knew it would turn the tide in our favor. Gavin's parents, brother, and a few others had sought refuge with us here in our mountain fortress. My fear was Payson, a man who pretended to be my guardian, was working with Lord Everett and the Lost King. It won't be long until he was upon us.

As I waited for everyone to gather in our hideout's main cavern, I picked at the food Cole set in front of me. My brain whirled with so many variables it was hard to eat anything. I was now the one person who stood, without a doubt, against Henry, the Lost King, bastard son of King Edward of Norden.

As if knowing I was thinking about his father, Gavin slid into the seat beside me and snatched a hunk of bread off my plate. He took after his father with matching deep blue eyes and dark blond hair, but Gavin got the curls from his mother. If you had told me that one day the Crown Prince of Norden would leave his role to be my ambassador, I would have said you're crazy. What man would do such a thing?

"You don't mind, do you? It looked like you were more interested in destroying the bread instead of eating it," Gavin said as I awkwardly stared at him without blinking.

"Oh, no, of course not." I fumbled, pulling my gaze from his. Looking down at my plate, I saw that I had, indeed, shredded the other hunk of bread. "Sorry, my mind is racing, and I can't seem to get it to slow down."

Gavin reached out and grabbed one of my hands, intertwining our fingers. "Love, we'll figure this out. Nine guardians and I are standing beside you, ready to do what we can. I'm sure the other clan leaders would also agree with your choice once you've explained it to everyone."

I sat up straight and turned slightly, giving him my full attention. "How in the world can you give such logical advice after you just lost your home, your title, and your family is on the run from your half brother?"

"Cassarah, don't you remember what I said at dinner last night?" Gavin questioned. "I already gave that up before the fight even started. Those weren't empty words. My choice to leave the throne was as much for myself and the fact that I couldn't imagine my life without you being a part of it, however or whenever that happens. Nothing about losing this battle has changed a thing for me. Has it for you?"

"No. As I said back at the castle, I want you to stay with me, but I know going to Sheca will change things. I wanted time to deal with my personal feelings for all of you. I'm not sure I still have that option," I answered with a sigh.

One of the many things rolling around in my head was thinking back on my dreams of Miranda's life and how she had to pick her consorts and declare them once she became queen. From what Zan told me, Sheca was as traditional as you could get about following the old rules.

"Selfishly, I don't think I'd mind if you couldn't wait, but as I said before, I won't rush you, either," Gavin assured me as he pulled my hand up and kissed the back of it, letting his lips linger.

"Aww, isn't this cute," Paxton gushed as he appeared out of the crowd. "I hate to break up this moment, but everyone is here and ready for your announcement."

Paxton was my newest guardian, whose twin brother, Payson, had tried to deceive me and sell me out to the Lost King. He was brash and impulsive, and his light crystal-blue eyes shone with mischief, along with an ever-present smirk on his face. In some ways, it irked me, but the sight of his black eye made me smile, remembering when I gave it to him yesterday. Like most of the Wind Fist clan, he had fair skin, light blond hair, almost white, but still had some golden tones to it. Now with his brother dead by Paxton's hands and his father, Porvan, locked up for being a traitor, he'd returned to the mercenaries after many years. It seems he was hiding out in Creisal, the kingdom along the coast, and somehow acquired himself a golden female dragon named Ninnat.

"How's your eye feeling?" I asked, not moving from my spot. Something about Paxton made me want to rebel and push his buttons just because I could.

"Just peachy. I have to admit, you can lay a mean right hook. Look at the color it turned." He grinned. "Trust me. I've been bragging about it to anyone who asks me what happened. It's not every day you piss off the queen enough that she clocks you."

I had no idea what to do with this man. Seeing as we've barely known each other for a full day, I had a feeling this thought wouldn't go away anytime soon. Turning back to Gavin, I gave him a soft smile. "Would you help me up to the platform?"

"Of course, love," Gavin answered as he stood and helped me to stand.

Without even trying to pick me up like my other guardians would have, he tucked my arm in his and let me lean on him as we walked. The sooner I could get this damn leg to heal, the better, but all I seemed to keep doing was making it worse. In the cavern where we all ate our meals together, there was a small stage of sorts at the head of the space for events like this. Having only been their queen for about a week, I hadn't made any official addresses yet. When I reached the spot, I found the rest of my guardians waiting for me, keeping the crowd at bay. Reaching up, I took Izel's hand as he pulled me onto the stage and made sure I was steady.

Izel was from the Jade Talon clan and the son of the clan leader, Xio. Izel had thick, straight, shoulder-length black hair that was currently pulled away from his face. His skin was fair and made for a striking contrast against his dark hair and eyes, which were almond-shaped and the color of coal. Even though his face was finer-boned, it didn't detract from the lethal presence he carried. I knew how kind he was despite his upbringing. He was one of the few of my guardians to have a Birthright, allowing him to open people's minds to suggestions. Not like the Lost King who can take over your mind, but more so to coax you into a state of being. He'd done it to me once when I was in far too much pain with my leg and sent me to sleep so I wouldn't have to suffer.

"Are you ready, Your Majesty?" he asked under his breath as he helped me to the front of the platform.

I knew arguing with him about the title wouldn't help, but he only used it in public. "Is anyone ever ready to uproot people from their homes or the security they think they have within these walls?"

"You will handle it with grace as you do everything else that's been thrown at you," Izel assured me, squeezing my forearm before stepping back and giving me space but not leaving me.

Glancing over the sea of faces before me, I took a few deep, calming breaths before I began to project my voice as best I could, hoping everyone could hear me. "People of the clans, I come before you as your queen with news from Royal City. We are at war with Utros and Errit."

The crowd gasped. They knew something was brewing, but the clan leaders had kept things quiet, and so had I until we knew the full extent of what we were dealing with. The murmur of voices filled the air, and people started to shift as fear started to bloom with the unknown.

"A man calling himself the Lost King is leading the fight. I've encountered him myself, and he is not an enemy to be taken lightly. When I left the fortress the other day with my guardians, we were in Royal City, brokering a deal with King Edward and Queen Mary to become allies. We were able to reach an agreement, but it was in vain. We were too late, and the Lost King was already inside the city. Norden has been lost to us, but the king and queen are still live, seeking refuge here with their allies," I shared, motioning to where they stood with the other clan leaders.

My guardians and I determined this was the safest place for them to be once the news was shared. I refused to let them hide. If we were true allies, then this mess would be dealt with together.

"Are we safe here?" someone called out from the crowd.

This was the part I worried wouldn't be taken well. "Payson, son of Porvan, the previous clan leader for the Wind Fists, turned his back on his people as his father had. I do not know what information he has given to the enemy, but as your queen, I will not risk your lives. We will have to move on from this place, and it will need to happen first thing tomorrow morning... early before the sun is up. We have a long journey ahead of us, but I know it will provide the refuge we seek."

This information set the crowd off. People started to yell while others surged forward as if they were trying to grab me off the stage. My guardians stepped in and blocked all their advances, but I knew I needed to calm them.

Placing my fingers up to my mouth, I let out a shrill whistle that caught everyone's attention. "I know you are scared, and the fact we must leave our home is the last thing you want to hear. As your queen, I haven't earned your trust yet, but I beg you to let me prove to you I have your best interests in mind. You are my people, and my sole responsibility is to keep you safe and protected from danger. Coming to this choice was not easy, but it is our only choice. If we stay here, we will be slaughtered.

"The Lost King is ruthless and has no scruples when it comes to killing those who stand in his way. The mercenaries are a huge threat to him because we know how to survive through the worst of things and come out the other side." I paused to watch them, seeing if I was getting through to them because this next part would either sell me as a crazy woman or a brilliant one. "We are going back to our roots, to the beginning where our people first founded themselves. Our ancestors are still waiting for us and our promised return we forgot about. The Dragon Queen is calling her people home to Sheca and the Dragon Castle!"

The space fell silent as they absorbed my words. I didn't even know if they knew about Sheca or the Dragon Castle. Sal knew of some bedtime stories, but that wasn't promising as a whole. Glancing at the clan leaders, they did not look happy about my idea. They believed me when I told them I had a plan, but I didn't tell them what that plan was. I still felt raw after Payson's betrayal, so I kept it to myself and my guardians. I knew when I was done here, they were going to have quite a few things to say to me, but I didn't care. This is what was best for our people, and nothing else mattered. Turning to my left, I signaled for Zan to join me, and Ezzu flapped her wings in reply.

Zan was blind, making his eyes a cloudy silver color, but his Birthright allowed him to see out of his dragon's eyes. I didn't know if it applied to all animals or just dragons, but since he had Ezzu, a miniature sassy female dragon who acted as his eyes, it didn't really matter. Zan, as attractive as he was with his dark brown hair braided away from his face and full beard, didn't lead with the best first impression. See, we didn't meet under the friendliest of circumstances—he tried to kill me—mistakenly thinking I'd somehow enslaved Vasin, my black dragon, and pair-bonded against his will. Once we figured things out, my magic decided he would also make a fitting guardian and placed my mark on him, just like it did the others. Zan was from Sheca and explained to me some of the history we'd lost over the years which is how I knew this was the right choice. Hidden away in the lands of Sheca was the other half of the mercenary clan we originated from. They were thriving where we were not.

"Many of you have seen this man around. He is one of my guardians, but he is also from Sheca," I shared. "Zan has been able to provide me with information we'd lost for so many years. This was always meant to happen. We just forgot our promise to return. Gather what you need. The journey will be tough, but we are tougher. Scouts will be flying ahead and behind to make sure we are protected and not caught unaware, but we must travel as quickly as possible. There is no argument you can make to sway my mind, but I will not force you to join us. Stay if you want, but know that you have chosen to leave the clans and, in doing so, you will not be allowed back. Times are too dangerous, and loyalty is valued most during a war—so consider your choice wisely."

Two

The Queen Has Spoken

After everyone dispersed to start packing, I was escorted from the stage to the private meeting room the clan leaders used. I'd spent most of my days since coming here in this room trying to figure out the best plan to survive this war. That was when we were still looking for a way to keep the danger at bay. Now that ship had sailed and left us to deal with a new set of problems. I took my seat in the middle with the best advantage of the map carved into the massive wooden table. The clan leaders sat across from me as if I were the one on trial, needing to defend myself from them. I glanced at Ballard, the steward of the clan in lieu of a king or queen, who'd also been my mentor for the six months I'd been with the clan. His kind brown eyes watched me with interest instead of anger like the others. Acton, Garold, and Xio hadn't known me for as long as Ballard. I could see how keeping this information from them might be seen as a slight.

"Your Majesty, would you care to further explain the journey you want to take us on?" Xio demanded, even though he posed it as a question.

I cocked my head and examined these three men who seemed to think I was subordinate to them. They had been running their respective clans for years and had become used to being the top dogs.

We'd butted heads, but I thought we were finally getting somewhere, but it seemed I was incorrect about that.

"What would you like to know?" I countered.

Garold scowled at me and slammed his fist on the table. "You withheld information from us that could have been vital to our survival, and you just announced it to the masses. I was beginning to think you had a level head for a woman, but it seems I was mistaken."

This made my eyebrows rise, but Dayson and May were already addressing the issue before I could say a word in my defense.

"How dare you speak to the queen like that!" Dayson barked at his father as May came up on the other side, boxing Garold in.

May pulled out a dagger and held it under her uncle's chin. "You will apologize for your rudeness. To question the queen's orders is mutiny during times of war." Garold gaped at her, eyes wide at her words. "Don't act surprised, Uncle. You know the law just as I do."

Garold was a tall, muscular man who would make most men look small, but Dayson was even bulkier than his father. Dayson's bronze skin partially covered in black, swirling ink added to the intimidating factor along with the shaved head, but for a thick section down the middle of his head braided in one long rope. May stood beside him, cousin by blood but raised as siblings when she lost her family. Her long blonde hair was about the only soft thing on her body, proving she earned her place as a fierce warrior. She also had the black ink on her skin, marking her as part of the Bronze Reaper clan, the most ruthless of our people.

"You two would turn on your own family for this queen?" Garold snarled, his gaze flickering between the two. "You've known this woman for a week, and already you would trust her with the lives of all our people?"

Dayson growled. "I don't expect you to understand, Father, but she's proven herself to me time and time again. Some of us wouldn't be alive if it weren't for her risking it all to get us out of the castle yesterday. She puts herself in harm's way without considering if it will protect others. So if she says we go to Sheca, then we go to Sheca."

Garold seemed to deflate a little. Not having had a chance to talk with all my guardians, I didn't really know what they'd told people about what happened last night. It didn't seem like much had been explained, but we didn't have the luxury to hash it all out. If they were going to fight me on this, then so be it.

"As I said to everyone in my speech, I will not force you to come with me. If you feel your chances will be better here, then so be it. But you will no longer be a clan leader or part of the mercenaries I rule over. Sheca is the only chance we have. Deep in my soul, I know it has all the information we need to rebuild ourselves into something more. During Miranda's rule as queen, everyone thought it was our golden era, but I don't believe that. It was a glimpse of what we could be. I want to surpass it. Just imagine for us to no longer be struggling people fighting for survival. The kingdom I want to create and rule will be a force to be reckoned with. Trust me long enough to get us there. Let me prove to you I'm a queen worth following," I urged, hoping this would be what finally convinced them.

"I believe our fellow clansman might have been hasty in his distrust in this move you are asking us to make," Acton spoke. "You have shared that you have a link to this group of people through this man of yours... Zan, was it?" I nodded when he paused for confirmation. "Might I ask him a few questions?"

Acton was the clan leader of the Hell Hawks and Jade's half brother, not that Acton acknowledged Jade as family. Out of all the clan leaders, he was the youngest and, interestingly enough, the most levelheaded as long as it didn't involve Jade.

I turned to Zan, to ensure he was comfortable with that before I answered. He must have already anticipated my attention since he was looking right in my direction. He nodded. "If Zan is comfortable with it, then please ask away, but I ask that you respect if there are things he cannot tell you. The people of Sheca do not recognize the authority of a clan leader."

This caught all of them off guard. Did they honestly think if we descended on a new civilization, the Shecans would cave to our ways? Granted, they were part of the mercenary clans, but they have been operating on their own for generations. Who knows how they will take me coming from nowhere to be their queen? Although I should be used to it by now. It seems surprising others is what I was born to do.

"Could you tell us a little about Sheca? What is the climate like or the way of life, perhaps?" Acton asked.

"I would be happy to share that," Zan answered with a smile. "Sheca is mountainous but also butts up to the Caleden Sea. Our land is very fertile and used for farming and grazing. It has a mild climate all year round but rains more often in the fall and winter months. My favorite time is early in the morning when the fog is trapped in the peaks of the mountains around us until the sun rises and they disperse. Shecans are hardworking people who are fully self-sufficient off what we grow and raise. Our contact with anyone outside our own people is practically nonexistent. We fled there to hide from the Norden king. Since that was the foundation of our civilization, we tend to be very private people. Much like you, we are skilled in fighting and other various abilities needed to be a valuable mercenary. Though for us, it's to defend our home rather than do jobs for money."

Now this seemed to be more to the clan leaders' liking. I knew from my queen studies they had been working for this very thing for generations, but being a hunted people, it made it hard to put down solid roots.

"How would you describe the journey from here to Sheca? Will our people be able to make it?" Xio questioned, narrowing his eyes at Zan as if he could intimidate him into giving him the answer he wanted.

"Do you doubt the fortitude of your people so greatly?" Zan countered. "I was led to believe you still keep to the same arduous training as we've always done, starting at a young age."

Before I could stop myself, I let out a huff of laughter, causing all eyes to snap to me. "I can assure you, Zan, from personal experience, their training is more than enough to get them through this trip."

"There are more people than there are horses. It will be slow going with all the children and elderly," Garold commented.

This made me bristle. He was trying to find fault with my plan, but I couldn't figure out why. What good did it do him to have everyone stay here when danger could arise at any moment?

"Then I suggest you give up your horse for someone who needs it," I offered, sitting up straighter. "Unless you plan to stay here."

The moment I said it out loud, I knew it was true. Garold believed that if he stayed behind, he might be able to convince more to stay, if not his whole clan, making him their permanent leader.

Garold crossed his arms over his chest and glared at me, ignoring that Dayson and May were still flanking him. "As you said, we are free to stay if we wish. I'm not convinced this is the best move for our people."

"What would you suggest instead?" I asked, leaning forward and resting my arms on the table before me. "I am happy to hear other suggestions from any of my people."

This was not the response that Garold expected, and it took him a moment to decide whether he would answer me. "If it were me,

I would stand our ground. This place is a fortress. Its secrets are known only to clan leaders and the king or queen. We could easily defend ourselves."

"Hmm, I see. Was Porvan privy to this knowledge as well?" I questioned.

Acton's lips twitched as if he was fighting back a smile. He understood where I was going with this.

"He was a clan leader until recently."

"Yes, and I believe he no longer is one because he'd betrayed our people on more than one occasion. Did it not surprise anyone that Payson left with us, but I returned with his twin brother, Paxton, instead?" I mused aloud. "It was because the apple didn't fall far from the tree, and Payson sold us all out to the Lost King, trying to offer me up as payment for him becoming a valued person in the New World order. Now, if I were to prove my loyalty to someone as crafty and suspicious as the Lost King, I would share whatever the most valuable information I had to share. What would you share with him?"

Clarity dawned on Garold when he took a moment to think it over. "The secrets to our hideout. One of the most guarded bits of information we have."

"Yes, that would be my line of thinking. Do you still believe it's best to hold our ground here and make a stand?" I inquired, resting my chin on my hand. "As you said, if you feel strongly about it, you may remain and test out your plan."

Garold shifted in his seat, no longer feeling as cocky about his plan as he once had. "How long will it take us to travel to Sheca?"

Trying to hide my smile, I turned to look at Zan, covering my mouth with my hand as if I were yawning.

"With as many people as we have, I'm guessing about five days. But if we can take some of the elderly on dragonback, it could help to speed things along," Zan shared.

I perked up at that idea, knowing we had the dragon riders with us, and gained Ninnat as well. "How fast can we get there by dragon?"

"Half a day."

Now it was Xio's turn to be upset. "Why such a difference? I know dragons can fly much faster, but half a day versus five makes no sense."

"If you account for the fact that you have horses for *maybe* half your people since they are only given to those able-bodied and working, this still leaves many on foot. The journey is through the mountains, and they are not forgiving, nor is there a path commonly used to make the footing easier. This is going to be a pilgrimage, to be sure, since we either use dragons or ships to get to where we need to go," Zan explained. "If we can shuttle the older people and possibly the children, it will bring that number down. It will still be a hard crossing for the horses."

I hummed in agreement as I pictured the landscape where I'd first met Zan and remembered how torturous it was. "I suggest that you and I fly out today and meet with the people of Sheca so they can prepare for our arrival. Then you can begin moving those who need it the most on dragonback while I lead the others the long way on horseback. I assume there is no way for us to use carts to transport our belongings?"

"That is correct, My Queen. We need to stick to the rule, 'if you can't carry it on your back, you can't take it.'"

I turned my attention to Ballard, knowing he would do as I asked without question. "I know there are things we *need* to bring that cannot be replaced. Could you work with Sal to gather and prepare those items so we can take them over on the dragons? They are stronger than horses and can take more at once, so we can refrain from using any as packhorses. The more people we can get moving faster, the better. I truly believe we don't have much time, and he does have his own dragons to use against us."

"Yes, Your Majesty. I will start on that right away with your leave," Ballard said, moving to stand.

With a wave, I sent him off and turned to my guardians. "I need a firm tally on how many horses we have and if there are any hidden away in the surrounding areas we can use. The guards need to make their way through the levels, making it clear that they must pack what they can only carry. We are not trying to be cruel. We just want to keep them alive. My hope is that we might get help from Sheca, but I won't rest our plans on it. Zan and I will fly to Sheca to see what we can do to pave the way for our people, then return to start the journey."

"Your Majesty, I don't think that is a good idea. Just the two of you can't go," Jade grumbled.

I couldn't help but smile at my outspoken guardian, who was always worried about my safety. Everyone kept trying to paint him in such a poor light, but I knew better. We'd saved each other one too many times for me to doubt him. His bright green eyes, which were such a striking contrast to his deep umber skin tone, held my gaze. Without him and his dragon, Tahir, I would never have survived to become queen when one of our own betrayed me the first time to the Lost King.

"I hear your objection, Jade, but this is how it needs to happen," I said, the finality of my choice clear in my tone.

Even though his expression didn't change, I knew he was upset with me. I trusted him to keep his objections to himself until we were in private. Turning back to the others at the table, I said my farewells. "If you'll excuse me, I have things to attend to. Any help you would like to give will be of great value if you choose to join us on our journey."

THREE
DO YOU TRUST ME?

I left the room and headed down the hall toward the cavern's front entrance.

"Vasin, get ready to head out. We are going with Zan to Sheca."

"WHY DO I FEEL LIKE THIS CHOICE IS NOT MET WITH AP-PROVAL?"

"It doesn't matter if my guardians agree with this choice. I am queen, and I've made my decision."

"NOT THAT I DON'T APPROVE OF YOU DOING SUCH A THING, BUT MIGHT I ASK WHY THEY DISAGREE?"

"Didn't plan on giving them the chance to argue with me. We don't have much time, and it's a half-day flight to Sheca. I need to meet with them and be back before everyone leaves in the morning. I refuse to make them leave their home without me doing so right beside them."

"ADMIRABLE, YET I STILL BELIEVE HEARING OUT YOUR AP-POINTED GUARDIANS MIGHT BE WISE."

I knew he was right, but after dealing with the clan leaders, I didn't want to have to justify every choice I was making as I was making it. If I was the queen, shouldn't I be able to make choices and have them do what I say?

"Cassarah, don't think you can run from me," Jade hissed as he easily caught up with me. "This is a reckless move, and you know it. We know nothing about these people other than what Zan has told us. Need I remind you he tried to kill you the first time you crossed paths? What happens if you're too far away and I can't get to you in time?"

Halting once we reached the entrance, I turned to face him, only to bump into his chest. Flustered, I stepped back, but he followed my movement, not allowing me to get any space away from him. My whole life I'd been raised to be a noble woman and not to show irritation or other *extreme* emotions. But I wasn't a noble woman anymore. I was a queen. "Stop that," I snapped and tried to shove him back.

Instead, he caught my hand and held it to his chest. "No, not until you give me a good enough reason for you to go with only one person as backup. Zan might be your guardian, but he has been a Shecan far longer. I can't say I trust him with you alone just yet."

"I know I'm new here too, but I have to agree with the Reaper," Paxton piped up. "Just because you made it through the events of last night, doing reckless things, doesn't mean it should be a pattern."

"I'm not going to justify myself when everything worked out. Everyone is alive and standing before me," I argued, scowling at Paxton.

Abbott stepped up to my left, drawing my attention. When we first met, I mistook him for a knight, with his long golden hair and light blue eyes. He had a gallant air about him. He was the best swordsman in all the clans and one of my teachers. He was one of the more mild-mannered of my guardians, but that was not to be mistaken as soft. That man could be a drill sergeant when he wanted to be. More than once, I'd been pushed to my limit and then some with his style of conditioning, but the moment I accomplished what needed to be done, he was my biggest cheerleader.

"Little phoenix, tell me you didn't do all the things he says you did last night," Abbot begged, his eyes filled with worry.

"That depends on what he said. If it was anything to do with jumping off a dragon, killing Lord Everett, and saving three of you and two dragons, yes, I did do those things," I answered. "If I hadn't done those things, you, Cole, and Izel might not have survived. Lord Everett was going to kill you along with Tahir and Ifra, and I couldn't let that happen if I could do something about it. You all are as important to me as I am to you. What I need most from everyone right now is a little faith in my choices."

Internally, I wanted to flinch at how I'd just sounded. It was as if my mother had taken over my mouth and spouted out things. I meant all of it, but there was no need for me to say it so harshly.

Jade let go of my hand to grip my chin, lifting my face until our eyes met. "Is that what you think this is about? You think we don't trust you?"

"I mean, that's what I was saying," Paxton said but was cut off by what sounded like a punch to the gut from someone. "Right, shutting up now."

The longer Jade held my gaze, I knew he knew that was exactly what I was thinking, even if I didn't want to.

He let out a huff and dropped his hand, backing away. "I can't talk to her when she's like this. She's all yours, Cole." Opening my mouth to stop him to explain myself, he held up a hand. "No, little bird, I can't be the one to speak reason with you right now. I'll let one of the others try."

His words felt like a dagger to the heart. I didn't understand why they hurt so much as I watched him head outside.

"Mouse," Cole whispered, placing his hands on my shoulders.

Pulling my attention from the direction Jade walked off, I met a pair of deep green eyes that belonged to my friend. When we first met all those months ago on my bedroom balcony, where my life forever changed, our friendship did not start off well. As a matter of fact, he hated me and did everything he could to make life harder for me in the first few weeks. Then we realized we had far more in common than we thought. Like Abbott, he'd been with me since the beginning and shared my love of history and languages, letting me share everything I learned in those early days. He was one person I knew would never lie to me, and I could see by the scowl on his face that the choice to go alone with Zan wasn't a good idea.

"You can't go with only one person as backup, Cassarah," Cole stated, using my given name, telling me he was dead serious. "Being queen means you can't take risks that will put your people in more danger. If they don't have you looking after them through this war, there's no hope for our survival. The clan leaders have already proven they aren't up for the task. Please think this through with that brilliant mind of yours."

I let out a puff of air in frustration. When he put it like that, I knew he was right. "Fine, Abbott and Izel can come along. I need people who aren't going to overreact if the Shecans say something crazy."

"Thank you," Cole murmured as he cupped my face and kissed my forehead. "I would rather have you take us all, but I get what you're trying to do."

With that settled, we headed out onto the wide ledge where Vasin and Ifra were waiting. Jade was working on the harness that Vasin wore. It acted like a saddle to ensure I didn't fall off him when flying. I've had the unfortunate experience of knowing what that felt like, and I preferred not to have a repeat if I could help it. The others lingered by the entrance, giving me space to talk to Jade as Zan started to put Ifra's harness on.

"I GATHER THIS ONE DIDN'T LIKE YOUR PLAN?" Vasin mused as I walked up to them.

"You know he didn't, and neither did you, I might add."

"True, but you don't get mad at me like you do with them."

"I get mad at you."

Vasin snorted as he tilted his head to look at me. *"Name one time you were mad at me directly?"*

I searched my memory and discovered he was right. I have been frustrated or disagreed with something Vasin had to say, but I was never mad. *"Okay, so I don't get mad at you. What does that have to do with anything?"*

"Nothing really, just wanted to point it out before I tell you that you should apologize before we leave. He was right to be upset with you."

Gaping at my dragon, I couldn't help but laugh at the corner he backed me into. It proved his point because I would be angry if anyone else had said that to me. Vasin gave me a nudge with his nose, sending me stumbling into Jade, who swiftly caught me before anything bad happened.

"This is not making me feel better about letting you leave without me," Jade grumbled.

"I'm going to bring Abbott and Izel with me. You were right. I shouldn't go with only one guardian into another country when we have no idea what I'm walking into," I said, resting my hands against his chest with his arms wrapped around me. "I shouldn't have doubted you were just trying to look out for me, not that you didn't trust my judgment."

"Little bird, I trust you completely in most areas, but when it comes to your safety, you seem to have blinders on. It's a lot harder being your guardian than I thought it would be," he teased, squeezing me. "Come on, help me get these last few straps buckled down."

Pulling out of his arms, I moved to the side and finished off the buckle he'd been working on before he caught me. "It's not true that

I only listen to Cole, is it? I feel like I try to keep an open mind about input."

"When it comes to things about the clans, yeah, you seem to be open to all suggestions. The few times it comes to your personal life, it's typically a tag team between Cole and Abbott. You've known them longer, so it makes sense. I wouldn't be too bothered by it. We each have our role to play," Jade explained as he finished the last buckle. "Looks like you're all set. We'll make sure things are running smoothly here, so we'll be ready when you return."

I didn't want to admit it, but I was starting to get nervous about what would happen if they wouldn't help us. Without Sheca to turn to, that didn't leave us with many options other than maybe trying Creisal since Queen Mary's sister ruled there with her husband.

"Cass, they will aid you in your hour of need. I reached out to the dragons that call that place home, and word is already spreading that the Dragon Queen is coming home. It would seem Zan shared the news when he returned for his things."

Why I didn't think of that before showed just how much I had on my mind. Of course, they would want an explanation as to why Zan was leaving. He was a soldier, after all. They would need to know why he was abandoning his duties at the drop of a hat. This would certainly help because they now know I existed and wouldn't be showing up out of the blue.

"Cassarah, we should be heading out if we want to make it there and back by morning," Zan pointed out.

Nodding, I turned to my other guardians. "Abbot, you'll be with me. Izel, you're with Zan. As for the rest of you, I'm putting you in charge of making this evacuation happen as smoothly as possible. We'll be back as fast as we can."

"Be safe, Cassy-bear," Dayson called as I climbed up on Vasin's back. "I'll make sure my father doesn't cause any trouble."

"With two of us keeping an eye on him, he won't have the chance," May added, knocking shoulders with her cousin and giving me a nod of reassurance.

Abbott settled in behind me, securing himself in for the ride before he placed his hands on my hips. I waved at the others before Vasin leaped off the ledge and shot us up into the sky in the direction of Sheca with a powerful beat of his wings. Ifra led the way, but I knew thanks to the dragons' ability to share memories, Vasin already knew where to go.

Flying quickly became one of my favorite things. It gave you a level of freedom you couldn't get anywhere else—the wind whipping through your hair, the scent of nature around you, and all the wide-open space you could ever ask for. There was the warmth at my back, a constant reminder of Abbott being close, something I was still getting used to after a life of being taught never to be alone with a man. I knew that the world wasn't what my mother had painted for my future, being forced into a loveless marriage just to gain status or money for my family. I was now given the choice of who I wanted to be with and a group of men who were all worthy of being loved wholeheartedly by someone. I knew they hoped I would be that someone. The fact I didn't have to pick between them made things more complicated. Never having been able to build a romantic relationship with a man, I didn't know what was expected. I knew for sure I didn't want what my parents had. My father loved my mother, but I don't think she was capable of loving anyone but herself and certainly not me.

Many of the kings and queens before me had taken more than one lover out of their guardians—Miranda went so far as to take five of hers. Granted, I found myself with eight men to pick from, and most of them had expressed interest in becoming a consort of mine. Zan and Paxton had only been with me a short time, but they knew the customs and that it was an option for me to pick them. I knew I wouldn't take a man who didn't love me or feel about me the same way I did for them. To trap someone in a loveless life or marriage was cruel and nothing I wanted to be a part of. Hopefully, I would be given time to make the right choice, but I had a gut feeling things would happen much faster once we reached Sheca.

Four

Welcome to Sheca

Just as the sun was setting, we crossed over a ridge of mountains covered in fog. When we came out the other side, there was Zan's home. An ancient-looking stone castle stood on a cliff that jutted out from the side of a mountain. It showed all the age of being abandoned for the past four hundred years. Below the castle was a winding path wide enough for us to see from the air that led to a village in the valley. Lush green vegetation set the land off from the cool gray mountains around it, with a river running through the middle, feeding the various crops. Homes were built into the mountainside off the main path to the castle, but there were others in the flat land of the valley itself.

People were working in the fields and gardens, pausing to look up as the dragons' shadows crossed over them. No one seemed surprised at the sight, leading me to believe it was more common here than it had been in Norden. As if they heard my thoughts, four dragons with riders appeared from the slopes around us, heading right toward us. Ifra let out a bugle, and Zan waved a greeting to them once they got closer. The other dragons returned the call as they wheeled to fly alongside us as an escort to wherever we were to land. I took a moment to reach out to the new dragons, trying to get a feel for their emotions or thoughts, but like Ifra when I first met him, they were closed off and unwilling to let me talk with them. Pulling back, I observed more of the town around me, noticing a town center at the base of the main road before it led out into the fields. The call of the dragons must have alerted everyone to our arrival since they started to flood the street, looking up at us. Kids yelled as they pointed at me, waving their arms excitedly, while the parents didn't appear to feel the same.

"What do you think Zan told them about you?" Abbott asked, his lips brushing my ear.

"He keeps calling me the Dragon Queen, but I don't really know what that means to him or them," I shared with a shrug. "I'm just thankful they aren't shooting at us or running to get their pitchforks."

Abbott chuckled at my worries. "I truly don't think Zan would bring you here if he thought you would be killed. He might be new to our group, but that man has more honor in him than anyone I've met in a long time."

Ifra circled and landed in a large open area, free from any grass or anything else we might damage or trample with how large the dragons were. It was two dragon widths wide and four dragon lengths long, leaving enough room for all of us to land easily.

"Picking up anything from these dragons that I should know about?"

"WHY DOES THIS REMIND ME OF WHEN YOU FIRST ARRIVED AT THE FORTRESS? I WILL TELL YOU WHAT I TOLD YOU THEN... YOU ARE THEIR QUEEN."

"Remind me not to bother asking you for a pep talk before things like this. You're not very good at them."

"MAYBE, OR I MIGHT BE AMAZING AT THEM, AND YOU JUST DON'T LIKE WHAT I'M SAYING."

"Still not helpful." I huffed as I began to undo the straps.

Abbott finished first and slid off, holding out his arms to me. "Careful as you slide down. The ground here is really rocky, but I'll catch you."

My heart warmed at how this man was always looking after me and keeping me steady, though there were moments I doubted myself.

"This is the type of support I was looking for."

"I am your pair-bond. He is your guardian and possible consort. It wouldn't be right for me to take his job."

Caught off guard by Vasin's words, I dropped more than slid down his side. But as Abbott promised, he was right there, his hands catching me around the waist before my feet could touch the ground. I smiled at him and placed a kiss on his cheek. "Thank you."

His eyes warmed, but he kept his face neutral as I heard the crunching of boots approaching. Looking over my shoulder, I spotted the four dragon riders approaching—all men of various ages, each holding a soldier's stance. Izel joined us, taking up a position on the other side from Abbott as Zan headed to greet the men, Ezzu sitting up tall on his shoulder.

"Naytan, I've returned with the Dragon Queen," Zan announced, making me stiffen at his words.

Please don't tell me he is going to betray me too!

"Last time I saw you, you said she didn't want to be our queen. Why should we care that she's arrived now when she's just like all the others?" Naytan grumbled, crossing his arms over his barreled chest.

He was the oldest of them, reminding me of Ballard in a way with salt and pepper shaggy-cut hair. Only this man had a thick, full gray beard and bushy eyebrows that were knit together as he glared at me.

"Now I really want to know what Zan told them about you when he was here last," Abbott muttered under his breath, placing a protective hand on the small of my back.

It would seem that it was my lot in life to dispel all the assumptions that people were going to make about me, no matter where I went. I wasn't lady enough to be a noble. I wasn't trained or skilled enough to be a mercenary. Now it would seem I wasn't worth their time because I didn't come the moment I found out they existed, even though we were on the brink of war, and I had another group to lead. Sometimes, a person could only take so much before it caused them to snap, and I was a thread away from doing so.

"You know that is not what I said or what I meant. Queen Cassarah had just been crowned and was dealing with a threat to our brethren that needed to be dealt with first before she could take the time to come here. We've waited hundreds of years for this moment. What do a few more days or weeks mean to us?" Zan defended.

Naytan grunted at Zan's words. "They always come before us. It's how we ended up forgotten here in Sheca in the first place. What need do we have for a novice queen who lost the battle at the Norden castle, having to flee back to the mountains? Let me guess... you came here to seek our help to save you from the Lost King because you're in way over your head, *little girl*."

Upon hearing this, that last thread snapped, and I charged forward, brushing past Zan right up in Naytan's space. "You know nothing about what happened at the castle or the Lost King. If you did, you wouldn't be talking about it so flippantly. Yes, we did lose that battle, but we lost it because the queen wanted to play politics when I told her we needed to move and move fast. They lost Royal City because of their stubborn pride, and the same thing will happen here if you don't get your head out of your ass and look at the world around you.

"You might have survived the last however many hundred years, hiding away behind your mountains, but that will no longer save you. The Lost King will stop at nothing until he controls everything he can get his hands on, and I'm the only one willing to stand up to him while taking the threat seriously. If you want to remain lost and forgotten here, then so be it, but know that this time it's because you decided to cut off your nose before hearing what I have to say." Finished with my tirade, my breathing was heavy with how heated I was about this entire situation. I was done taking shit from people who didn't even know me.

Naytan looked at me with a calculating gaze before he signaled with his hand, causing the other three men behind him to draw their weapons. This caused everything to turn to chaos as Vasin roared, flaring his wings as he came to my rescue, and my guardians drew their weapons. However, I didn't move a muscle as Naytan drew his sword, never letting his gaze drop from mine.

"Do not threaten us, child. We've survived far worse than the likes of the Lost King," Naytan sneered as he stepped back and lifted his sword.

Sensing the danger I was in, my Birthright flared to life, causing me to glow in a blue light as my bow materialized in my hand and the quiver on my back. The marks on my guardians also began to glow from where they stood, backing me up, their weapons at the ready. I wasn't going to fight Naytan and his men, there being no need to prove myself to them in that way. Never did I want to be known as the queen who led with an iron fist or would savagely kill those who didn't follow her every whim. Naytan was scared and protective over the people he'd been guarding his entire life.

"Put your weapons away," I ordered. "There will be no fighting between us."

One of the men behind Naytan scoffed. "I don't think she's very bright if she won't even fight back."

"What good would killing you do? It would only serve to create more problems. Since I have an extremely pissed-off black dragon at my back, I'm not worried about the four of you," I shared, releasing my hold on my bow so it dissipated. "Now, seeing as you are the soldiers of this land and not the people who speak for everyone, I will take my leave to talk with them. Somehow, I feel they might be more agreeable to deal with."

Zan started to cough, covering up what I might guess to be laughter as I turned on my good foot and headed off toward the center of the village.

"You dare to turn your back on me?" Naytan yelled.

"Go, Cass, I'll deal with the rabble."

"Thank you. I knew you'd have my back."

The sound of cursing and growling behind me made me smirk to myself, knowing that Vasin could be intimidating to others.

"Your Majesty, are you sure you're all right?" Izel asked as he walked beside me.

Glancing at him, I nodded. "No harm done other than being irritated that I wasted so much time arguing with someone who wasn't going to do me any good. I just snapped when he badgered me as if he wanted to provoke me into fighting with him. What good would that do anyone?"

"I should have warned you that there is a group of zealots among the people who believe we should choose our own ruler and break forever from the mercenaries completely," Zan informed me. "Let me take you to the village hall where the viceroys work. There are three of them who guide us as a people or handle issues that arise that cannot be handled between peers."

"Please tell me they are going to be more willing to hear me out before they write me off." I sighed as we approached a simple stone and wood building with a bell tower attached to it.

Zan turned his head in my direction and offered a comforting smile. "Lawrence and the others are good men who have been eagerly awaiting the arrival of the Dragon Queen. They are our scholars as well as our leaders. You can't advise the future if you don't know the past."

"I like these men already." I grinned.

As we made our way up the few steps, a guard at the entrance nodded to Zan before he opened the door, allowing us to enter. The building was dimly lit by lantern light, making shadows dance on the walls. But instead of it being spooky, it was comforting. Much to my surprise, the building was a library filled to the brim with books and scrolls, along with desks for you to read at or work from. Already, I was fantasizing about getting lost in this place, discovering everything it had to tell me.

"I'm sorry, but we are not taking any more audiences for the day, but we will be of service tomorrow after eight bells," a soothing voice called from somewhere in the row of shelves.

"If Thomas let them in, then it must be important," another man said.

"Eleazar, if we make an exception for one, then we will have to for all. These are the rules we have established, and we must follow them," the first voice countered. "I'm sorry, whoever you are, but Thomas shouldn't have let you pass. We will speak with you in the morning."

Hearing the two men bickering made me smile and set me at ease. "What if the person is the Dragon Queen?" I called out.

There was a pause then the shuffling of feet as two men appeared out of the shelving, wearing robes with hoods covering their faces.

The man in the green robe with gold stitching headed toward a set of armchairs by the fire where a man in a blue robe was sleeping.

The sleeping man spluttered awake, his arms thrashing about as he fought off his supposed attacker. "What the bloody hell, Lawrence? It better be important for you to wake me up after I just fell asleep."

"Mathew," Lawrence hissed as he pointed at us. "She's here!"

When waking up, Mathew had knocked his hood back, and I saw he was an old man with a wrinkled face and short white hair... well, what was left of it. He shot to his feet with surprising ease for a man his age and brushed out his robe before pulling the hood up again, collecting himself. Then the two of them were joined by the man in the red robe, I guessed to be Eleazar, before they approached and fell to their knees in front of me.

"Your Majesty, it is an honor to be in your presence," Lawrence said, his head bowed.

Shocked, I looked at my guardians, but Zan just shrugged while the other two seemed as caught off guard by the whole interaction as I was. Thankfully, I didn't sense any danger from them. I reached out and touched Lawrence on the shoulder. "Please, this is unnecessary, but your greeting humbles me."

Lawrence looked up at me, hope shining in his hazel eyes that didn't match his weathered face and thinning beard. "I can't believe you came. Zan wasn't sure if you would, but we prayed to the gods they would guide you to your true place and destiny here."

"There is much that I want to ask you and hope to learn, but why don't we find a more comfortable place to do that," I suggested, hoping they would listen to my request this time.

Thankfully, they rose and pulled back their hoods so I could see their faces better. Each of these men had experienced a long and full life, but the glint in their eyes told me they weren't to be underestimated. "If you will follow us, we can't talk in the meeting chamber," Lawrence offered, leading the way.

FIVE

TRUTH AND MORE SURPRISES

The meeting room was an office of sorts with three desks and a small seating area with a couch, a few armchairs, and a roaring fire to keep the chill out. I sat on the couch with my guardians standing behind me while the viceroys sat in the armchairs opposite me.

"Are you hungry, thirsty? I imagine the trip here was a long one if what Zan told us is accurate," Mathew asked, reaching for a bell on a small table next to him.

"Something to drink would be lovely. Flying always seems to make me thirsty," I answered, giving them a smile at their thoughtfulness.

Mathew rang the bell, and a few moments later, a woman appeared, wiping her hands on her apron. "Working late tonight again? Do I need to make supper too?"

"Ann, if you could bring us something cool to drink for our guests as well as some bread and cheese to tide them over before dinner," Mathew requested.

Her whole countenance changed when she spotted me, standing straighter and bobbing a curtsy. "Straightaway... anything else I can get you, ma'am, milady, Majesty, miss..."

"No, thank you. What was requested will be wonderful," I answered, trying to ease her nervousness.

After bobbing a few more hasty curtsies, she left the room in a flurry.

"Forgive her. Once people found out that Zan was leaving us to become a guardian of the Dragon Queen, it spread like wildfire," Lawrence said as he folded his hands in his lap. "It has been a prophecy that we have waited generations to be fulfilled."

Little did these men know that they were drawing me in with every word, making me want desperately to know everything about this prophecy. "I absolutely want to know more about that, but I have come for a specific purpose. Having already met some of your soldiers, I understand you know about the Lost King and what happened in Royal City?"

"Yes, since Zan's departure, we felt it was wise to keep ourselves more informed of things happening outside our valley," Eleazar concurred.

"Unbeknownst to me, one of my guardians was an impostor and spy for the Lost King, reporting everything we were doing. This leads me to believe he's also given the location of our hidden mountain fortress where the mercenary clans have been hiding. I've come to request your help by giving refuge to my people," I stated, searching each of the men's faces.

They shifted in their seats and looked at one another, confused, until Lawrence spoke. "Your Majesty, why would you feel the need to make such a request to us? This is your home. These are your people, and we are your subjects who have humbly kept your throne ready for your return."

"What?" I blurted, my brain having trouble processing all of this. "You are willing to hand me over your entire kingdom just like that?"

"Perhaps we need to start at the beginning," Mathew suggested. "I assume you aren't heading back tonight?"

"Actually, I need to be back by first light to accompany my people as we leave our hideout," I answered. "But we have a few hours before we need to return since I wasn't expecting this to be so... simple."

Eleazar muttered something under his breath as he got up from his chair and headed to a cupboard. He produced a key from somewhere in his robes and unlocked the door, revealing a collection of old books and scrolls. Carefully, he removed two scrolls wrapped in what looked like bright red velvet and returned to set them on the low table between us.

"These are the first scrolls ever written by the first king, King Yash, just after he established the mercenaries here in Sheca. As you know, he was the first man to build a bond with a dragon. He said that when the venom entered him, he saw a vision. This vision was of our future and what our people would one day become. King Yash foresaw a time when our people would need a champion, but he didn't see who that champion would be. Of course, we never got a timeline of when that would happen, but we did get events and other signs to look out for. This second scroll is that of our third king, King Cardon, and his vision that predicted the name of the champion... the Dragon Queen," Eleazar said as he opened one of the scrolls.

Peering at the scrolls in the light of the fire, I could tell they were written in the old tongue. They had a slightly different way of being written, making reading a little more challenging.

"Vasin, is this version of our language in your memory?"

"IT IS OLD, TO BE SURE, BUT WE DO NOT FORGET SOMETHING ONCE IT IS PULLED INTO OUR MEMORY BANK. THIS DIALECT DATES BACK TO THE BEGINNING OF OUR MEMORY."

"So, you can help me if I get stuck?"

"Yes, Cass. You will not miss out on any secret those scrolls possess."

I couldn't help but grin that he knew me so well. When I processed what I was reading, my smile faded into a frown as I read the signs of the champion. My gaze flicked up to Eleazar studying me as I read. "This can't be... how could this be true?"

"Now, do you see why we do not doubt you are the Dragon Queen? Your arrival has been foretold hundreds of years before it could ever be possible," Mathew interjected, his voice filled with excitement.

The guys shifted behind me as they tried to get a better look at the scroll, but I didn't think Abbott or Izel could read it. Shifting, I turned so I could see them as I explained what I'd just read. "The scroll starts with predicting the hour of need that would bring forth the champion. Our countries will be hunting the mercenaries, forcing us back into hiding. A great evil will arrive out of the East, but we won't know until it's too late because of the fighting within our borders. It goes on to explain the signs that the champion has arrived. A black dragon will reappear after a century without one, on the verge of dragons abandoning us as a lost cause. The champion will be found among people who'd lost the knowledge of their heritage. Upon their coronation, they will unite the mercenaries and end the reign of evil to create a time of prosperity, the likes we've never seen before..."

"So, the queen is a scholar," Lawrence commented with a kind smile. "Not many besides us can read these ancient words. Many believe them to be the ramblings of a madman, but we know the truth the others chose to turn a blind eye to. The time of darkness is coming, and the hour of the Dragon Queen is upon us."

"Why don't they believe?" Izel asked as he came to sit beside me.

"Because they are fools," Eleazar snapped. "They let resentment cloud their judgment even though it's been four hundred years since we were left here. Many want to release us from our history and blaze a new trail as a new people independent from the mercenaries who forgot us. Our wise king knew we would be needed. It's written clearly here in these scrolls. We weren't abandoned. We were being protected for when we would be needed. If we had all left together, then who would be here? Who would you have to turn to in your hour of need when hope seems to be fading away? They choose to be ignorant, and that will be their downfall," he finished, slamming his fist on his armchair.

Ann entered the room with a tray of cups but paused when she saw the scroll on the table. "I'll just set these on the side table for you. Do you still want me to bring some food or just wait for dinner?"

"Might be safer just to wait," Abbott offered. "None of us will waste away before then."

Having been on the receiving end of Abbott's full attention combined with a smile, I couldn't blame her for the blush that colored her cheeks. It was rather overwhelming. I didn't appreciate her flirtatious look in return and how her walk had a little more sashay to it.

"Would you like us to continue, or should we change topics to another subject less historical?" Mathew asked, drawing my attention back to him. He had a knowing twinkle in his eye that told me I hadn't been as subtle in my disapproval of Ann's actions as I thought.

"I would greatly love to learn all the history here in Sheca, but I think right now, we need to focus on the future before the rest of my people arrive," I suggested.

"Very well then," Lawrence said as he stood from his chair to grab another book out of the cabinet. This one was bound in leather with gold writing on it, announcing it as the concordance of royal decrees. "Tell me what steps you have taken as queen so far."

"Steps?"

"Yes, I assume you have gone through the full coronation since you have your guardians. Who have you chosen as your consorts? I see these men don't hold that mark. Are there more back with the rest of your people waiting for you?" Lawrence inquired, looking down his nose at my guardians.

Shifting in my seat, I looked up at Zan, confused, but he just shrugged his shoulders as unsure as I was. "I think it might be best if we assume I've completed nothing. My coronation was not planned and happened more on the spot out of necessity. When I came to the clans around six months ago, I was tasked with a year of training in all things mercenary on top of learning the history and role of being queen. I'd been kidnapped by the Lost King and was rescued by one of my other guardians who brought me to the fortress where I was announced as queen. My Birthright picked my guardians out of necessity, not in the typical fashion of one from each clan."

Now it was their turn to look stunned and confused. Eleazar sputtered as he tried to find the words to express his displeasure at what I'd just told him. "Gods above, that... whatever that was, is absolutely no coronation!"

"Calm yourself, my old friend. We don't know how things have changed in the past four hundred years," Mathew chimed in, trying to soothe Eleazar. "You do not wear a crown, either. Is there another mark to establish you are queen?"

I pulled out the pendant I wear all the time since I'd been given it. "This is the symbol of royalty and also a key to unlock certain rooms or things meant for our eyes only."

"May I?" Mathew asked, holding out a hand.

Slipping off the necklace, I handed it to him and watched as he studied the design. It was of a dragon curled around a sword, and the tip of the sword was the key.

"Do you know what you have here?" Mathew asked, his voice full of reverence. "That's foolish of me to ask. I'm sure you don't, seeing as you didn't know we existed until meeting Zan. This, my dear girl, is the key to the Dragon Castle." Upon hearing the shocked sounds coming from his friends, he handed over the necklace for them to inspect.

"This is proof that the king always planned to return. Why else take the one and only key to the castle with you?" Eleazar announced as he looked down at it in his hands, rubbing a thumb over it. "It's been locked up for four hundred years, an impenetrable fortress that dragons can't even access once it's been secured. It's one of the reasons we use this building to conduct our work and not the castle as it should be."

Just when I didn't think more surprises could pop up, they kept coming. I was going to assume that everything had more meaning to it than I was told so it would make it easier for me when things like this happened.

"You're telling me that castle we saw when we flew in hasn't been touched in four hundred years?" Izel asked, leaning forward, resting his elbows on his knees. "How is it still intact if no one has maintained it?"

"We might not be able to get inside, but that doesn't mean we will let it fall into ruin," Eleazar grumbled. "We've maintained what we could from the outside."

I could tell the others had more questions, but they could wait a little longer. "Back to the coronation, what is it that you require?"

Lawrence flipped through the book's pages before handing it to me. "Here is the outline that has been laid out for us."

Taking the book, I settled it in my lap and read over what was written, surprised at the level of detail listed. This reminded me more of how things were done in Norden, but with a few differences. "Do you still have everything needed for this to happen?"

"We have some, but the rest of it is locked away safely in the castle. Now that we have the key, we can gather those as well," Mathew said, giving me an excited smile. "We will be the first to see the inside in over four hundred years. Think of all the things we can learn!"

Before the others could get too excited, Ann poked her head into the room. "Dinner is ready if you would like to come to the dining room."

Thankful to have the break, I stood and followed the others out. I knew this place would hold secrets, but I didn't know just how many there would be. It seemed that around every corner there was something more. We haven't even broached the subject of dragons or Birthrights, either. It might be better to wait for those revelations once we've gathered our people here and have had time to dive into everything once the castle is reopened.

Six

You Have How Many Dragons?

Dinner was a delightful change of pace of roasted chicken, vegetables, fresh bread, and some wine. I hadn't had much experience with wine, seeing as my mother didn't let me have it except for special occasions. I sipped at it slowly, remembering the night I overindulged in drinking with my guardians. It was nice to see everyone relaxed and enjoying the meal. The viceroys shared stories of what life was like here in Sheca. Hope filled me as it seemed like this might be what we'd been looking for all along—a place to start again and build up our people, no longer looking over our shoulders, wondering when the next attack would happen.

I was thankful I kept Sheca a secret until the time was right. Payson knew that Zan came from somewhere else but didn't know the exact location, giving us more time before the Lost King turned his attention to us. If I were him, I would have sent a group of dragons to attack the fortress, knowing we would all be hidden away there. The Lost King making his move on the fortress and discovering we were gone would tell us just how much time we had before he started looking for us. My hope was he would have his hands full dealing with Royal City and taking over Norden. That would give us the chance to regroup. Only time would tell.

"Your Majesty."

Lawrence's voice had me refocusing, and by the look on his face, I could tell it wasn't the first time he'd tried to get my attention. "I'm sorry, it's hard not to get lost trying to stay one step ahead of danger."

"Such is the life of a wise ruler." He nodded in understanding. "I was only hoping to offer whatever assistance we could to you as your people journey to here."

"What would be most helpful is getting a group of dragon riders to accompany us. If we can have them take some of the important supplies and maybe some of our elderly, it will free up horses," I explained. "Even then, I would love to get a few waves of dragon riders so we can move people faster through the treacherous mountains."

"Then it shall be done. How many men and dragons were you hoping to send in the first wave?" Mathew asked.

"How many do you have to spare?" I countered.

Mathew grinned as he sat back in his seat. "Roughly six hundred or so."

My fork fell out of my hand as I stared at him, stunned. No one had that many people bonded to dragons. Even back in the days when they were more common, it never grew to that number. Yet here we were in a secret town, and a third of their population had a dragon. "How?"

"I think it's best we discuss that in greater detail once we've gotten you and your people settled. Let's just say we understand the true dynamics of a human and dragon relationship," Eleazar answered with a chuckle.

Baffled by this turn of events, I looked at my guardians, unsure how to use this information and hoping they would have ideas.

"What if we had a group of, say... a hundred come with us to take the supplies we need and those who can't easily make the journey? Then we can find out the exact number of horses we have and send a second group to meet us along the way to gather those left. We'll still need to have some people take the long journey, but I think it will be faster with everyone on horseback and a smaller group," Izel suggested.

"Sounds like a logical plan. Ann!" Lawrence called, and seconds later, the woman appeared. "Could you please ask Alsten and Naytan to join us?"

I groaned internally as I heard him mention Naytan's name, knowing this conversation was going to be a battle. Thankfully, the viceroys had been wonderful and on my side from the beginning, unlike the clan leaders—another problem I would have to deal with later.

"Unfortunately, Cassarah was already greeted by our pigheaded second-in-command," Zan shared once Ann left the room. "Things did not go well, so I wouldn't expect much help from him."

Much to my delight, Eleazar rolled his eyes upon hearing this. "Good thing he isn't the commander of our army, now isn't it? Alsten is much more levelheaded and agrees with the prophecy of the Dragon Queen."

"The way Naytan talked, you think that no one here wanted Cassarah or the rest of us, for that matter," Abbott commented, taking a large gulp of wine. "I would be remiss in my duties if I didn't ask if he's a threat to our queen."

Lawrence nodded his approval at Abbott's protectiveness as he refilled his glass with wine, telling me this wouldn't be a pleasant conversation with our military commanders. "As we've mentioned before, there is a group of those who wish to break from our ties to the mercenaries... the most outspoken of them being Naytan. Is he a threat... that is to be seen? I would suggest keeping an eye on him. There is always the chance he might come around once we prove the wait was worth it. They have been living under the cloud of being a forgotten people, which always breeds discontent. Take that information and do with it what you will. You are the ones charged with her safety, and while we advise, it doesn't mean we are right. Too long have we lived in our own bubble here in Sheca. We have only just started to expand our reach once we learned of you, Your Majesty."

Remarkably, it didn't take long for the two men to arrive, and Naytan looked none too happy about it. Alsten, on the other hand, seemed eager to meet me. I was surprised to find he was far younger than I would have expected to be leading the kingdom's military.

"Viceroys, Your Majesty. You called for us?" Alsten greeted with a bow, elbowing Naytan when he didn't do the same. Begrudgingly, he gave a halfhearted bow, refusing to look at me.

Eleazar noticed as well and shoved his chair back. He marched up to the man, poking him in the chest. "Naytan, you listen up, and you listen good. I know your father filled your head with all this nonsense about breaking ties, but now that the Dragon Queen is back, that ends now. Do you hear me?"

"They are a threat to everything we are. How can you stand by and let a child like her swoop in and destroy everything we have worked for?" Naytan snarled. "You might see her as the one who will save us all, but I see nothing but destruction in our future."

With a heavy sigh, I stood, planting my hands on the table, grounding me before I spoke. "Then you may leave."

Everyone looked at me like I'd just spoken a different language rather than telling a man to go away.

"What?" Naytan shot back.

"If you do not want to be here under my rule, then go. Leave this place and your post as second-in-command. Take any who will follow you and be gone," I said, spelling it out for him. "Once my people are here, I will be going through the official coronation to be your queen. When that is completed, I will do what is best for my people in whatever way necessary. Not everyone is going to like it, so I will always offer the option to leave. If you don't want to be under my rule, then start your own kingdom or join another that will make you happier. You will not stand here and tell me to my face that I will be the ruin of this kingdom and its people."

We all waited for his answer as he stared at me like I was some problem he couldn't figure out. "You'll let me walk away just like that?"

"What good does it do me to keep you or kill you? If you stay, you will only be a problem, always trying to prove that I'm the enemy. If I kill you, what sort of first impression does that give to everyone else? I will not be known as a queen who throws a fit and kills those who don't agree with her. I have far more important things to do," I informed Naytan before turning my focus to Alsten. "Commander Alsten, I am in need of about a hundred of your dragon riders to come with me tonight. I am evacuating everyone, and I have supplies and people I would like to have brought here in a speedier fashion."

Alsten shook himself out of his surprise and schooled his features to be more serious. "Of course, Your Majesty. I can get my people gathered right away. How many do you think you'll need for just supplies? We have a special harness that works better for that need."

"I'm not sure..." I started, looking at Abbott and Izel for assistance.

"Let's say fifteen to be sure," Izel responded. "How many people can a dragon take comfortably? We are looking to move elderly and children out first via dragon."

"Dragons could easily take their rider and two adults or three children, depending on size since they have to fit around their wings."

"Good, then eighty-odd dragons will be more than enough for the first wave of people. Can they be ready to fly out in the next hour or so?" Abbott asked as the bell tower rang eight bells.

"We can be ready in half that time if needed," Alsten responded smartly, drawing himself to attention. "Our people are highly trained and disciplined in more than just the standard abilities of a mercenary. We have always maintained the knowledge we would need to be ready for the return of our king or queen and the protection they would need."

"Speaking of protection..." Mathew cut in. "How many guardians did your magic call?"

"Seven men and two women," I answered. "There is also Gavin, who was once the Crown Prince of Norden but stepped down to become my ambassador and consort."

Eleazar almost choked on his wine. "Are you saying you made a treaty with the royalty of Norden?"

"Yes, the king and queen will also be joining us as my people rescued them from the battle at the castle," I disclosed, frowning as the others gaped at me like fish.

"Do you still doubt her, you fool?" Eleazar muttered, glaring at Naytan. "How many more of the signs do you need her to fulfill right in front of you or from her own lips?"

Naytan didn't answer, but he did look even more uncomfortable with the situation he was in.

Feeling just the slightest pity toward this man, I raised a brow at him as I caught his eyes when he glanced at me. "You're still here? Does that mean I can expect you and your dragon to be ready with the others?"

Zan snorted but tried to cover it up with a cough. Naytan didn't seem to like my question much either and took this moment to leave the room. *Guess we'll just have to see what he decides, won't we?*

"I will get the men ready, and we will await your signal. Zan knows what it is. Our roost is built into the mountains. It's not obvious how many of them we have on call to us. Not that all of them live here. Many fly free until their partner calls them," Alsten shared.

"There seems to be a lot I need to learn about this place, but let's get the rest of our people to their new home first," I said with a smile.

Alsten gave a quick bow and left to get the dragon riders ready.

SEVEN

BY DRAGON AND BY LAND

T rue to his word, Alsten had the riders ready when we took off. Ifra shot out a ball of flame as the signal in the night sky. It was colder flying back without the warmth of the sun, but Abbott's warm body kept me from getting too cold. He felt me shiver as the winds picked up, so he wrapped his arms tightly around my waist, pulling me into the shelter of his broad body. This had me thinking back to what the viceroys had asked about who my consorts were. I had no idea there was another mark they got when that happened. Was it given by magic like the guardian symbol or did I provide that proof? Either way, after reading the coronation rules, I would have to announce at least one of them. No king or queen is allowed to hold the throne without the chance of continuing the line.

It would seem they followed the rule that the offspring of the king or queen would rule if there weren't another black dragon to make a different choice. So like a normal royal situation, I would have to prove to my people I was making an effort to provide for their needs with a child. *Did I want kids?* Now that I had a choice in the matter, I found I wasn't sure what answer I would give. All my life, it had been assumed. I was a woman, therefore, I had children. What other purpose could I possibly have? Did the men in my life want kids? Do I ask them that before I make my choice? How many do I want to pick? Can I choose some and see how it goes and add more later? No. That would be cruel and unkind to those I didn't pick right away.

"Cass, you are going to make your brain burst thinking that hard. Trust your heart. You know these men were handpicked for you by the power inside you. The gods would not have chosen poorly for their favored child, the Dragon Queen."

"What does that mean? Have you known all along I was this person?"

"Of course."

"So you just didn't bother to tell me I was some prophesied queen who would change the world?"

"Cass, if I did that, then you wouldn't have become who you are today. Just like there is a reason you needed to lead the life you did and go through those hardships before coming to this point."

"The viceroys mentioned gods earlier too. Why don't others speak of them in Norden?"

"They once did, but like all things, if you lose faith in something and choose to cut it out of your life, it fades out of existence. Now that doesn't mean it still exists in the world because you choose not to believe it. This is the case of the gods the people of Sheca speak of. All of this will be explained once we get you and our people settled."

"How is it that so much has been forgotten?"

"It is human nature to wipe out all that it fails at or chooses not to accept. It's easier to pretend it never happened than to face what you've abandoned."

As much as I wanted to deny what Vasin was saying, I knew it was true. My family did it as they tried to hide the fact we were once mercenaries. They refused to acknowledge that part of our family because they were ashamed of what others thought. Now, here I was, queen of the whole lot of them *but* with the advantage of knowing both sides of things. Just in our short visit, I could tell there was much to learn from the Shecans.

The night around me was quiet, and even though there was a strong wind, the sky was clear, making this an easy journey home.

"Vasin, have the dragons find places to land in the area around the fortress since they won't all fit on the ledge. We will have them come four at a time to be loaded up, starting with the dragons outfitted for packing supplies," I instructed as we landed just as the sun began to warm the night sky.

"IT IS DONE."

Scouts shouted our arrival, and I was soon faced with Becka holding out a mug of steaming liquid. Her red hair was bright in the early morning glow, making her easy to spot, but I never feared she wouldn't be somewhere close by. After being my handmaid for most of my life as well as my best friend, I knew she was one person who would always have my back no matter what happened. "Here, this should warm you up and keep you awake."

"Bless you. I didn't really consider I wouldn't be getting any sleep doing this," I mumbled as I lifted the cup and took a tentative taste.

The beverage was bursting with flavor, and I registered it was the same thing Alto had given me after my hangover. I gulped it down greedily, not caring that it scalded my tongue, knowing it would fuel me for another few hours. "Where is everyone?" I asked as we headed inside.

"Ballard, Cole, and Sal are working with a group to gather the supplies we can't leave behind or have land in the enemy's hands. Dayson and May are dealing with the horses and getting them ready to head out while Jade and Paxton are checking to make sure that people are only taking what they can carry," Becka reported.

My brows shot up at how things seemed to be going in a quick and orderly fashion. "Seems like you have a handle on things. Where do you need help?" I asked as Abbott, Izel, and Zan joined me.

"Zan, are you sure there can be no wagons?" Becka pleaded. "We have far fewer horses than we originally thought since some clans don't keep as many of them."

"No need for wagons when you have dragons," Zan announced. "A hundred dragons are waiting in the area to take supplies and people back to Sheca. Cassarah also arranged for another wave of them to come if we need them."

Becka's jaw dropped open. "How can that be?"

"Welcome to what we've been telling ourselves since we arrived there," Abbott muttered, running his hands through his hair. "I'm gonna go find Ballard and Cole and fill them in on the change."

"Zan, you should stay with Cassarah and Becka. I'll go help Dayson and May," Izel suggested.

"I'll make sure no one gets any crazy ideas and tries to attack our queen," Zan said with a salute and grin.

Since Zan arrived, I haven't had time alone with him. None of the guys felt comfortable with him doing that yet. So, the fact that Izel was giving him this opportunity was somewhat of a big deal.

"So what can the three of us do?" I inquired, turning to my two companions.

"I would say let's go check in with the stables, but those are at the base of the mountain, and it's a long way there just to come all the way back," Becka mused out loud as she looked over a sheet of paper with notes written on it. "To be honest, things are going smoothly. It's just the act of getting everyone out of here that will be the trick."

"Did we get a headcount of how many people would benefit from being flown out of here?" I asked. "It might be a good idea to start separating those who will be leaving from up here so we don't send them all the way out that entrance."

Becka snapped her fingers together and grinned at me. "This is why you're the queen. Brain like a fox you have, Cassarah. Okay, so new plan. We'll review who is in the staging area that May set up for those they have checked so far. We can direct them to the stables or the ledge for their exit. Are you thinking of just elderly and those who can't make the journey or kids too?"

"You two would offer a better suggestion on that. I haven't spent much time with children, but I imagine they would be easier to have ride double on dragons if we needed," I pointed out.

"That is a good thought," Zan agreed. "Let's start with those we *know* won't be able to make it on foot or horseback and go from there. We have plenty of dragons at our disposal. It's more about the best situation for the ground travelers."

"Perfect, I like this plan," Becka cheered as we headed off to start the process.

May had set up a staging area for those going to Sheca to ensure they were bringing along things that wouldn't slow them down. Once they passed through, they would be supplied with food rations for the day and sent to the third section to eat a bowl of hot porridge and wait. We headed to the third section and decided it was best to mark people's hands with an 'S' for stable or 'D' for dragon so as more people were added to the mix, we wouldn't get lost in who we talked to. Time flew by, and the sun was already halfway up the mountains when we were finished, but it was all worth it. According to Becka's numbers, we would be short about two hundred horses instead of the three hundred we originally thought before the extra dragons were provided.

"This is going to make things so much easier. If we can keep the kids on the horses and have the adults walk, it will save us time," Zan said as we reviewed the work we'd done.

"I had no idea we had so many elders and children in the clans. When I read about how our civilization was dying, I didn't think of it in actual humans, just numbers on a page," I commented, watching the kids running around the space oblivious to what was really going on.

Zan stepped closer, bumping his shoulder against mine. "Just think how many more will arrive once everyone gets settled in Sheca... those who haven't found marriage partners yet might as well as some who have been holding off because of other fears that may no longer be an issue. This move will be good for both factions. They just don't know it yet."

"By the way you're talking, you sound like a hopeless romantic," I teased, nudging him back.

"That's because I am. Even though I have Ezzu and can function like a normal person, people always see me as broken or needing to be taken care of because I'm blind. If not for that, I could have been a higher rank in our military, but they didn't want to take the risk that I'd miss something important. Although now that I see the big picture, I should be thankful they didn't. Otherwise, I never would have been on patrol and found you."

This caused me to give him my full attention. Even though he refused to look at me, Ezzu's golden eyes were peering at me, letting me know he could see me. "Zan, I might not know much about you yet, but I do know you are far from broken, and no one needs to coddle you. From what I've seen, you have the heart of a warrior and are deeply loyal to your heritage, willing to protect it with your life. It seems that whatever you give that loyalty to, you protect with everything you have. The man who attacked me, trying to save Vasin, does not think of himself as defective or disabled in any way, so why should I treat him any different?"

Zan shifted to face me, and I felt he was searching for something in my expression before he reached out and took my hand. "You, Cassarah, are one of the few people I truly believe sees me as a whole person who can be useful. I see your honest heart in everything you do, putting others before yourself. These people have no idea how lucky they are to have you as their queen, but they will soon. I'll make sure of it."

"So does that mean I am one of the lucky few who have earned your loyalty?" I asked, giving him a soft smile as a blush heated my cheeks.

"I have a feeling you will have much more than that the more time I get to spend around you," he whispered, giving my hand a gentle squeeze before he let go. "I think it's time we get these people moving, don't you?"

With a nod, we headed out to find where they were working on supplies so we could get those loaded up first.

EIGHT

SO THE JOURNEY BEGINS

When we entered the strategy room, we found a huge argument going on with the clan leaders, King Edward, and Queen Mary, with Gavin trying to defuse the situation.

"Surely, there has to be a mistake. Why would I allow another to ride with me on my dragon?" King Edward demanded. "What if they try to harm me? I've seen the looks they have been giving us. We aren't welcome here."

"Father, it makes sense to allow those who can't make the journey to go first," Gavin argued, standing up to his father.

"As clan leaders, we need to arrive first so we can be there to greet our people and make sure they are being taken care of. There is no way the queen meant for us to take the long route. We know nothing about this place, and to send our children off without their parents is ludicrous," Xio stated.

The group was so absorbed in their argument they hadn't noticed I was there yet, but it gave me time to set the ground rules for the dragons.

"Vasin, make sure every dragon knows that if one of my guardians doesn't escort a person to them, they are not to take them anywhere. It appears our so-called leaders are throwing a temper tantrum."

"Are they allowed to remove or retaliate against such advances? If someone gets bit or hit with a tail, I don't want them to be in trouble."

"I'm fine with them being able to defend themselves."

"That will please a fair amount of them."

Lifting my hand to my lips, I let out a shrill whistle that Becka had taught me. It did the trick splendidly, grabbing all their attention and shutting them up. "It seems there is some confusion about what's happening with our evacuation. Would anyone care to tell me what the issue is so I can clear it up?"

"Ah, Queen Cassarah, you're back." Queen Mary sighed with relief, making her way over to me. "It seems your guard here is telling us the dragon riders are only taking the elderly or children, including us."

"That is exactly what I expect to happen," I answered.

Queen Mary blinked at me as she processed my answer. "Surely, you don't think that is a wise move. What about our safety?"

"What about theirs? As a queen, you should understand putting your people ahead of your own needs. Doing this will show my people that the agreement we had to become allies wasn't just a bunch of pretty words while you bide your time to betray us as your ancestors have done before. If you no longer want to be allies, then you are free to get on your dragons and fly to your sister if you think she will offer you the protection you need at the standard you require," I expressed with a tilt of my head, waiting for her reply.

"Your Majesty, do you really intend to cast off an alliance with the Norden royalty so easily over refusing to take someone with them?" King Edward demanded.

"I'm not sure what the confusion is." I turned my gaze to Gavin. "Was I unclear in what I said?"

Gavin tried to hold his face in a neutral expression, but I could see his lips twitching. "No, I think you explained yourself clearly."

"All right then, the choice is yours, Your Majesties. Are you an ally, or are we parting ways here?" I inquired.

"Your Majesty, is this wise?" Garold pressed as he stepped up next to King Edward.

Letting out a heavy sigh, I looked up to the heavens and then back at the people before me. "Vasin will be taking two or three people himself as I ride with the group traveling by ground. I expect my fellow leaders to do the same or at least allow one other person to travel with them. If you do not wish to help an elder, then what about a child? Do you view them as a threat to your lives as well? I promise even though we train our children to fight, it's to protect themselves and not to be killers where there is no payoff."

A snort came from somewhere to the left, and my guess was it came from Cole. Apparently, lack of sleep and dealing with self-entitled nobility made me short-tempered and petty, but even monks have their limits of being gracious to those around them.

"You plan to ride with them the whole way?" Acton asked, curiosity in his tone.

"Clearly, I am not explaining myself well if I need to keep repeating what I've said. Yes, I will be riding the entire three days with my people." I huffed. "If I expect them to make this journey, how can I place myself above them just for my own comfort? When I first came to the clans, I was asked to prove myself as one of you. I had to complete the same training everyone else does. Mercenary first, queen second. This is the way I want my people to see me. Otherwise, how can I ever expect them to trust me? Now, are there any more questions?" When no one answered after a moment, I nodded. "All right, we need to take whatever supplies you want out of here to the ledge so we can load up the first group of dragons.

Then we can commence with the people." Grabbing a small crate of books, I turned on my heel and left, refusing to discuss this issue further.

With the dragons' help, we were able to take much more with us, allowing for more food to be taken along for those of us traveling through the mountains. Once that was all completed, they were sent off and began the trip back to Sheca, where the viceroys were working on setting up placement for our people once they arrived. I'd been a little worried that people would be scared to ride on the dragons, but that was soon tossed from my mind. The excitement on their faces, young and old, was priceless as they greeted their dragon and rider. We fell into a good rhythm of settling and buckling them in before they took off, making short work of the whole ordeal.

King Edward and Queen Mary each took two children with them as if they hadn't tried to refuse the idea. I was glad to see that when push came to shove, they made the right choice for the future of their people and mine. Vasin was the last to get settled in since he would be going without me. He was the only one I trusted to take Sal. As much as I'd love to see the first meeting between him and the viceroys, I knew I couldn't go with them. Instead, a little girl took my place, strapped and ready to fly with excited giggles and all.

"When you get there, ask for the viceroys. They are the men in charge and are aware of the whole situation. Plus, I feel like you will find kindred spirits among them," I said with a grin.

"Don't you worry about me, Cassy. I'll make sure nothing goes wrong while we wait for you and the rest to arrive," Sal assured me with a wink.

"I know I don't need to say this, but keep me apprised of how the journey goes."

"Don't fret, Cass. I will look after the old man and the rest of them. You focus on those in your care.

THE JOURNEY WON'T BE WITHOUT CHALLENGES. ONCE I'VE DROPPED THEM OFF, I WILL RETURN TO KEEP A LOOKOUT JUST LIKE THE OTHERS OF YOUR DRAGON-RIDING GUARDIANS."

Hugging his large head, he hummed his pleasure before pulling away and leaping off the ledge. Jade, Paxton, and Zan flanked the group, keeping an eye on how things went as they too carried a passenger to Sheca. I was now left with those of us who would be making the long trek through the mountains. Becka and I walked arm in arm as we made our way down to the stables. When we reached them, my leg was throbbing, having been on it way too much today and not having slept. Would I be able to make it through a long day's ride?

As if reading my mind, Alto walked up to me with a knowing look of disapproval. "Your Majesty, you are not doing yourself any favors by being on your leg so much."

"Once we get to Sheca, there will be time to rest. Until then, we need to keep moving forward," I explained.

"Don't make me have to slip something into your food to make you take it easy once we get there. I won't have you push it to the point we might have to remove part of your leg due to infection." Alto scowled at me, hands on her hips. When I nodded my understanding, she motioned for me to give her my hand. "Chew these roots if the pain gets bad. It will ease it without making you sleepy. Since I know you haven't slept yet, these roasted beans will keep you awake. Typically, we brew them and drink the liquid, but since we don't have that luxury, this will have to do."

She pressed a small leather pouch into my hand before heading off. I glanced at Becka, knowing she was the one to tattle on me. She just grinned and tugged me over to the front of the procession of horses. Inali, my black mare, was saddled with packs filled with supplies, ready to set out on our journey. She snuffled my pockets, looking to make sure I wasn't hiding any treats from her and snorted when she didn't find any. I smiled at her as I rubbed her silky ears, trying to make up for not bringing her anything.

"Cassy-bear!" Dayson called out, walking up with his arms wide, letting me know he was going to hug me. His strong arms wrapped around me, and he picked me up off the ground, making me squeak in surprise. "Now I see why Cole calls you mouse. You sound just like one." He chuckled, setting me down. "Did everything go well? I heard about the dragons. That is a major help, seeing as we had far fewer horses than we originally thought."

"Things went fine in Sheca, but it wasn't a long enough visit to really get a feel for what things will be like," I shared with a heavy sigh. "Day, there is so much we don't know. The things they were telling me about being queen and my purpose were overwhelming and strange yet made perfect sense at the same time. Being there was like tasting a dessert before it's done baking, and now, I have to wait to get a real piece of it."

Dayson's eyebrows rose higher the more I spoke. "Sounds like we better get these people hustling so we can get you back there. Are you sure going with us is the best choice? Sounds like it might be better for you to be there already."

"No, this is the right move. I already sent Vasin off with Sal and had to tell Gavin's parents they couldn't be selfish, so neither can I."

"Love, the last thing anyone would call you is selfish," Gavin announced as he walked up to us. "My parents deserved to be scolded. They have been tucked away in their castle for too long and don't know what the real world is like anymore. Even though it's been a short while, being here with the clans has opened my eyes to so much."

"I shouldn't have been that hard on them," I countered. "They just lost everything, and now I'm forcing them to look after people they've been fighting against for decades, if not centuries."

"You didn't force them to do a damn thing. Hell, you gave them an out, little mouse," Cole said, joining our group. "All you asked them to do was prove they weren't just allies in name only. If you were in the same situation, would you hesitate to help them by allowing *one* person to ride with you on Vasin?"

"Of course not," I answered.

"Exactly. You aren't asking anything from them that you wouldn't do yourself," Cole pointed out. "Now that we have that settled, I'm to tell you everyone is ready to move out at your signal."

I looked around the space and saw people mounted up and the rest lingering behind with their packs at the ready. "Then we should be off."

Double-checking my tack just as I'd been trained, I grabbed hold of Inali's mane and tossed myself up on her back as if I'd been doing it all my life. Inali pranced in place, far too well-trained to actually step out of her position until given a command.

"Would you look at that? You'd never know she couldn't do that six months ago. I wonder who taught her that?" Becka mused as she settled on the back of her red roan gelding behind me.

Laughing, I gave a light kick of my heel, and Inali was moving out into the bright morning sunlight. Cole pulled up next to me, acting as the guide out of the fortress and steering us in the right direction for our journey to Sheca. Zan sketched out a map for us to follow for the first part since tomorrow we would have a few dragons to lead the way as they scouted, making sure we weren't being followed. Thankfully, the ground was rocky enough that it would be hard to follow our trail from the fortress. Vasin said they would help keep it hidden as well.

This was it. I was bringing the two factions of mercenaries back together after four hundred years apart. I hoped they could learn to be a united people once we got there.

NINE

THREE PEOPLE, ONE TENT

The day started out fairly easy, but the real struggle began once we got into the deeper part of Restless Mountains. The ground was unsteady, so we had to pick our way the best we could, stopping often to make sure those walking could keep up. Many of the group switched out at intervals to give those walking a break which helped to keep people from getting too tired. I was the only one who had to stay on horseback because none of my guardians would let me walk on this unreliable footing. Even Ballard threatened to tie me up like a sack of potatoes if I didn't comply, so I helped by letting some of the older kids we had with us ride with me.

By the time the sun faded to the point we had to find shelter before it got too dark, I struggled to keep my eyes open. Even with the help of the beans Alto gave me, my body was exhausted and was going to force me to rest whether I liked it or not. Thankfully, we'd just made it over a ridge and into a fairly flat pass before the next mountain slope we had to cross over. It gave us a place to rest for the night. The weather was much colder now that we were higher up in the mountains with snow lightly drifting around us. I was thankful to whoever packed my bags because wrapped up with my bedroll was a fur-lined cloak that kept most of the chill at bay. The group was silent as we set up our meager tents, struggling to pound in the stakes to keep them up. Some just tied the lines to rocks instead. We didn't build a fire since we each had our ration packs of dried meat and hard tack bread that softened in water.

Once everything was set up, I tumbled into my tent and wrapped myself in my blanket, missing Vasin's warmth. Even if he were back by now, it wouldn't have made a difference. The pass was too narrow for him to land with everyone else here. What surprised me was when Cole and Gavin showed up outside my tent just as I was on the verge of falling asleep.

"Cassarah, you awake?" Gavin called.

Groaning, I peeked out of the tent, blinking up at them. "What's wrong?"

"Nothing, well... we didn't have enough tents like we thought for some of the families, so we gave up ours," Cole explained.

"Wait, does that mean you don't have a place to sleep?" I asked, my tired brain struggling to keep up.

Cole and Gavin looked at each other then back to me. "See, we were hoping we could bunk with you..." Gavin hedged.

I blinked at him a few times as my brain registered what they were asking. "You want to sleep in here with me in this tiny tent?"

"Hey, more bodies make for a warmer night's sleep," Cole pointed out. "We would have found somewhere else, but there isn't room. You wouldn't want us to sleep out in the cold and chance freezing to death, would you?"

Scowling at him, I crawled back and flopped on my mat. "Hurry up before I change my mind."

They both scrambled to get in at the same time, making them mutter at each other as they didn't fit. Cole shoved Gavin back, entering first. He settled on my right but cursed at Gavin. He *accidentally* stepped on Cole as he got situated on my left side. The tent was really meant for one person, *maybe* two. With the three of us all packed inside, I was pressed up against Cole's chest while Gavin was at my back. Even though I felt exposed, we were fully dressed with cloaks and blankets between us. But my brain had been trained at a young age that this was inappropriate, and I couldn't seem to relax.

"Goodnight, mouse. We'll make sure no one else bothers you tonight," Cole whispered, pressing a soft kiss to my forehead.

I grunted my acknowledgment of his words but still couldn't seem to relax even though I was much warmer than I was before. A hand started to drift up and down my back in a soothing motion as Gavin started to hum some song I knew but couldn't place. Finally, my tired body won out over my worried mind, and I drifted off to sleep, dreaming of a dance I'd seen Miranda and her men attend right after they'd married. The whole night, her face had been beaming with the love she had for all her men who took turns twirling her around the ballroom in the castle. *Could I really love more than one man that much?* I knew I didn't want to lose any of them, and even though Paxton had only been around for a day or two, he seemed to fit the space his brother hadn't been able to. Even Zan, who'd come from another kingdom, had managed to find his place among my men in a way that just seemed to work. But could they each be okay with sharing *me* with each other? Soon enough, even my brain gave up trying to fight sleep, and I sighed into the warmth surrounding me, feeling safe and cared for.

Gentle fingers brushed along my cheek as I nuzzled into the warmth I was lying on, which made it hiss as my nose touched skin. "Damn, mouse, your nose is freezing," Cole muttered.

I froze as his voice rumbled under my ear, making me realize I was sprawled out on his chest with my face buried in his neck. Something shifted against my back as an arm and leg pulled me tighter. I got a cold nose to the back of my neck, followed by a deep sigh of warm air hitting my skin. Gavin had managed to wrap himself around me as I'd done to Cole who was practically bearing the weight of both of us. Carefully, I maneuvered my hand so I could push myself off Cole, but he didn't seem to like that idea very much and pulled me back down.

"Nope, too cold for you to move," he said, brushing my hair off my face. "Besides, you're kinda cute when you sleep. Did you know that you are an extremely aggressive cuddler? Once you were out, you latched on to me like a dog would a bone with meat still left on it."

"Don't act like you didn't enjoy every moment of it," Gavin voiced, lifting his head to peer over my shoulder. "She tried to roll over to snuggle with me, and you wouldn't let her. I don't want to hear you complain about shit."

"Oh, sounds like the prince is a little jealous about that," Cole taunted.

Gavin grinned at him and shook his head. "Nope, I have a whole new appreciation for Cassarah's assets and how they seem to fit in all the right places." Cole tried to smack Gavin, but he ducked behind me, using me as a shield.

"Well, that's my cue that it's time to get up," I announced as I wiggled out from between them. "We've got another long day ahead of us, so make sure you guys get the tent packed away once you're done arguing."

They looked at me, stunned, making me chuckle to myself as I slipped out of the tent. The sun was still hidden behind the mountains, telling me we hadn't slept in too late. As much as I wanted to get to Sheca, everyone needed their sleep. Showing up to Sheca half dead wouldn't do us any good in the long run. If we took longer than three days, so be it. The whole point of this was to keep my people safe. Pushing them to the limit wasn't doing that.

Taking in a deep breath of the cold morning air, I stretched, feeling far more rested than I should have for the condition I was in. Others were up and getting things packed away while kids huddled together, still wrapped in blankets, gnawing on their dried meat. A fire was lit this morning, but it was only to melt the snow so we could fill our water bags and give some to the horses. I made my way over to Inali, brushed her down, got her ready for another long day, and packed my things before I ate my meager breakfast. A shadow cast over the camp, making me look up. I saw Vasin and the next wave of dragon riders swooping in, making the children jump to their feet and wave excitedly. Tahir and Jade landed in a precarious space long enough for Jade to hop off before Tahir took flight again. Jade took a moment, scanning the area until his eyes landed on me. A smile grew on his face as he headed in my direction.

"Good morning, little bird," he greeted. "We've come back with another hundred dragons to take the rest of the kids and others without horses."

I moved forward, intending to hug Jade, having realized how much I missed him, but Paxton took that moment to fall out of the sky and land beside us, spooking Inali in the process. She reared and let out a shrill whinny, unsettling the other horses as they responded to her distress.

"What the fuck do you think you are doing?" Jade snarled at Paxton.

"Making an entrance, of course," Paxton said proudly. "I figured I would take a page out of our Queen's playbook and leap off my dragon instead of having her land, and it worked out quite well if you ask me."

"Seems like nothing has changed about you after all these years," Cole snapped as he walked up to Inali with a bag of grain, trying to settle her. "Always thinking about yourself, not giving a rat's ass as to who or what it might hurt in the process."

"Glad to see you are the same self-righteous asshole. Is Grandpa Ballard still greasing the wheels to get you the best jobs?" Paxton countered, a grin plastered on his face.

Cole dropped the bag of grain, but Abbott grabbed his arm, shaking his head. "It's not worth it, Cole."

"Ah, I wondered when the abandoned orphan of the Bronze Reapers was going to show up. Speaking of which, where is the lug and his cousin?" Paxton asked, looking around.

"You looking for us?" Dayson called, whipping a snowball at Paxton, dodging it at the last second.

"Now the gang's all here!" Paxton cheered. "My apologies. I didn't get a chance to greet all of you properly after saving our new queen from my twin. You see, the clan leaders needed their pound of flesh first, and then our lovely spitfire decided we needed to be on the run. Just so busy, busy, busy, but I have been looking forward to the warm greeting from you all after coming back from the dead and all."

He talked so fast that my brain had difficulty keeping up with everything he was saying, but it seemed everyone else was tracking just fine. None of them seemed thrilled to have him back from the grave, dashing my thoughts that things were going well between them. Had they been playing nice for my sake up until now? What changed from yesterday to today? Or was I the one who didn't see their true feelings until now?

"Wait, what did you say about the clan leaders?" I asked, cutting off whoever was going to speak next.

Paxton turned, giving me his full attention. "You didn't know? I thought for sure you asked them to interrogate me after you clocked me in the face to teach me a lesson."

"What did they ask you about?" I pressed, not liking that they would go behind my back and question one of my guardians. Sure, Paxton might have some history with the clans, but once he bore my mark, he was mine. They should have known better. They didn't do that with Zan, so why would they with Paxton... because of his father and brother? Still, why didn't they tell me?

"The typical... where I was, how I was not dead, did I plan to betray the clans and turn them over to Creisal since I'd been hiding out there. Oh, and they also wanted to know how I acquired Ninnat since she's a golden female and all," Paxton shared with a shrug. "I'm sorry I didn't tell you sooner. I honestly thought they would have told you what happened."

My hands balled into fists, wondering what else they might have done behind my back. The clan leaders had been spending a lot of time with King Edward and Queen Mary while Gavin hung out with his brother, Philip, who'd gone with the first group of dragons. It wouldn't do me any good to have this battle here. Once I was officially crowned in Sheca, I could restructure how things would work, blending the two groups together.

"Is there anything you told them that I should know about?" I inquired, rubbing my hand over my forehead.

Paxton dropped his gaze and kicked a stone with his foot before answering. "I was a spy for the Creisal, gathering useful information about the other countries. I knew about Henry and his movements before he infiltrated Norden."

My eyes widened. "Are you telling me that we could have avoided what happened at the castle if you'd actually come to find me right when you got your guardian mark?"

"I didn't know what it was at first," Paxton argued, trying to defend himself. "Once I did more research, I figured it out and then came to find you. But I was in Errit, talking to an old mercenary about it. I was too far away to get back any sooner than I did. You have to admit, it was pretty perfect timing too."

"Why can't things ever be simple?" I demanded, tossing my hands up in the air.

"Vasin, can you come get me? I need some space and advice."

"I can do that, Cass. Give me a moment to find a place to land."

Grabbing my rations, I marched off without giving any explanation to the guys. I felt someone following me and peered over my shoulder to see it was May. She kept a few paces back and didn't try to stop or talk to me, just keeping an eye on me. Vasin was in the air wheeling, looking for the best place to land which was easier now that most of the tents had been packed up. Once he was safely on the ground, I sped up. Reaching him, I hugged him, relieved to be able to escape everyone just for a bit.

"Can we fly around for a bit just until the other dragons have picked up the people they are going to take?"

"You may stay with me for as long as you like. I will never turn you away."

I climbed up and was strapping in when Paxton came running up. "Cassarah, wait! Please let me explain things to you better."

"Not now, Paxton. I just need a little space," I answered.

He tried to push the issue, but a snarl from Vasin stopped him dead in his tracks. "Cassarah, I'm sorry. I fucked up. You're right. I did know what the mark meant, and I ran from it. But I won't anymore. It's why I'm here with you."

Meeting his gaze, I could tell he was being earnest about his words, but I just needed some space. No matter what I was dealing with, it just seemed like the hits kept coming. Flying with Vasin helped to ground me. He was a wise sounding board who wasn't trying to manipulate me. That is what I needed right now. Paxton must have seen that in my look because he backed up and hung his head in defeat as Vasin took off.

Ten

Thank the Gods for Dragons

Vasin didn't press me to talk right away, allowing me to enjoy the sights around us as my mind calmed. It wasn't really the fact that Paxton didn't come to find me right away. It's not even that the clan leaders talked to him behind my back. What got me in that moment was the overwhelming feeling I was in over my head. I was twenty-one, unmarried, with no family around me, and they expected me to rule over a whole kingdom! I'd just wrapped my head around dealing with the small group of mercenaries hidden away in Norden. Now I was heading toward Sheca and a whole new ball of yarn to untangle. Every time I felt like I was getting a footing in what I was doing, it changed, and I was starting all over again. This time there was far more pressure, seeing as there was a prophecy written about me from hundreds of years ago that I had to live up to. It frustrated me even more that I kept having these moments of self-doubt. You'd think I'd be over that after all I've been through.

"Cass," Vasin spoke, nudging me to tell him what was wrong.

"How do I make all this progress and keep tumbling back down to where I started? Every time I get overwhelmed, I run. Why can't I get to the point where I can stand my ground and face whatever comes?"

"Do you truly think you are that scared girl who was secretly taken from her bedroom in the dead of

NIGHT? I CERTAINLY DON'T. WOULD SHE HAVE BEEN ABLE TO DO WHAT YOU DID BACK AT THE CASTLE, SAVING THOSE MEN OF YOURS? WHAT ABOUT FLYING OFF TO ANOTHER KINGDOM WITH THREE MEN AND A DRAGON TO BACK YOU AND BEG THEM FOR THEIR HELP?"

"I wasn't going to beg." I scoffed.

"YET ANOTHER BIT OF PROOF TO SHOW YOU HAVE GROWN FROM WHO YOU USED TO BE. THE CASSARAH I MET ON THE SANDS OF THE ROOST WOULD HAVE NEVER THOUGHT LIKE THAT."

He had a point. Going off to Sheca on the word of my guardian was an incredibly risky move, but I didn't hesitate once. *"So why am I running now?"*

"ONLY YOU CAN SAY, BUT PERHAPS EXPLAINING TO ME WHAT HAPPENED MIGHT HELP YOU UNDERSTAND YOURSELF BETTER."

"The morning started off really well for being in a small tent with three of us in it. I slept well and was warm. Gavin and Cole bantered some, but it wasn't out of anger. It was how Becka pokes fun at me. You know they don't mean any real insult, but they want to get a rise out of you for some odd reason."

"THEY SPENT THE NIGHT IN YOUR TENT?" Vasin's tone was that of a disapproving father, which made me chuckle.

"It happened because they gave up their tents to others. Apparently, I was the only one with space left."

"I DOUBT THEY LOOKED VERY HARD."

"Aren't you always the one telling me to let down my guard and take a chance for them to see the real me?"

"YES, WELL, I DON'T BELIEVE I TOLD YOU TO INVITE THEM INTO YOUR BED—"

"We had all our clothes on plus cloaks and blankets. Besides, I never would allow myself to end up in a compromising situation. I might

not be a noble lady any longer, but I was raised like one. My virtue will stay intact until I am properly joined to my partner."

"OR PARTNERS."

"How can that even happen if they hate each other? Just because Cole and Gavin are becoming friends doesn't mean it will happen with the rest of them."

"HAVE THEY SHOWN YOU PROOF THEY CAN'T BE FRIENDLY TO EACH OTHER?"

"There was a heated argument between Paxton and the others the moment he showed up this morning. I was talking to Jade when he literally dropped in from the sky, spooking the horses. Jade yelled, then somehow, all the others got involved in the argument as well. Seems like they have some history with each other from way back in the day."

"I SEEM TO REMEMBER WHEN ZAN SHOWED UP THAT JADE DIDN'T TRUST HIM EITHER. OUT OF ALL YOUR GUARDIANS, JADE IS THE MOST OVERPROTECTIVE, AND IT PRESENTS ITSELF WITH ANGER OR LASHING OUT. COULD IT BE BECAUSE ALL THEY RE-MEMBER IS THE BOY HE ONCE WAS? MAYBE THEY ASSUME HE IS THE SAME AS AN ADULT WITHOUT GIVING HIM A CHANCE?"

Hearing it spelled out that way, it was easy to see how that could happen. Many of my guardians seemed to have a quick temper when it came to me. Could it be as simple as having them get to know each other to calm things down? How did I do that before I was forced to pick my consorts?

"Vasin, you know the rules of coronation in Sheca. I have to pick."

"MY ADVICE ON THAT IS TO SIT DOWN WITH THEM AND EXPLAIN THE RULES AND THE POSITION YOU ARE IN. YES, TO BE CROWNED QUEEN, YOU HAVE TO AT LEAST HAVE ONE CONSORT, AND THAT RELATIONSHIP MUST BE CONSUMMATED, BUT THE LAW ALSO ALLOWS YOU TO TAKE AS MANY CONSORTS AS YOU WISH AFTER THAT. MY GUESS IS THEY WOULDN'T WANT YOU

feeling forced into a relationship with them if you're not ready for that. They care a great deal about you, Cass. Give them a chance to show you that."

"*So you don't think they'll be mad if I don't take them all right away?*"

"*Do you want to take them all?*"

"*No… at least not right now. I don't really know Zan and Paxton as well as the others. Cole and Abbott have been with me since the beginning, showing me time and time again I can trust them. I could see a deeper connection turning into real love like they talk about in books. Same with Jade. He gets under my skin and sees the real me. Even if we argue, I know it's because he's looking out for me or pushing me to do the right thing. Izel also has a special place in my heart along with Dayson. They are new and growing slower than the others, but I see what they can be with more time. Zan is such a mystery. He keeps holding back because of things I need to learn about Sheca, but he is easy to be with and so smart. Paxton, though, is the wild card. I mean, how can I even say there's a chance for a relationship when I've known him for all of two days, most of which we've been apart.*"

"*What about Gavin?*"

Just hearing his name made me smile. "*Gavin is my prince charming. I know that once he gives his heart to someone, it will be forever and in the most beautiful way. I just don't know if I feel worthy enough for that kind of love when I have feelings for other men too. That's the biggest part of this. I know I can choose more than one, but should I? Is that fair to them? Being queen in the middle of a war doesn't give me a lot of extra time to invest in multiple men. It would be selfish of me to promise them part of my heart when I don't know that I'll ever have time to give it.*"

"*My sweet, tenderhearted Cass, you are looking at this all wrong. A healthy relationship goes both ways.*

YOU ARE NOT RESPONSIBLE FOR THEIR HAPPINESS JUST AS THEY AREN'T RESPONSIBLE FOR YOURS. TOGETHER, AS A TEAM, YOU LEARN TO BUILD EACH OTHER UP AND SUPPORT ONE ANOTHER, BUT IT DOESN'T ALL FALL ON YOUR SHOULDERS. SOME DAYS YOU MIGHT NEED MORE ATTENTION FROM THEM, AND IN RETURN, THEY MIGHT NEED YOUR UNDIVIDED ATTENTION. IF YOU BUILD THE RELATIONSHIP ON THE RIGHT FOUNDATION, THEY WILL UNDERSTAND AND RESPECT IT, KNOWING THEY WILL GET THE SAME IF THEY NEED IT. IF ONE OF YOUR PARTNERS CAN'T DEAL WITH THAT, THEN THAT'S ON THEM, NOT YOU."

"*How do you make it sound so simple?*"

"*BECAUSE I'M LOOKING AT IT FROM THE OUTSIDE WITHOUT MY FEELINGS OR HEART ATTACHED TO THE SITUATION. IT'S ALWAYS EASIER TO BE ON THE OUTSIDE LOOKING IN THAN IT IS TO BE IN THE MIDDLE OF IT.*"

"*All right... since you're on a roll from your omniscient perspective, how would you deal with the clan leaders? I just found out they pulled Paxton into an interrogation and never once told me about it or what they learned from it.*"

"*I WOULD INFORM THEM THEY ARE NO LONGER NEEDED TO SERVE THE ROLE AND THAT THEY ARE IN UNDER THIS NEW RULE OF THE DRAGON QUEEN. ALTHOUGH, I SHOULD ADD THE CAVEAT THAT YOU WILL BE CREATING A GROUP OF ADVISERS INSTEAD. IF THEY WOULD LIKE TO PUT THEIR NOMINATION IN FOR THAT ROLE, YOU WILL CONSIDER IT AND INFORM THEM IF THEY GAIN THE POSITION OR NOT. PERSONALLY, I WOULD MAKE THE VICEROYS ALONG WITH SAL AS YOUR HISTORICAL ADVISERS LIKE THEY HAD SAL DOING PREVIOUSLY, IN ADDITION TO OTHER ADVISERS WHO CAN HELP IN OTHER WAYS.*"

"*Now why didn't I think of that?*" I huffed, seeing it as the perfect solution for what I would need and not to ruffle too many feathers along the way to a new way of doing things. *"Too bad I can't make you one of those advisers. You could teach them all a thing or two."*

"Yes, well, they wouldn't listen or trust my words the way you will. Such is the pair-bond between dragons and their humans, which I will forewarn you, there is much for you and the others to learn about."

"Delightful. Just when I thought I had enough on my plate to worry about."

"Since you are already bonded to a dragon, it won't be as large of a revelation as it will be for the others. I just wanted to alert you to the subject coming up in the near future. It explains how they have so many dragon riders versus what is happening in the rest of our world."

"That actually sounds like it would be beneficial, unlike some of the other dramas I've faced the last few days. If they had told me it would be this hard to be queen, I might have taken my chances in the wild."

Vasin just chuffed at me as he wheeled back over the camp below, watching people getting on dragons. *"Now that we've traveled this far, how long will it take for them to get back to Sheca?"*

"You could do two trips in a day if you wanted them to send back another group of dragons."

"If we could get everyone not on horseback to Sheca, then it would make the journey easier, and people would be less tired, making it safer."

"Does that mean you wish to return to camp?"

"Might as well. I won't let the rest of my people go alone with the clan leaders. It would prove they are still more in power than I am. It will already be hard enough to retrain them all out of that mindset after so many decades of them leading."

With a hum of acknowledgment, he descended into the pass, landing in an open spot that the previous dragon left open. I saw two teenage girls next in line to be placed on a dragon, so I waved them over once I slid off Vasin's back. "Come, let me introduce you to Vasin. He'll take good care of you on the way to Sheca." As they approached, the girls looked warily at Vasin, but he just settled on the ground, tucking his wings away, trying hard not to look intimidating. "Would you like to pet him? He loves to get his eye ridges scratched," I suggested as he swung his large head over for me to show them what I meant.

"He wouldn't eat us for touching him?" one girl asked, a quiver in her voice.

Smiling at them, I wrapped my arms around Vasin's snout and placed kisses on his scaled forehead. "Not at all. He is a gentle giant as long as you respect the fact he is an intelligent being. People get in trouble when they treat him like a horse or another pack animal that doesn't share the same level of understanding. He is like you and me in how he thinks, so treat him the same way, and you'll never go wrong with any dragon."

"Hello, Mr. Dragon... I mean, Mr. Vasin," the other girl greeted, bobbing a curtsy.

Vasin gave a soft, pleased trill as he nodded his head in return before extending his leg to make it easier for them to climb on. Giving one last confirming glance at me, they scampered up, and I helped walk them through how to attach the harness straps.

"Make sure to tuck your cloaks nice and tight around you. The wind gets even colder the higher you go," I warned, then gave them a wave as Vasin took off to join the other waiting dragons.

I felt someone step up beside me. The familiar presence alone told me who it was, so I relaxed. "Wasn't sure if you were going to come back or just leave us to deal with a group of sulking grown men for the day," Becka said.

"If I'm being honest, I wasn't sure if I was going to either, but then talking to Vasin always seems to put things into perspective," I shared. "How many do we have left on foot after this group heads out?"

"Hmm, I think a little under a hundred, but there won't be any more kids so that will help. This also means we will have plenty of tents if you don't want uninvited guests again," she mentioned with a sideways glance. "Unless you *enjoy* having them keep you warm."

Snapping my head to face her, I scowled. "What exactly does that mean?"

"Seems I was mistaken on how things went down last night. One could only hope you might be able to actually relax if a man blessed you with a few mind-blowing orgasms. Don't look at me like that. The men might be a pain in the ass to deal with, but orgasms are always worth it," Becka answered before she gave me a wink and headed off to the horses.

Unsure what to do with that statement, I decided to leave it alone. I wasn't ready to deal with that part of what it meant to be in a relationship. I was just trying to wrap my head around the emotional aspect, making me anxious. Thankfully, there were still a few more days before I had to cross that bridge.

Eleven

Let's Try and Make Friends

The second day was much like the first, but the ground was steadier since we were descending the mountain slope. The next peak we had to cross wasn't as steep or high so the last part of our journey would be easier, especially as we now had everyone on horseback. The second wave of dragons came to take the last of those on foot, leaving us with my guardians to watch over us in the air. Vasin suggested it might be wise to have someone hide near the fortress to let us know if the Lost King was ready to attack us like we assumed he would. Having this information would also let me know how much time we had before he would start looking for where we went and if he knew about Sheca.

I called a halt to our trip early when we found a basin with a river and flat land that fit all of us. This time, we lit fires and people gathered around them, warming themselves and chatting. Having spent most of my time with the clan leaders or my guardians, I felt like it was a good idea to travel and spend time at the various fires, listening to stories and learning more about my people. I don't know if Becka and May talked to the guys, but they gave me space, letting my two female guards keep an eye on me as I wandered through the camp. I settled at one that was mostly people around my age, trading stories of their first missions and the things they screwed up on.

"There I was hanging from the rafters, trying to pick the lock upside down, when the owner of the safe walked in on me. We both just stared at each other for a moment, shocked to find one another there. I almost burst out laughing at the look on his face," one man shared, chuckling as he told his tale.

"What did you do? Were you able to finish the job?" another asked, fully invested in the story.

The storyteller leaned forward as if he were going to tell us a secret. "I was in the wrong house. The one I needed to steal from was his neighbor. I misread the address of the home. All the houses in Errit are packed so close together it was a simple mistake. So, I hightailed it out of there, waited a few more days for things to settle down, and then went to the house I was supposed to be at."

Everyone cracked up while those closest slapped the man on his back in approval. Then all eyes turned to me, and I realized they were waiting for a story about my first job, but I didn't have one, not really.

"I haven't had an official first job yet. There was a group of us who went on a training exercise... capture the flag, and during that event I was kidnapped. Guess you could say that was a major failure seeing as I was far too trusting of those around me. One of my own clan was working for the Lost King and sold me out to gain favor. I woke up to find myself tied up in the back of a wagon, almost to the border of Errit, with no idea of what was going on," I recounted. This seemed to surprise everyone, but I guess those from the other clans didn't really know all that much about me.

"How did you get free?" someone asked.

Thinking back, that time seemed so long ago but, in reality, was only a little over a week. "From the information that was given to them, they knew I could communicate with Vasin silently through my mental connection being his pair-bond. To stop this, they drugged me for most of the trip. Once I woke up, they made sure I didn't try to reach out to him. I managed to do something they call a waking trance, where you keep your eyes open but zone out like you would when meditating. I reached out, searching for my connection with Vasin, but I was too far away. I then caught a flash of something's presence and assumed it was Vasin. The distance made it hard to connect. Well, it seems I actually was speaking to Tahir, Jade's dragon."

"No way!" one of the women called out. "You can talk to other dragons? I didn't think that was possible outside of the black dragon."

"Is that why they call you the Dragon Queen because you can communicate with other dragons besides your own?"

"I can't believe the Grim Reaper saved your life. He never does something without there being payment involved," a guy sneered.

It didn't take me long to see that the clans had a very poor opinion of Jade, but I knew who he really was and that there must be some reason that everyone saw him this way. Someday he would tell me his story, but I wouldn't press him for it. That didn't mean I would let others speak ill of him for no reason.

"Without even knowing who he was helping, Jade saved my life that night. Once I was free from the wagon, he had no reason to take it any farther, but he landed and came to check on me. Once he found out who I was, his only goal was to get me back to the clans safely," I defended.

"What she isn't telling you all is that our queen has a bit of a stubborn streak and wouldn't let me keep her safe until she understood what was going on," Jade interjected from where he appeared out of the shadows. "If she hadn't pressed the issue, we never would have discovered the Lost King or saved Prince Gavin."

"Are you telling me the two of you and a dragon attacked their camp?" the man who'd sneered at Jade helping me asked.

"That's exactly what she's saying and what we did. Of course, her blowing up the supply tent wasn't part of the plan but worked out well for causing a distraction," Jade boasted.

This seemed to get the whole group riled up, shooting questions at me left and right about the attack—how we managed to do it, if that's where I hurt my leg, and how we made it out of there alive. It would seem that this story I viewed as a failure was quite the opposite to them. Some of them moved closer, trying to get my attention from the others, making me start to feel very uncomfortable. I didn't think they meant me any harm, but the intensity I was getting from them was too much for me, and I didn't know how to stop it.

"Okay, that's enough story time from the queen," May cut in, silencing everyone. It seems they feared my guardian enough not to push the matter and gave me my space. "If you would like to hear more, then learn to mind your manners and not barrage her with stupid questions. She might look like you but remember she has us and a black dragon backing her up, so don't get any smart idea about cornering her." Turning to me, she held out a hand, helping me to my feet, and gave me a small smile as her eyes sparkled with humor.

May didn't give a rat's ass what other people thought of her as long as they didn't cause trouble. I had no doubt that if they started something, she would end it faster than they could remember their name. May was no lady-in-waiting like Becka could be. No, she was a warrior through and through, reminding me how lucky I was to have her at my back. She was hard to get to know, not really one to share or have *girl talk* with, but she proved to be in my corner with situations like this. Having her at my back meant I was safe no matter where I was, and that was something you didn't often find in another person.

We moved to another fire, and this one is where I found the clan leaders with their partners or other family members still with us. Ballard's wife, Helena, stood and hugged me, making me feel welcome as she pulled me to sit next to her.

"Goodness, child, you are a hard one to spend some time with these days," Helena teased as she squeezed my hand. "How exciting is it that we get to venture into a new land? Well, I guess it's new to us, seeing as this is where we originally came from. Is there anything you can share? I know what's said in your meetings is for the leaders' ears only, but I'm just bursting with curiosity."

I frowned at her as I looked at the other men around the fire, stopping on Ballard last. "They haven't told you anything?" I asked Helena, even though I was looking at her husband.

"Oh, it's nothing to fret over, dear. I'm used to finding out with everyone else what's going on around us," she shared, patting my hand, trying to ease my distress.

"Nothing that Zan or I have shared about Sheca was meant to be kept hidden from everyone." I shifted my gaze to Acton. "You weren't asking on behalf of your people you so claim to protect?"

"Your Highness—" Acton started to speak, but I held up a hand to stop him.

"No, I don't want to hear excuses from you or anyone else. You call me your queen, but I don't actually think you believe it or respect the title when it comes to me. I was just informed that Paxton was taken in and interrogated by you, but not once have you mentioned it to me. Now why would that be? Did you not question him in an effort to protect our people, or was it for some other reason that you felt the need to drill him for information? A trusting person might see these small missteps as nothing to worry about, but I am not that trusting or that stupid, which you would know if you paid attention to things other than your own status." I rose to my feet and looked all the clan leaders in the eye for a moment. "Consider this your final warning. The title of clan leader is no longer needed. Once we get to Sheca, things will change. You can change with them, or you can be left behind outside the circle of protection I offer. That is up to you. Goodnight," I retorted.

I went to walk away then paused as Helena reached out to me. "Might I have some of your time tomorrow?"

"I would enjoy that," I answered with a smile. "Until tomorrow, rest well and stay warm."

Deciding I was done interacting with people, I headed to the fire located near where my tent was set up, surrounded by my guardians. I plopped down on a folded blanket waiting for me, dropping my head into my hands and letting out an irritated grunt. Becka and May settled in beside me, lending their silent support while the rest of my guardians appeared out of the night to join us. After some time, I was tapped on the shoulder and handed a cup full of hot, sweet-smelling liquid. I took a sip, and it burned the tip of my tongue. I had to blow on it, but the warmth was welcome. It was thick and rich, made with chocolate and something else that added a bit of a kick to it that warmed my tummy when it hit.

"Make sure to drink that slowly so you don't get a hangover tomorrow," Dayson advised. "It's something we Bronze Reapers drink on those cold winter nights up in the mountains when we're snowed in for the day. Drink too much of it, though, and you'll be tossing off clothes faster than you realize, standing in the middle of a snowbank buck-ass naked."

May snorted. "I think you're the only one dumb enough to do that."

"Ha! I recall a time not so long ago when I caught you behind the woodshed with your tongue down someone's throat while his manhood was seeking shelter in a different hole," Dayson shot back.

"You're forgetting we ended up back at his home, where his wife joined in on the fun," May said with a grin. "Ah, the things *chatla* will open your mind to once it breaks down your inhibitions."

Intrigued, I leaned in and whispered, "You take both male and female partners to bed?" I'd heard of people doing this, not caring if they were the same sex or not, but it was never spoken about in the environment I grew up in.

"It's simple, Cassarah. I like who I like and love who I want to love. If they are willing, then so am I. The world puts too many rules in place. I feel like it's my duty to show others there is another way to live. It's not for everyone, but sometimes all a person needs is to know other like-minded people are out there," May explained. "Like you, not all women can take more than one love and have things work out. But you, you have such a large heart, you can't help but share it. The world will tell you it's odd or different, but I say follow your heart because your head isn't always right."

I sat there stunned at what she'd just said and how it seemed to hit home on one of the things I'd been worried about. I knew it was more accepted for me to take more than one lover, but that didn't mean everyone would agree. It had been centuries since Miranda and her men lived, and from what I've seen, most people only kept one partner. Yet here was May, unattached as far as I knew, taking life by the reins and doing what made her happy.

"Woman, I think that is the most I have ever heard you say at one time," Becka joked. "How much *chatla* have you had?" May just gave her a look that sent Becka into a fit of laughter as she brushed off the visual threat. "Down, girl, down. I'm just impressed, is all."

May's response was to grunt and sip her drink, ignoring my best friend completely. The interaction brought a smile to my face as I enjoyed the warm drink... carefully.

TWELVE

MEN AND MORNINGS

That night I spent it alone in my tent and discovered how much of a difference not having two other warm bodies in the space made. I swore I shivered throughout the night until I finally gave up and headed out of my tent to make some hot water, hoping it would help. The sun was far from rising and warming up the freezing air, but moving around had to be better than being a shivering ball on the ground. The fire was a glowing bed of coals as someone packed it in, preserving it to use in the morning which I was thankful for. I found a pot to heat the water in and trudged over to the river, slamming it on the ice to break it.

"You're awake early," Izel said, his calming voice fitting for the early quietness.

Dipping the pot, I filled it fairly full, unsure if anyone else would want something warm to drink. "I was so cold I couldn't sleep."

"One of us should have been with you. I knew the temperature was going to drop, I could feel it in my bones," he muttered to himself.

"Too late now. I'm already up, and moving around seems to be helping."

Izel took the pot from my hand and tucked me into his side so he could wrap part of his cloak around me as we walked back. "What were you planning to make with the water?"

"Nothing, really. I just hoped it would warm my hands along with my insides." I chuckled. "Not the best plan, but it was all I could think of to get warm fast."

He started to build up the fire and then set the pot in the center of the hot coals to heat. Without saying a word, he left and entered his tent. He returned with one of his packs and a blanket. Before I could object, he sat down, crossed his legs, and pulled me onto his lap, where he settled his cloak around my shoulders and added the blanket over my lap. Cocooned in warmth, Izel took one hand, started to rub the warmth back into it, and then moved to the next. "Better?" he asked, his lips brushing my ear.

Licking my lips which had suddenly gone dry, I managed a breathy, "Yes."

Once both hands were back to their normal temperature, he wrapped his arms around my waist and pulled me tight against his chest, dropping his chin over my shoulder in a tight hug. The silence between us was comfortable, and even though sitting in his lap wasn't what I would normally have allowed, it was the warmest I'd been all night since I went to bed. Izel was a man of honor, but I could tell from where I sat that he was pleased with me being this close. I might not have ever experienced a man before, but I did study anatomy and had lessons on how children were made. I wasn't completely ignorant. As if he sensed where my mind had wandered, he shifted his head so his nose ran up along my neck until it reached behind my ear, where he placed a soft kiss.

I let out a sigh as my body relaxed into his, giving him the encouragement he needed to place another kiss a little farther down, taking his time and allowing me the chance to object as he kissed along my neck then back up to trail down my jawline. Turning to face him, he caught my lips with his, allowing me to set the pace, never once pushing me for more, just enjoying the sensation between us.

His hands released their hold and slipped under my shirt until they rested on the bare skin of my ribs. I tensed, and he paused, holding perfectly still, waiting for me to decide whether we continued. I pulled back and looked into his stunning dark eyes that held such tender emotions as they looked back at me.

Just as I was about to speak, Dayson emerged from one of the tents, scratching and yawning loudly. He caught sight of us and froze as if he wasn't sure what to do now that he spotted us. "Ah... I'm gonna go back to bed... yeah, that's what I'm gonna do..."

"Day," I called, shifting so I was once again sitting with my back to Izel's chest. "It's fine. Come join us. The water is boiling."

Izel pressed a lingering kiss to my neck and let his fingers play along my ribs before he removed them and lifted me so he could stand. He took a moment to adjust things before he stepped out from behind me. "I have tea leaves and thought I would make a pot. You want some, Dayson?"

"Of the tea or..." he asked, his eyes flicking to me then back to Izel with a knowing smirk.

"I cannot speak for others, but I can offer you tea at the moment," Izel answered, not at all playing into Dayson's suggestion.

The large man let out a sigh. "Then tea will have to do, but I'm going to claim your spot since you got up."

Not catching on to what he meant, I let out a yelp as Dayson scooped me up and settled on the ground with me perched in his lap. Too stunned at the turn of events, I lost my chance to get up without causing a fuss as the blanket was tucked in around us.

"Man, no wonder why you two were so snuggled up. This is the warmest I've been in days. These mountains are fucking cold," Dayson grumbled, and he buried his face into the crook of my neck.

Once again, I squeaked as his freezing face touched my skin, making my body shiver in response to the abruptness in temperature change. "You're freezing!"

"Why do you think I'm huddling for warmth, Cassy-bear? A man could lose his nose in weather like this if left cold for too long. I had to find someplace warm to hide it," he answered, his words muffled by my skin.

"I'll bet that's not the only thing of yours that wants to find a warm place to hide," Paxton said as he poked his head out of the tent Dayson just left.

Izel grabbed Paxton by the hair and yanked him out of the tent before I could even understand the true meaning of Paxton's words. "You dare to speak about your queen in such a manner? Being her guardian means you protect her from anything that could harm her body and mind. Cassarah is an honorable woman and will be treated as such. Do you hear me?"

It was moments like these I was reminded my guardians were more than meets the eye. Izel was quiet and observant, but I knew he was lethal with any blade he could get his hands on. Paxton was still alive because Izel wished to keep him that way, and that made me oddly trust him even more. While Paxton and Cole were rasher with their emotions, Izel was beyond controlled. You didn't know what he was thinking or feeling unless he decided to show it.

"What the hell, man?" Paxton spluttered as he kicked out, hitting the back of one of Izel's knees. Unfortunately, he wasn't fast enough, and Izel dropped and swiveled to put Paxton into a headlock with his other leg resting on his throat. The more Paxton fought, the more he would just cut off his air supply.

"You aren't the master of your own life anymore. Once that mark showed up on your arm, Cassarah became your master. It is better to curb this attitude of yours now than to have it cause problems for us later when her life might be in danger," Dayson spoke up after he lifted his head to see what was going on.

Paxton tapped furiously at Izel's leg, trying to get him off by showing he was giving in to the takedown. When Izel stood, freeing Paxton's airway, Paxton gasped and rolled onto his side, coughing as he sucked air back into his lungs. Finally back to breathing normal, he pushed himself up and glared at the two men. "How dare you assume to know a damn thing about me or what I think. Yeah, I might not have been thrilled to have the mark show up on my arm and be dragged back into this mess, but it's because of people like you assholes. Since when did all of you become so uptight? Doesn't anyone know how to take a joke anymore? Or is it just because I said it?"

He had a point. Dayson had also been making suggestive comments before Paxton appeared out of the tent. Hearing what was happening might have made him feel more comfortable to make such jokes, thinking I was all right with it.

"Paxton, what do you know about me?" I asked, drawing all their attention.

"Ah, well..." Paxton started running his hand through his hair. "Not a whole lot. Just that you are paired with the black dragon and didn't grow up in the clans."

"If I didn't grow up in the clans, where might you guess I was raised?" I questioned, curious as to what his thought process was.

He looked at me with his pale blue eyes like I was asking him to tell me what the weather was in Sheca. "In Norden somewhere, maybe a farmer or someone in Royal City. I don't know what this has to do with anything?"

"It has everything to do with everything, Pax," I announced, getting a raised brow from him. "I was raised as a noble woman, and I'd just been presented at court to the king and queen when the dragon eggs started to hatch. Cole had to come and steal me out of my home because my parents refused to give me up since the Crown had shown interest in me. My value has always been in my virtue and who I marry, along with having a boy to secure the lineage of whomever I was married off to."

Paxton gaped at me then looked at the other two men. "You've got to be shitting me! A noble woman turned queen of the mercenaries… how the fuck does that even happen?"

"You said it yourself. The black dragon chose me, the first in centuries to appear, in fact My parents refused to believe the pair-bond with Vasin was real and locked me away, hoping it would be forgotten. Well, that is until Queen Mary thought it would be a good idea to make me a potential bride to one of her sons."

As if on cue, Gavin appeared, having refused to leave with the rest of his family and taking the long way with us. "Isn't it interesting that the first time I met you was the day you came to rescue Vasin from Lord Everett? I should have known then that being around you would never be boring. Seeing as I'm now one of *your* consorts, things worked out the other way around, didn't it?"

"Hold up. The crown prince is a consort to *our* queen?" Paxton blurted. "I seriously shouldn't have run off to Errit. I'm behind on everything."

"See, I'm not the crown prince anymore. I gave that up to my brother so I could be the ambassador between our two kingdoms," Gavin explained. "I never wanted to be king, so this turned out for the best."

Paxton rubbed his hands over his face as he tried to wrap his brain around all of this. "Okay, so Cassarah was raised as a noble woman then was brought to the clans… how did that go?"

"Not at all how I thought. I was given a year to learn everything you all spent your childhood training for. I was to go on a job to prove I could be one of the people. Getting kidnapped by the Lost King put a bit of a wrench in that plan, but it led us to discover his presence. When I blew up his camp and saved Gavin, I found out the clans had moved to the mountains. From there, I think you know the rest with the alliance and then the battle we lost," I answered.

By now, the rest of my guardians had awoken and joined us as Izel passed out cups of tea to everyone. They seemed to catch on to what we were talking about and were content to listen in as Paxton came to terms with everything I told him.

"No wonder the clan leaders don't respect you. Their worst nightmare rode in on the back of a black dragon and stripped them of everything in one swift moment. It also makes more sense why you wouldn't be as comfortable with vulgar language and the like from us. I apologize if I made you feel uncomfortable. I might have been around the snobs of Creisal, but I didn't make any friends there for a reason. You'll have to be patient with me as I learn how to act around a lady, but feel free to hit me again if I offend you. Sometimes it's the only thing that gets through my thick skull," Paxton said with a sigh.

"Don't worry. We will be more than happy to help you out with that," Cole answered with a grin.

"Leave it and drink your tea," Jade ordered, cutting off whatever Paxton was going to say next. "We have the last stretch of this jour-ney, and then we'll be in Sheca. There will be time enough later to deal with our own issues once we get everyone settled."

They all grunted their agreement and did as they were told, mak-ing me smile behind my cup at how they would work together for the good of our people.

Thirteen

Hidden Enemies

I couldn't be more thankful to be out of the peaks and on the last leg of the trip into the valley. The weather turned warmer, and I could finally shed my thick cloak and let the sun warm my face and thaw out the rest of me. We'd decided to break for lunch to give the horses a rest with the downhill work they were doing as we zig-zagged over the terrain. Vasin and the other of my men with dragons went ahead to Sheca to let everyone know we were almost there. While we rested, Helena came to join me, reminding me that she'd asked to speak with me today, piquing my curiosity.

"It will be good to be someplace we can finally settle into. It's been many years since I've spent my days on horseback, and my rump is reminding me of the good old days," Helena said with a chuckle.

"I couldn't agree more. Even though I'd been training, I don't think I was ready for this long journey, either," I shared, tearing off a chunk of dried meat to chew on. "I also wouldn't mind having something else to eat. Three days of leather is about all I can manage."

We fell into a simple silence. I could tell she was on the verge of telling me what she wanted to talk about but was searching for the right way to start. Shifting so I was facing her, I reached out and took her hand in mine, causing her to look at me. "Helena, whatever it is, you can tell me. You and Ballard have been nothing but kind and welcoming to me since I arrived. If there is something I can do to help, I will."

"Bless you, child, but I'm not worried about me. It's you I'm worried about," she said, patting my hand. "The other clan leaders don't agree with this plan of combining our groups, and I fear they are going to cause trouble."

I knew they weren't fans of the idea, but the fact she was worried enough to bring it up caught me by surprise. "Helena, what do you know?"

"Strictly speaking, I don't *know* anything because it is forbidden for my husband to tell me what happens between clan leaders." She paused and looked around as if to make sure we weren't being overheard. "Although the other night, Ballard might have been talking in his sleep and mentioned something about finding a way to keep you from becoming queen. They know that he supports you. They have been leaving him out of the loop on a fair amount of things, but he did catch part of a conversation they were having with the Norden king and queen about how it might be better for them to ally with someone other than the child who was ruling at the moment."

"Are the rest of the leaders in agreement on this choice?" I asked, fear sitting in my stomach like a rock.

"That's something I don't know and haven't been able to glean from other sources. But I can tell you that Acton is not voicing an opinion either way. He keeps his thoughts to himself for the most part, where Xio, Garold, and Porvan have always been more vocal. No matter what the vote was, no one ever knew which way he would lean until he gave his official vote. From what I know about Acton, he doesn't rush into his choice and gives people a fair chance to prove themselves," she explained, watching my expression closely. "My biggest fear is that they won't follow the rules and will make a deal without taking it through the proper channels. Things are tense with the king and queen when it comes to you. I heard about how you handled things with them before we all left, and that did not go over well with them."

Reaching out, I pulled Helena into a hug. "Thank you for coming to me about this, but for your own safety, I need you to stay out of it. Now that I have the information and know to be on the lookout, I'll take it from here. You and Ballard have given so much to these people, and I know you want the best for them as do I."

"Cassarah, you remind me so much of my daughter, Cole's mother, and I don't think I could bear losing you like we did her," Helena shared, pulling back to cup my face in her hands. "Promise me you will be safe and don't trust anyone but your guardians and Gavin. Not even me or Ballard when it comes to the clan leaders. They have remained in power for as long as they have for a reason, but once they view you as a threat, nothing will stop them."

"I won't let them take this from me. I've fought too hard to get where I am to have it stripped from me so easily," I told her, my voice firm with resolve. "I am the Dragon Queen, and they will come to respect that."

Moving on to lighter topics, I shared with her what I knew about Sheca and the people I'd met so far until Cole came up to us. "Sorry to be the one to cut in on girl time, but if we want to make it there with any light left, Zan said we should be heading out."

"That's a fair call. This break took longer than I planned," I agreed, holding out a hand for him to help me up.

His hand wrapped around mine, but I should have been prepared when I saw the glint of mischief in his eyes. Tugging on my hand with far more strength than he needed to, I stumbled right into his chest with a squeak as he closed his arms around me so I didn't bounce off him. "Would you look at that. It seems I caught myself a little mouse. You know it's getting rather hard to do that these days."

"Don't tease her, dear boy, or you'll end up at the end of the list when she wants to spend alone time with someone," Helena teased, patting him on the back as she headed off.

Ignoring his grandmother, he kept his attention on me. "What did she want? Looks like you had quite the conversation when she first sat down with you."

"How would you know that? Were you stalking me?" I gasped overdramatically.

"Mouse, you should know by now that even when you think you're alone, we always have eyes on you. What kind of guardians would we be if we left you unprotected?" Cole pointed out.

After what Helena just told me, I was more grateful for this than they realized. "We can't talk here, but tonight we all need to gather so I can share what your grandmother shared with me," I whispered.

"Are you in danger?" Cole demanded, his body going rigid.

"I have a feeling that I'll always be in danger, Cole, but I don't think this danger will act in the next day or two," I answered, letting my head fall to rest on his chest. "Let's just pray we can get to Sheca in one piece so we can deal with the rest of the problems we have going on around us."

Cole tightened his hold and wrapped his body around mine as if he could infuse me with his strength. It was exactly what I needed at that moment, giving me the courage not to be okay for a moment as I gripped his shirt in my hands like a lifeline. "You sure you want to take on more of this craziness by becoming one of my consorts?"

"No place I'd rather be than guarding your back and keeping the crazy at bay. Not that your front isn't nice too, but it's not as romantic to say." Cole smirked as he pulled me back, bent his head, and placed a soft kiss on my lips. When he pulled away, I chased after him, wanting more. This caused him to chuckle. "Sorry, little mouse, but we have to keep it proper for the prying eyes around us and the fact we laid into Paxton about being respectful."

Sighing, I pouted a moment then stepped out of his arms. "You lot are going to need to deal with that situation. I can't have you fighting among yourselves."

"I agree. Discord between us makes us weak, but we'll get it figured out soon enough. I promise," Cole said with resolve. "Come on, Your Highness. Let's get you to your new kingdom so we can finally get a bed to sleep in tonight."

This caused me to laugh which was the goal, lightening my worry as we all mounted up and continued on our way to our new home.

We made excellent time with everyone—man and animal—refreshed from our long break and the ground leveling out, becoming softer under foot. The sky was clear, and even as the sun was waning, the air was warm, giving us a boost as well. The dragons above started to dart about, playing in the air currents, making me smile as I could feel Vasin's joy at having other dragons around. They were a creature of community, and even though he was my pair-bond, I couldn't give him the connection the others of his kind could.

Zan had flown ahead but came back, only this time he was on horseback, wearing a wide grin as he rode alongside me. The entrance to the valley, in true mercenary fashion, wasn't one you could spot easily, so having him navigate made it much easier. Working our way through the tight zig-zag pass of the final mountain ridge that guarded the valley from sight, I couldn't help but gasp at the sight before us. Seeing it from the air was stunning, but there was something about viewing it from eye level that showed the true vastness of the land before my very eyes. Everything was so green, and the earth under our horses' hooves smelled so rich and fresh that it astounded me this could have been kept a secret for so long.

The wide dirt road led us into the village where everyone was out, lining the path, waving and shouting their greetings. It would seem that what the viceroys had shared about most people being excited about finding the Dragon Queen was true. Flower petals rained down from the rooftops where kids tossed them from windows, trying to get a better vantage point for our procession. As if she knew what was going on, Inali started to prance under me, tossing her head so her mane blew in the wind like a conqueror returning from war. I couldn't help but laugh as I waved to all the people we passed until we paused at the end of the village right before the road took us to the castle.

"Wait here. The viceroys wanted to come out and make a statement before you ride up to unlock the castle," Zan said, keeping his voice low. "They feel like it's the easiest way to prove your claim as the Dragon Queen."

"Is it really going to be that simple?" I asked, feeling nervous about the situation.

"Guess we'll find out together," he answered, sitting up tall as the three older men came out of the main building wearing the same different colored robes as when I'd first met them. I noticed Sal was with them, now wearing a black robe made in the same style as the others.

They walked up to a small deck that was built off to the side of the building for announcements such as this. Lawrence stepped up to the railing and raised his hands, drawing everyone's attention as the bell rang in the loft above. "People of Sheca, today is a day many of us thought we'd never see. Not only has the Dragon Queen herself come to take her rightful place, but our people are also now whole again as those who left have now returned home. In honor of this auspicious day, we will celebrate with a feast for all those who call the valley of Sheca their home. But that is not all. Our queen will once again open up the Dragon Castle, declaring our kingdom whole once more!" The crowd burst into excited yelling and clapping. Some even started to jump about, unable to contain their joy at this news. "Queen Cassarah, will you do the honors of showing us your key to the castle before you make the trek up there?"

Surprised by the request, I pulled it out of my shirt and slipped it off, holding it up for everyone to see—not that they could see it well. Part of me was leery, not wanting people to steal it, but since it never left my neck, I guess it wasn't that big of a deal. As the crowd settled down, a wagon appeared, and the four men climbed into it and led the way up to the castle. I fell in line behind it with my guardians. Peering behind me, I saw the rest of the people following us, not wanting to miss out on the big event.

Though the trail was clear and easy to travel, it was deceptively farther than I originally thought. Thankfully, we made it back in time to still have a fair amount of sunlight left because once we got to the top of the overgrowth of plants, it made it tricky to navigate, not knowing what might be hiding under the tall grass and moss. The castle was free of any clinging plant life, but the drawbridge didn't get quite the same attention. The wagon stopped before it, and they all got out. I dismounted and walked up to see what we were dealing with. Many of the boards looked fine, weathered and warped, but only a few were to the point of rotting.

"The drawbridge was redone about seventy years ago, according to our records," Mathew shared as he tapped a foot on one of the slats. "I think if we cross on foot, it will be fine, but it should be at the top of the repair list, don't you think, Your Majesty?"

Peering over the edge at the depths below that would end in almost certain death if you were to fall, I said, "That is one thing we can absolutely agree on."

I went to venture forward when someone grabbed my shoulder and pulled me back. "Not so fast, little bird. I think your guardians should be going ahead of you to check for the safest route," Jade decided, his voice rumbling in my ear, not wanting us to be overheard. "It wouldn't be good for people to see you taking unnecessary risks, let alone us allowing it."

"As usual, Jade, your overprotectiveness is deserved," I said, looking up at him. "Does that mean you volunteered to go first?"

He narrowed his eyes at me, telling me the smirk I was trying to keep off my face wasn't happening. "You're lucky you're as cute as you are, you know that? I'm going to end up with a head full of gray hairs trying to keep you out of trouble. I can feel it. Come on, Dayson, you're doing this with me," Jade called as he stepped around me, pushing me against another of my guardians. "Izel, I trust you'll keep her out of trouble long enough for us to get across this damn bridge."

"I will endeavor to do my best," Izel answered, making me giggle.

Jade grunted as he stepped onto the bridge after Dayson. "Follow where we go and nowhere else. You hear me, little bird?"

"Who's supposed to be the one in charge here?" I inquired as I started to cross.

"When it comes to your safety, that would be us," Cole called from behind. "Now do as you're told, *Your Highness.*"

Crossing the bridge was uneventful, and there was only one section of boards we needed to be careful of. Otherwise, it wasn't in terrible shape. Jade and Dayson hacked away at some of the bushes and other greenery that tried to take back ownership of the path to the front of the castle. Finally, we reached the first obstacle—the metal portcullis that sealed the entryway to the castle itself.

"Do you know where the key is supposed to go at this point?" I asked, turning to the viceroys.

"First, you have to break the magical barrier, then you can find the place to put the key... or at least that is what the texts say," Eleazar explained.

Okay, so clearly they did not have the answer to my question, but I knew who would. *Vasin, how exactly am I supposed to get into the castle?*

"You will need to use your magic to break the protective shield over the metal first, then it will open for you. Once you are inside the courtyard, the key will open the door to the castle directly."

"All right, how do I break the shield?"

"Fight magic with magic, dear Cass. It's the only thing that can break it."

"Sure, why not."

Taking a few steps back, I fell into my archery stance and looked at the others with me. "You might want to back up. I'm not sure how this will go."

Wisely, they heeded my words and backed up so they were more directly behind me. Taking a deep breath, I called on my Birthright and drew back the shimmering blue arrow from the bow my magic produced. Letting out my breath, I sent the arrow sailing right into the middle of the portcullis, praying it wouldn't explode on us like the doors of the roost had when I freed Vasin. The arrow buried itself into the metal and stopped, just sitting there doing nothing. *Maybe it needed more magic?* I drew back and hit the same spot, but this time I pushed more power into it, and that did the trick. As if the seal on a water skin had been broken, air burst from inside, knocking us all off our feet as a shimmering blue light floated on the wind like snow. The portcullis had vanished, and we now had entrance into the Dragon Castle.

Fourteen

Feasts and Foreboding

"**Y**ou all right?" Abbott asked as he reached down to pick me up.

"Fine, just wasn't expecting that. Although, compared to the other times I broke a seal, that was fairly tame," I answered, dusting myself off.

"Does this sort of thing happen around you often, Your Majesty?" Lawrence asked, sounding a little concerned.

Looking back, I found my guardians helping them to their feet, their robes in disarray, making them look rather flustered. "I wouldn't say *often*, but surprisingly more than I expected."

"We will keep that in mind the next time we decide to join you on an event like this," Eleazar muttered, shaking out his red robe.

My gaze was caught by Gavin, whose eyes shimmered with laughter at the situation. I gave him a knowing smile before I turned back to the castle. Now that the protective shield was off, the abandoned-looking castle was gone, and in its place was something that looked like it was just built. Unlike the castle in Norden, where it was spread out over vast amounts of land, this one went up almost like it was trying to blend into the surrounding mountains. The spires got lost in the clouds hanging around the mountain peaks that the sun hadn't quite chased away while its cream-colored stone stood out against the cold gray around it.

Passing through the gateway and into the courtyard, I felt like I was transported to the time when this castle was left. The cobblestone under my feet showed no signs of aging whatsoever, and as I tilted my head back to see the main portion of the castle with its glass windows and red-painted wooden shutters, I was awestruck. The castle was made out of some kind of cream-colored stone accented with a wrought-iron railing and art in the form of the mercenary crest of the dragon wrapped around a sword. Besides the castle's main structure, the outbuildings were closed up so I couldn't tell what they were. I was dying to explore them. I found the main entrance with its thick wooden doors reinforced with metal and a large crest set into the stone above it with an inscription written on the arch just below it—*Though Disgraced, We Rise.* In those words, I could feel the true heart of the first king who created these people and had been chased out of his kingdom after saving them all. They had been disgraced, looked down upon, and seen as a threat to be hunted. Here in Sheca, they rose again to create a kingdom that has prospered without aid for five hundred years. Now I was going to unlock all their secrets and make it even better than it was before.

In the center of the door, I could see the keyhole. I stepped up the stairs and stood before the next stage in my life. Once this was open, there was no returning to how things had been. Slipping the key off my neck once again, I inserted it and turned, the lock moving smoothly like it hadn't been left sitting all these years. With a click, one part of the lock opened revealing another that I had to pull the key out and lay it flat to fit into the space and rotate in a clockwise manner. Then a *thunk* sounded, and the door started to give. It was a heavy door, and it took me putting my entire body weight behind it to push it open, revealing the entryway to the castle. Darkness greeted me as I peered past the door since all the shutters were closed so only small shafts of light filtered in.

"Your Majesty, I'm sure you are eager to explore the castle, but I think it's best if we leave it for tomorrow. The sun is fading fast, and I, for one, would rather make it back down alive for the feast," Eleazar spoke from behind me. "We came to do what we needed. Now, let's celebrate with the feast our people have been hard at work making."

As much as I didn't want to leave the castle, I understood that once I stepped through this door, I wouldn't be emerging for quite some time after. Locking the door now that it wasn't protected by the magical barrier, I followed the others back through the court-yard. The guys insisted on the same procedure of crossing the draw-bridge, muttering about needing to get it fixed *soon*. Being the valiant men they are, they assisted the viceroys and Sal back into their wagon where Lawrence once again stood to address the people.

"You have now witnessed the Dragon Queen unlocking the Dragon Castle's magical barrier. The exploration of the castle will begin another day because we have a feast to attend!"

The crowd sent up another roar of excitement as they turned to head back down to the village. Giving them a chance to get a head start, I stood next to Inali and stroked her neck as she relaxed after our journey.

"Are you doing all right?" Gavin asked, coming to stand next to me.

I answered with a shrug. I didn't really know how I felt. What I did know was that spending the night at a feast with people I didn't know if I could trust wasn't my idea of a good time. I still didn't get the chance to talk to my guardians about what Helena said yet, and it looked like this might be the best time. Once we returned to the village, I would be surrounded by people who wanted my attention.

"Cassy, are you coming?" Sal called from his place in the wagon.

"You go on ahead. I just need a moment after using that much magic," I offered as an excuse.

He narrowed his eyes at me, knowing what I did wouldn't take it out of me, but he just nodded, keeping his thoughts to himself.

Once we got some distance from them, I turned to face all of my guardians and Gavin. "We need to talk."

"That is never good," Paxton groaned, causing the others to glare at him. "What? Trust me when a woman says, *'we need to talk,'* nothing good comes out of her mouth."

Becka just rolled her eyes and looked at me. "So, is he right?"

"Well, what I have to tell you isn't great news..." I offered.

"See! What did I say... nothing good, ever?" Paxton grumbled.

"Love, I think it's best if you just say what you need to say since some of us can't handle the tension," Gavin suggested, nudging me with his shoulder.

I let out a sigh. "Helena told me that the clan leaders are working with King Edward and Queen Mary to keep me from becoming queen and making an alliance among themselves."

Clearly, this had not been what they were expecting me to say by the stunned expressions on their faces. Many of them quickly morphed into anger, especially Gavin, whose hands balled into fists and his jaw clenched.

"Are you positive?" Izel pressed.

Knowing that their fathers were the clan leaders, I could see why they wouldn't want to believe this bit of information, but I knew Helena wouldn't have brought it up if it wasn't important. "She couldn't tell me much since they have been edging Ballard out of the conversations. What she could tell me sounded pretty legitimate. I had an altercation with them before we left the fortress, and they were not happy with me forcing their hand. Garold wanted to stay behind with whoever didn't want to leave, but he hadn't thought that whole idea through."

"Can they do it? Could they keep you from becoming queen?" Abbott asked.

"No," Zan interjected. "With everything that's just happened, there is no way they will change the opinion of the viceroys or the majority of the people here in this village. If they tried, it could turn into a battle between both factions of our people."

"Fucking hell," Cole muttered, rubbing his hands over his head. "How did we jump from one fire into another?"

I turned back to face the castle, taking in its beauty in the setting sunlight. "I should have been prepared for this, especially after what I told them last night. It will have only made matters worse, calling them out like that."

"Last night? What did you do last night?" Paxton asked.

"She told them they were losing their positions once she became queen," Jade shared, crossing his arms, his face tight with anger. "They were withholding information from the people to make them more wary of coming here to Sheca and hiding the fact they questioned Paxton. When our little bird learned about it, she spanked them like the children they are acting like, setting them straight."

Paxton let out a long whistle in amazement. "Damn, spitfire, you sure have some balls on you to draw the line in the sand like that. I would have waited until I was queen, then told them to kick rocks."

"Yes, well, sometimes my anger gets the best of me, and I lash out. Something you have personally experienced, I believe," I stated.

"Got to be honest, I'm a little sad it's fading so fast. I feel like I might need to piss you off again so I can keep it," Paxton mused out loud as he stroked his cheek.

"Fucking idiot," Cole muttered under his breath. "So what do we do now? How can we go and have a feast with everyone when anyone could come out of nowhere and stab you in the back?"

"Hence, the reason that I am bringing this up to all of you," I pointed out. "Ballard is against it. Porvan is no longer a clan leader, but I have a feeling Garold and Xio are driving this movement. Acton is the only one no one has a feeling about, so maybe I should see if I can get a chance to talk to him alone?"

"Huh," Jade barked. "That pompous prick won't support anything if it involves me, including you becoming queen, little bird. He has a large grudge against me for what happened to our father, but he doesn't know the whole story. In fact, he refused to let me explain myself at all."

"So what you're saying is it would be best to have you elsewhere when I try?" I ventured.

The look he sent my way was a halfhearted glare at best. He knew I wasn't trying to be mean. I needed to talk to Acton to get the information I needed on the situation since they were blocking Ballard out.

"Looks like we better get down to the feast then so we can get ahead of this problem," Gavin suggested, moving toward the horse he'd been riding.

I reached out and grabbed his arm, turning him to face me. "They are your parents, but they are not you. What they do doesn't reflect on who you are to me or anyone else in this group. You've made it very clear your intentions are in support of me and my people. I'm also willing to bet so is Phillip. Don't go looking for more in this matter unless you are ready to see that side of your parents because once you see it, you can't unsee it. I should know."

Gavin pulled me into a hug and kissed my forehead. "You are more than I or this world deserve."

"It's because of people like you who believe in me. Without that, I wouldn't have the chance to do anything to help these people," I shared as I pulled back from him. "Let's get this over with so we can get to bed and explore the castle tomorrow."

"Sounds like a great plan to me, Your Majesty," he said with a wink.

With the villagers already in full swing of the feast, it wasn't hard for us to filter into the crowd, get some food, and find a place to eat. Those I'd traveled here with didn't really pay us any mind, but the people of Sheca were another story. Person after person came up to our table bowing, sharing their names, who they were, what they did, and how honored they were to have the Dragon Queen back in Sheca Valley. This meant that my plan to move through the crowds until I found Acton wasn't going to work, but as I kept an eye out, I couldn't spot any of the clan leaders or King Edward and Queen Mary. Phillip had joined us earlier, saying we were far more interesting to spend time with than his parents but didn't mention them leaving for the night.

"Vasin, are the king and queen's dragons still here?" I asked, fearing they might have left while we were all distracted.

"THEY ARE NOT HERE, CASS, AND I MIGHT MENTION THAT NAYTAN, ALONG WITH A FEW OTHERS, HAVE LEFT AS WELL."

"Goddammit! Could this be it? Are they planning our demise as we speak? Did the other clan leaders leave with them?"

"NOW THAT YOU ASK, YES, THEY DID. I'VE BEEN KEEPING AN EYE OUT AROUND THE BORDER LANDS TO MAKE SURE THE LOST KING DIDN'T SEND DRAGONS TO SEARCH FOR US. GIVE ME A

MOMENT, AND I WILL FIND THEM. IT IS EASIER FOR ME TO STAY HIDDEN THAN THE OTHERS."

I searched around me and found three of my guardians right away. "Jade, grab the others. We need to get out of this crowd and over to where the dragons can grab us."

"What's wrong?" he countered.

"No time, just grab the others and meet us at the edge of the village," I ordered, shoving him on his way. "Izel, Zan, let's go. We've got a problem to deal with."

Fifteen

Deal with a Dragon

My adrenaline coursed through my veins as I pushed through the crowd and emerged on the other side. I moved as quickly as I could to the edge of the village without looking like something was going on. Darting behind one of the large barns with bleating sheep, we waited for the others to show up. Zan tried to get me to tell them what was happening, but I refused. It was easier to give the information once to all of them. Besides, I still needed to hear back from Vasin on what the hell was happening. Anxiety prickled along my skin, making it hard not to fidget, but I did my best by wrapping my arms around myself to keep them still. Finally, Jade appeared with the others, all of them looking worried. Unfortunately, Phillip came along with them.

"Cassarah, what the hell is going on?" Cole demanded, coming to stand right in front of me.

"They're gone," I answered.

Cole placed one hand on my shoulder, and the other gripped my chin, forcing me to look at him. "Who's gone? You're going to need to spell it out for us."

"The clan leaders, Gavin's parents, and Naytan, the sec-ond-in-command of the military here in Sheca," I explained, his touch grounding me. "What if they are going to the Lost King?

Giving me and Sheca up in exchange for getting their kingdom back and me gone?"

"Slow down, Cassy-bear," Dayson murmured, stepping up behind me and putting his hands on my waist. "We don't know anything yet other than they aren't here. Do we know where they went?"

"Vasin is looking for them. He can fly unseen now that it's dark out," I answered.

"Okay, that's a good start. Now why is this freaking you out so badly?" Dayson questioned. "You've faced a lot of things and not been this bothered, why now?"

I tilted my head back to look up at him, letting it rest on his chest and taking a moment to soak in his strength. "If they destroy Sheca, it will have been all my fault. There will be no one left to stop him. Us coming here was our last hope to survive through this war, and I don't know who I can trust."

"You can trust in me, Queen Cassarah. I was present during a few of these talks. What do you need to know?" Phillip asked, stepping forward. "I believe an alliance with *you* is the best thing for me, my kingdom, and all our people. Tell me how I can fix this."

Stepping out from between my two guardians, I faced the young crown prince, searching his face but only finding it full of earnestness. "What was their plan?"

"Originally, it was going to be Garold staying behind with those of the Bronze Reapers and Jade Talon, and they seemed to think they could get the Wind Fists as well. If they could have a large enough group, then they would have a spy go along with you to find Sheca. If it were worth the trouble, they would attack it and take it over for themselves. Then you showed up with a hundred dragons and made a very compelling argument about how that plan wouldn't work if they wanted to avoid the Lost King. Ballard has been arguing with them the entire time, but he is only one person and doesn't have the same standing as he used to, according to them," Phillip shared. "I honestly don't know where they went tonight. There was no new plan in place. There had been talk of stealing the key from you, but you're too well-guarded and always wearing it. That doesn't matter now that you've opened the castle. I don't see how they can make a case for you not being the rightful ruler of this kingdom."

"*Cass, I found them. They are just outside the valley headed for the border of the Unclaimed Dragon Lands. I think I know what they are doing, and we need to get there before it can happen. I'm coming back, but you'll need to get all your people on a dragon now!*"

"Zan, who can we trust here that are dragon riders? We need to get to the Unclaimed Dragons Lands border quickly," I explained.

He took a moment to think that over and nodded. "Give me a moment to find them, and I will be right back. Come on, Ezzu, it's time to go hunting." The little gold dragon gave a battle cry before she leaped off his shoulder into the night sky with Zan hot on her heels.

"What did Vasin tell you?" Jade commanded.

"Back off, man. Give her a minute. Can't you see this is freaking her out?" Dayson growled, stepping in to block Jade from me.

This couldn't be happening now. I needed them to all work together, not stand here arguing. "*Enough*! We can't do this right now. Whatever issues you have with each other, you'll need to deal with later on your own time. Right now, we need to stop whatever chaos the clan leaders are trying to cause. Anyone have a problem with that?"

"No, Your Majesty," Abbott answered, shoving the two men apart. "As your guardians, we shall do our duty to you and the people under your protection to keep them all safe."

Hearing Abbott's tone, I remembered all too well from our days of training together, I wasn't surprised when they all agreed with him. "Wonderful. Now, Jade and Paxton, will you please call your dragons? We need to get moving as soon as Zan is back." The gentle whoosh of air above me was I all needed to know that Vasin was back and preparing to land. "Don't be alarmed... it's just Vasin."

Wind whipped around us as he dropped to the ground in more haste than I had seen from him before, shaking the ground under our feet. *"CASS, CLIMB ON AND BRING ANOTHER WITH YOU. WE DON'T HAVE TIME TO LOSE."*

"ZAN SHOULD BE BACK WITH OTHERS—"

"No time, let's go!"

Rattled by his intensity about this matter, I grabbed who was closest to me—Dayson. "You're with me. Let's go."

"Cassarah, where are you going?" Jade called after me.

"Vasin said we have to go now, and I'm not going to argue with the dragon. The rest of you will be able to catch up to us easily enough once Zan and the rest get here," I answered as I climbed up on Vasin.

My ever-cautious dragon didn't even wait for me to buckle the first strap before he tossed himself into the air and shot off in the direction we needed to go. Dayson wrapped his arms around me as I was flung back, not ready for the speed Vasin was going. Dayson seemed to have managed to get at least one strap done, keeping him attached to Vasin as we flew at crazy speeds.

"Vasin, you need to tell me what is happening. I can't go into this blind. I need you to give me something to work with here," I begged, feeling my pair-bond's panic.

"NAYTAN TOLD THEM THE SECRET ABOUT DRAGONS AND WHERE THE MAGIC OR AS YOU CALL IT, BIRTHRIGHTS, CAME FROM. IF THEY ARE AT THE DRAGON LANDS, IT MEANS THEY ARE LOOKING TO TRAP DRAGONS INTO AN AGREEMENT WITH

THEM SO THEY CAN GAIN POWER. WE CAN'T LET THE CYCLE REPEAT ITSELF WHEN WE ARE SO CLOSE TO BEING FREE LIKE WE ONCE WERE."

"None of that makes any sense," I argued. "What is the secret?"

"THE REASON YOUR BIRTHRIGHT IS SO STRONG IS BECAUSE I BIT YOU. THE VENOM FROM A DRAGON IS WHAT TRANSFERS THE MAGIC INTO A PERSON, BUT THE ONLY WAY THEY SURVIVE IT IS TO BE BONDED TOGETHER FOR LIFE. IF THE DRAGON REJECTS THE PERSON, IT WILL KILL THEM AND THE PERSON THEY BIT... ONLY FOR THE DRAGON, IT DOESN'T HAPPEN RIGHT AWAY. THE HUMAN WILL DIE INSTANTLY, BUT THE DRAGON WILL BECOME WILD, AND THEIR MINDS WILL SLOWLY BEGIN TO ROT, TURNING THEM INTO MINDLESS BEASTS, VANISHING INTO THE DRAGON LANDS WHERE THEY WILL DIE YEARS LATER. THIS IS WHY THERE WAS AN AGREEMENT WITH THE DRAGONS THAT WE COULD CHOOSE WHETHER WE WANTED TO BE BONDED WITH A HUMAN. WE WERE SUPPOSED TO KEEP OUR FREEDOMS LIKE THE DRAGONS DO HERE TO LIVE OUR LIVES AND HELP WHEN WE ARE CALLED ON, BUT THE OTHER KINGDOMS TURNED US INTO SLAVES TO WIN THEIR WARS."

"How could they control a dragon?"

"BY CONTROLLING OUR PAIR-BOND. WHEN WE PICK A PERSON, OUR SOULS SPEAK TO ONE ANOTHER, AND WE TRULY ARE BONDED TO THAT ONE PERSON FOR LIFE. IF ANYTHING HAPPENS TO YOU, THEN THE SAME FATE WILL BEFALL US AS IF WE HAD REFUSED THE BOND, KILLING US SLOWLY. IF YOU AND I HAD BEEN A NORMAL DRAGON AND HUMAN BOND, THEN WE WOULD HAVE BEEN SENT TO A TRAINING CAMP WHERE THEY BRAINWASH YOU INTO BELIEVING WHATEVER THEY SAY, KEEPING YOU IN LINE WITH WHAT THEY NEED FROM US."

"Birthrights have been dying out, though, and the queen seemed genuinely scared when you bit me."

"THAT IS BECAUSE WE FIGURED OUT WE COULD STILL BOND WITHOUT ADDING IN OUR VENOM, ALLOWING OUR SOULS TO BOND INSTEAD. ONCE THE MAGIC DIED OUT FROM ALL THE PEOPLE, THEN THERE WOULD BE NO PULL TO CONTINUE BONDING WITH HUMANS. IT'S WHY FEWER OF US HAVE CHOSEN SOMEONE. THERE ISN'T A CONNECTION TO OUR PAST THROUGH THE LINGERING MAGIC IN YOUR BLOOD."

"So the magic of my ancestors called to you?"

"IN A WAY, YES. YOU ARE STILL THE ONE AND ONLY PERSON WHOSE SOUL CALLS OUT TO ME IN A BOND THAT CAN'T BE IGNORED, BUT IT IS FAR STRONGER BECAUSE YOU HAVE THE MAGIC ALREADY BOOSTING THE CALL. BEFORE THE FIRST PERSON WAS EVER BONDED TO A DRAGON, THERE WAS NO MAGIC IN THE WORLD. WE INTRODUCED THAT WHEN THE FIRST DRAGON MET THE FIRST KING OF THE MERCENARIES. THEY BUILT A FRIENDSHIP OVER TIME, AND THE BOND GREW NATURALLY, BUT THE DRAGON FELT COMPELLED TO KEEP HIS FRIEND ALIVE LONGER AND KNEW THE MAGIC WOULD PRESERVE HIS LIFE. SO HE BIT HIM, AND THEY CREATED THE FIRST PAIR-BOND KNOWN TO DRAGONKIND, ALLOWING US ALL TO CREATE A BOND AND OUR LINKED MEMORY THROUGH THE AGES."

Whatever I expected Vasin to say as he explained what was going on, this was nothing I could have imagined. Dragons were the source of our Birthrights—I mean magic—seeing as who we were born to no longer mattered since they weren't the one to provide the magic. Could this be why I have a link to Miranda? Was it because of the magic lingering in from my ancestors so I had a shared memory like the dragons do? Then a thought struck me, and I understood why Vasin was so worried about what was about to happen.

"Vasin, are they going to the Dragon Lands to try and gain magic from being bitten?"

"Yes, Cass, that is exactly what they are trying to do."

"How, though? Don't dragons know the dangers of doing that? Isn't this the whole reason they are trying to break away and live in the Dragon Lands?"

"If any of them hold magic within them, it makes the call to your pair-bond extremely hard to ignore. Imagine if I turned away from you, knowing what we could and do have, the need not to be alone is so strong it ruins us every time. Part of me thinks it's the feeling the first dragon had when he chose to build this bond with the first king."

"I would guess since Izel has a Birthright that Xio would too, but I don't know about Garold."

"I do believe that is his son sitting behind you..."

Shaking myself out of our mental conversation, I leaned my head back against Dayson's shoulder so I could yell into his ear. "Do you know if your father has a Birthright?"

"Not really, unless you count being able to start a fire no matter what stones you strike together as a Birthright," Dayson answered.

"Did you get that ability too?" I pressed.

"Sure did... comes in handy when you're out on jobs but not really all that helpful in real life."

Dammit, it looks like two of them had magic enough to call to a dragon. Wait, is that how Tahir and Jade ended up together? His Birthright was much stronger than anyone else's I've seen in a long time. So many things were now making sense as I fit the pieces together. Could I do more with my magic then produce a bow? I can break spells, but I never considered the fact that I might be able to do more with it. Would the Dragon Castle hold answers to this?

"Cassy-bear, what's going on?" Dayson challenged. "I can feel how tense you and Vasin are."

"There is a lot more going on with dragons than we ever realized, and the clan leaders are about to destroy decades of progress," I answered. "Just trust me when I say we need to make sure they don't have a chance to bond with a dragon."

"Bond with a dragon? They can do that? I thought it only happened at hatchings."

"Day, I don't have time to explain more. We're almost there, and it's going to be two of us against the lot of them and their dragons. Vasin is good, but he is still growing and hasn't gotten his fire yet which puts us at a slight disadvantage."

"Just slightly, you say? Well, I eat those odds for breakfast. Don't underestimate me just yet, Cassy-bear. I've got plenty of tricks up my sleeve," Dayson assured me with a smirk and a wink.

Let's just pray that will be enough until the others show up. They are going to kill me when they find out what's going on.

Sixteen

Stop Them!

V asin didn't go for the gentle circling glide to land. Instead, he dove and, at the last moment, flared out his wings, bringing us to an abrupt halt before his feet touched the ground in the middle of the group of people. Everyone scattered with lots of swearing and screaming as a hulking black dragon descended upon them out of nowhere. The other dragons around us let out deafening roars as they came to the aid of their pair-bonds, so I pulled my feet up under me and used Dayson to steady myself as I stood on Vasin's back.

I drew on my magic and the ability I used to connect with other dragons and thrust it out around us, grabbing their attention. *"Calm yourselves, please. We are not here to hurt you or your pair-bonds. All we want to do is stop these people from trapping dragons they wish to use for power. Feel my intentions and look at Vasin's memory about who these people are. Don't let them do to others what you've been fighting against all this time."*

The dragons were reluctant to believe me, but seeing that I was reaching out to them in this way when no one had been able to do this before made them curious. I wasn't going to second-guess the situation, and seeing as they calmed, I was going to take it as a win. The human part of this wasn't as agreeable to what I was doing and tried to advance on Vasin, but even though he might not have his fire yet, his teeth, claws, and wings seemed to serve him well.

"Cassarah, what are you doing here?" Ballard called, his voice full of panic. Glancing at him, I saw his hands were tied in front of him, and he had a massive bruise on the side of his face where something had hit him. "You can't be here alone. It isn't safe!"

Part of me relaxed to know that Ballard hadn't gone along with this, but it also fueled my anger at how he was treated. "Would anyone care to explain why you are all meeting out here when you should be enjoying a feast?" At my words, the soldiers stopped attacking and looked back at the clan leaders, Gavin's parents, and Naytan, standing back at a safe distance. "I'm surprised to see you can make friends so quickly, Naytan, but I might caution you on your choice of friends. Seems that when they decide they don't like you, they make plans to stab you in the back."

"You should never have come here, little *girl*. *This* situation is far too much for the likes of you to be able to handle," Naytan spat.

"That is your belief in the matter, but I know for a fact that you aren't the right person to be able to handle this either... none of you are." Shifting my gaze, I turned to the king and queen. "Tell me, are the rumors true that you are looking to dissolve our alliance in favor of a deal with these men? Did the fact that they are willing to betray their own queen not give you any pause to the fact they could also turn on you? If this is how you run your kingdom, it's no wonder it was taken from you."

King Edward did not like that one bit as I watched his face start to turn purple with his building rage. "You dare to speak to your king in such a manner? I'll have you head for that!"

"You and what army?" I asked, truly curious how he thought he would back up that threat. "I don't remember rescuing more than you and your sons from the castle. Did you manage to regain some of your military without me knowing?"

"Cassarah," Dayson whispered behind me. "Let's try to stay alive through this. Making them even more angry isn't going to help."

Ignoring my guardian's advice, I kept my gaze locked with the once king of Norden. "These men with you are from Sheca, making them my subjects. In helping you with whatever plan you have to remove me from my throne, they are doing so in an act of treason and shall be faced with death. If you do not have an army or even your own men to defend yourselves with, how do you see this as a valuable alliance? The clan leaders have now sealed their fate and will no longer be of use to you. All that is left is me. No one knows you are still alive after that battle. I could kill you and place your son, Phillip, on the throne, who is proving himself to be a valuable asset, unlike you two."

My words were cold and ruthless, but I was done giving them chances to prove themselves when, time after time, they betrayed me. Never would I be safe in my lands if I let these men continue to walk freely, thinking they have the power to usurp my rule. I could feel the other dragons listening to my words and, being the wise creatures they are, understood my choice was one of sound logic. They retreated, leaving me to deal with the humans. The only dragons who fought my touch were the king and queen's dragons. The need to protect their pair-bond was all that mattered to them, even if they didn't have the backup of the others.

"That's some big talk, little girl. Who's to say I can't just shoot you down where you stand and end this right now?" Naytan said, signaling to the soldiers. "If they are going to die for treason as it is, what do we have to lose?"

Out of the group of six men, four raised their bows while the other two drew their swords ready in case shooting me didn't work. "You can take that chance, but what makes you think I came alone?"

As I spoke, I could feel Tahir, Ifra, and Ninnat were right upon us just in time to prove my point and settle this once and for all. The dragons that belonged to the soldiers snarled and gnashed their teeth at the newcomers, but they backed off, leaving us more room for the fifteen dragons that landed with doubled-up riders. I now had thirty people to back me up, and by the looks on my guardians' faces, they were pissed as hell.

"What is going on here, Naytan?" Alsten barked as he leaped off his dragon's back. "You were warned what would happen if you didn't come to terms with Cassarah becoming our queen."

"I took your warning under consideration and decided I didn't care. I won't bow to some child claiming to be the savior of our people. It's not right, and you won't ever convince me otherwise," Naytan snarled.

"CASS, I NEED YOU TO STEP DOWN NOW THAT THE OTHERS ARE HERE. IT SEEMS I'M IN LUCK OF FINDING A LATE-NIGHT SNACK."

As much as I wanted to preserve life, Naytan made his bed, and there was nothing I could do to change his choice. With Dayson's help, I slid off Vasin's back with him right behind me, ready to spring into action once our feet hit the ground if it was needed. Someone pushed through the crowd of guards and dragons that just landed, surprising me when I saw it was Phillip.

"Mother, Father, what have you done?" he demanded. "Are you so determined to get out of this alliance with Queen Cassarah that you would stoop to this level? Do you not realize that this whole thing is your fault? The Lost King claims to be my half brother, and I'm inclined to believe him. If you'd kept better tabs on your firstborn, Father, then we might have avoided this whole issue, but instead, you hid him away like the bastard you believe him to be. Now look at us, chased out of our kingdom and at the mercy of the kindness of these people you are slapping in the face with this kind of stunt."

"Son, you aren't king yet, but when that day comes, you'll understand why we are doing this. There is more going on here than just an alliance with Sheca. Here in this land they are so close to are thousands of dragons up for the taking. We can bring back the days when we were feared for our dragon army and crush those who oppose us," King Edward explained, his eyes wild with excitement. "Wouldn't you want your own dragon, son?"

"I would be honored if one picked me to be its pair-bond, but I don't want a dragon for the power it would provide. I've also done my own research in the lore of the black dragon, and I know their bond to their chosen human is far deeper than what I've seen from you and your dragons. What they have was created by choice and honoring that bond not by stealing or lying," Phillip countered. "It's time to back down, Father. Surrender from being king and live to see another day. If you don't, I can't help you."

"Never!" the king shouted, triggering his dragon to open its jaws and hurl fire at us.

Vasin moved forward, spreading his wings, blocking the flames from hitting us, but I could still feel the heat of his on the wind that blew around his wings. The king of Norden just declared war on me and almost killed both his sons in the process. I could hear the queen screaming on the other side, but our view was still blocked, and I didn't trust being able to move from behind Vasin. The other dragons and their riders didn't hold back. They moved in ready for battle, teeth bared and swords brandished. Dayson grabbed my arm, pulling me away, but when I didn't move fast enough for him, he tossed me over his shoulder and darted behind a boulder. Phillip was right on our heels, diving out of the way as a dragon tail sailed through the air right where he'd just been. I tried to wriggle out of

Dayson's hold as he set me on my feet, but his arms were like bands of steel keeping me trapped against his chest.

"Cassarah, I can't let you go out there until things have calmed down. Trust our people to take care of it. They are trained to deal with situations like this, and we can't afford to have you get hurt right now," Dayson said, trying to reason with me.

"Why... why would they do this? It doesn't make any sense?" I stammered, rattled at how fast everything just evolved. "He could have killed everyone with his dragon reacting like that."

Phillip sat on the ground and started to laugh, catching me completely off guard. "If you truly knew my father, the man behind closed doors, you wouldn't be so surprised at this. The Lost King didn't get his crazy out of the blue. Let's just say he didn't fall far from the tree."

"Are you saying your father truly didn't care if he killed everyone?" I demanded, shoving out of Dayson's grip. This time, he let me go, but he wasn't far away.

"The kingdom is ruled by my mother... pretty much has been their entire reign. Good King Edward is always thinking that someone is out to get him or that there is some conspiracy to take the throne from him. It's even been bad enough that Mother had to keep us away from him when we were little. She managed him well, and he had a personal doctor in the castle who would keep him medicated with some herbal remedy or another to keep him calm. My guess is that since he has been off whatever concoction they were giving him, his mental stability cracked," Phillip explained. "I'm surprised Gavin didn't tell you about the family secret, seeing as you wanted an alliance with them."

Gavin never would have divulged something like that unless he felt it was necessary, and since I've mostly been interacting with the queen, there wouldn't be a need. Although, now that Phillip shared this information, it connected the dots of seeing how his father has been unraveling. Every altercation I'd seen has been from the king, although the queen seemed to agree with him, but I doubt she was feeling that way at this moment. She might be pragmatic when it comes to ruling, but she is still a mother, and I've seen how she looks at her sons.

"This is why you wanted him to step down and let you take over. The stress of war and not being medicated would be too much for him to handle," I said as realization hit me.

"Gavin knew he didn't want to be king, and I was better suited to it, even if I was younger. Over the past two years, Father has become even more unstable, and it's harder to keep it a secret. Once the wolves smelled blood, they would be ready to attack. So to keep that from happening, we've been trying to find the best way to get him to step down. Mother didn't agree with our plan, saying she could still rule like she always has, but we knew there would come a day when Father did something like this, and we would be screwed." Phillip sighed, dropping his head into his hands. "Now my father has declared war with Sheca and their new queen."

Looking over my shoulder at Dayson, he just shrugged his shoulders, not really having anything to add to this situation. It was then I noticed the sound of battle had quieted, so I moved to peek around the boulder blocking us. My heart broke at what I saw, causing me to step out to take in the scene before me. Queen Mary sat on the ground sobbing as she clutched her husband to her, and even in the dark, I could see the blood pooling under him. Naytan and a few of the soldiers with him were also dead along with King Edward's dragon and one other, while the third was still breathing but was bleeding out. Carefully, I made my way over to the dragon.

"Cassarah, what are you doing?" Dayson yelled.

"Don't even think about walking up to that dragon, Cassarah," Jade shouted at the same time.

I didn't bother to argue with them, feeling the pain this dragon was in from the wounds and having lost his pair-bond. He bared his teeth at me, but that was about all the strength he had at the moment to threaten me with. Reaching out, I placed a hand on his head and closed my eyes, taking in all he was feeling, the sadness at being unable to protect his person. Interestingly enough, I found he also wasn't in agreement with what had happened here tonight, but he would support his pair-bond no matter what.

"Would you like me to end your pain?" I whispered to the dragon. "You honored your bond, and if you want, I will set you free from it so you can find them once again in another life."

The dragon's acceptance told me everything I needed to know. Calling on that part of me that held my Birthright, I forced it through my hand that touched the dragon's head, and within seconds, his breathing stilled, and he was gone. Never would I leave anyone to suffer if I could do something about it, no matter what side of the fight they were on. No one deserved to die alone, afraid, and in agony, especially not one such as a dragon.

Stepping back from the once-majestic creature, I faced the others who all paused to watch what I was doing. That's when I noticed the clan leaders bound and on their knees in front of my guardians, and Alsten was looking worse for the wear. Taking a deep breath, I steeled myself for this interaction, knowing that I might have to call for the death of one or all of these men. If it came to that, I don't know how I was going to look my guardians in the face, seeing as these men were their family, but such is the life of a queen.

SEVENTEEN

THE CHOICES THEY MADE

"Was this worth it? Lives were lost tonight that didn't need to end, but because of your selfishness, this is where we are at," I spoke as I walked in their direction. "Did you really think being able to gain a pair-bond with a dragon would change matters? A quarter of their people here have dragons, and it doesn't make them any more important than those who don't. Someone, please explain to me what your plan was because I just don't see it, and I'm not one to miss things like that."

Garold and Xio stayed tightlipped, but Acton surprised me as he spoke up after a few moments of silence. "Tell me how would you feel if someone you didn't know anything about appeared out of nowhere and took everything from you? We have been groomed from a young age to take over these roles, spending our lives learning how best to take care of our people. Then it's all stripped from you in a moment like it was all a dream. I was willing to work with you, to give you a chance to show us why the black dragon chose you, but then you decided to bring us here and cast us aside. If I were in your position, I would want the counsel of those doing the job far longer than you have. Snubbing us and allowing others to fill that role is foolish and shortsighted."

Hmm, it seems that the half brothers are more alike than they think. Jade is just as blunt about how he views things, the only difference being that he likes me. Acton made a fair point, but he was missing half the story in his narrative which led me to make the choices I did.

"If things had happened as you say, I could easily see your point," I mused aloud. "Let's get a full perspective on this situation, though, before you choose to die by your beliefs in this matter. Picture living a life where your role was set, you knew your place in life, and you believed everything you've ever been told about who you are as a person. Then one day, you get paired with a black dragon, having no idea what that means to the world, only knowing you now have disrupted the plans so carefully laid out for you all your life.

"Sometime later when you think life couldn't be turned even more upside down, a group of mysterious men show up and tell you that your dragon means you are queen to a group of people you've never really heard about besides the idle gossip. At the request of people you don't know, you decide to go with them, leaving behind *everything*, never knowing if you'll see your family again or if they'll want to see you after abandoning them. When you arrive at this new life, you discover it wasn't quite what they said. Now I have a year to learn a whole new skill and prove I can be queen. I do as they ask, spending day after day learning what you all spend a lifetime learning. Then I get betrayed by the very people I'm supposed to be proving myself to. When I'm rescued and have no place to go, I return to these people I don't really know and haven't proved myself to yet, so they try to kill me.

"Somehow, this leads me to becoming crowned queen along with calling eight guardians to protect me. I'm lost, overwhelmed, and floundering, trying to keep up with everything that has happened in my life up to that point. I hear there are clan leaders, and I'm overjoyed to have people I can lean on to help guide me through what it means to be the queen to a people I was still learning about. Only they prove to be someone I can't lean on. Instead, they are questioning me on everything, making me feel small and insignificant. They claimed to be looking out for their own people, but I discovered within my first two days there was a traitor among you. This leads to more hostility from you all, even when I offer olive branch after olive branch, trying to work with you.

"The final straw came when you decided to use the people you claim to care so much about as a means to undermine me and lie to them. So tell me, Acton, would you trust them to guide you in this new era? Because I most certainly wouldn't. *That* is why I am dissolving the role of clan leader on top of the fact we don't have multiple clans anymore. We are united once more, and that is what is going to make us stronger. Due to your actions here tonight, you will no longer be part of what I am trying to do with the clans." I was so worked up by my rant that my heart was beating rapidly and my breath was shallow and quick. My anger at them for pushing me to make this call coursed through my veins, making my hands shake.

"Why couldn't they see I didn't want this but left me with no other choice?" I demanded from Vasin, needing to know I wasn't wrong in my thinking.

"Cass, we can't change how people see us, but what we can do is show them who we really are. You have given them chance after chance to show you a different way to end this. It's their doing that we ended up here."

"Am I doing that bad of a job they just won't give me a chance?"

"This is about power, not about you. They do not want to give up the control they have, and the clan leaders know that the longer you are in power, the more the people will grow to love you. When they lose that last trump card, they lose everything. You are

DOING THE RIGHT THING BY REMOVING THEM FROM POWER AND STARTING FRESH WITH THIS NEW WAY YOU WANT PEOPLE TO INTERACT AS ONE."

Even though what Vasin was saying made sense, I still wasn't feeling any better about this position they put me in.

"Your Highness, what would you like us to do with them?" Alsten asked, his face neutral as he awaited orders.

Taking a moment, I looked at my guardians who all stood just behind the clan leaders, and I met their eyes, praying they would understand what I had to do. "I, Queen Cassarah, sentence them to death for acts of treason against the Crown and the people of Sheca. They will not receive a hearing and will be put to death by beheading at dawn tomorrow."

"So it shall be done," Alsten stated as he bowed. "Men, take these prisoners to the cells and lock them up for the night. They have an appointment they can't miss tomorrow."

"General," I called out. "Please allow them to say goodbye to any family members as long as it is supervised."

Alsten nodded and headed out with his men, taking Acton, Garold, and Xio with them none too gently. I watched them fly off, and a part of my spirit broke the farther they got, knowing this would affect so many more people than just me. Tomorrow, people would be losing a son, father, brother, or lover, and who knows how they would respond to the event.

"Dayson, Izel, May, do any of you feel the need to head back?" I asked, refusing to look at them as I spoke. I knew there was no love between Jade and his half brother and that neither one of them would welcome a visit from the other, so I didn't offer. Plus, Jade had Tahir if he felt differently than I assumed.

"There will be time later to speak with them," Izel answered first, sounding much closer to me than he had been moments ago. "Are you all right, little warrior? You didn't get hurt in the fight, did you?"

This caused me to snap my head in his direction, shocked he would be asking me that right now. "I'm fine. Vasin and Dayson made sure I was protected."

"I'm glad to hear that. It would have been worse if they managed to harm you with their asinine idea," Izel muttered, his face lined with anger. "How could they be so stupid to pull a stunt like this?"

"That's what I want to know. My father might be a loose cannon, but he isn't one to make rash choices unless there is something else we are missing in all of this," Dayson interjected.

Watching them all, I couldn't get over how calm everyone was acting, even Gavin and Phillip as they sat with their mother who refused to let go of her husband. For all that they were an arranged marriage, it seemed they had found a way to find love. This made the whole thing even worse. Now the queen was never going to see eye to eye on anything after my people killed her husband, whether we were in the right or not. Unsure of what to do, I walked over to the queen and her sons, needing her to know I never wanted this to happen.

"Your Majesty." I started, kneeling across from her but with plenty of space between us. "I am so sorry," I whispered, tears pooling in my eyes and my throat constricting with held-back tears.

She lifted her face streaked with blood and tears, a look of devastation written on her face as she gazed at me. "You're sorry? My husband is dead because of you, and you dare to apologize to *me*?"

"Mother, that isn't fair. Father attacked her first. She had every right to defend herself," Gavin explained as he touched her arm.

The queen shoved him away, knocking him to the dirt in his surprise. "Don't you dare try to justify this, you traitorous bastard.

You turned your back on our family and your role as prince for *her*. Why should I trust anything coming out of your mouth!" she snarled. Phillip made a move on her other side, but he got the same treatment from his mother. "Both of my children have betrayed me, leaving me with no husband or sons to call my own. I am alone and will seek revenge on those who have hurt me and destroyed my life along with my kingdom!"

Even though she was screaming at all of us, I could see in her face that her pain was talking. She'd just lost her husband and wasn't in any place to be reasoned with about what she was spouting at all of us. We needed to get her someplace safe and kept under a watchful eye so she didn't hurt herself or others as she grieved. Standing, I walked over to her dragon who was as distraught as her pair-bond, but she didn't lash out at me, knowing I wasn't the one who started this.

"I need your help. We need to get her and her husband back to the village. Would you take them there? I know your pair-bond wants to run and hide away from all this, but that isn't what's best for her right now. All I want to do is keep her safe." The queen's dragon nodded in agreement and sent me some emotions to let me know she was worried about her pair-bond. *"I will do everything I can to help her, but it will take time."*

The dragon hummed in agreement, and I turned back to Gavin and Phillip. "She will take your mother back to the village along with your father's body if she won't leave without him."

Gavin nodded, giving me an appreciative look as he grabbed one arm of his mother and Phillip the other, helping her to her feet.

"No, we can't leave him!" she cried, fighting against them.

"Mother, we are not leaving him. We just need to get you on Petra's back first, then we can figure out the best way to get Father back as well," Gavin assured her.

Abbott and Dayson stepped forward and hefted up the king's body, following after the queen. They set him back down beside the golden dragon and stepped back, available if needed, but I appreciated they didn't push the matter, not knowing how the queen would react. It didn't take Gavin and Phillip too long to get their parents settled, and once that happened, the rest of us climbed onto our dragons, ready to head out. Gavin climbed up behind me, wrapped his arms around my waist, and buried his head in my neck as we took off. He didn't say a word, but I could feel his tears against my skin as Vasin took his time flying back to the village.

When we landed, the queen was put in a room with the windows locked from the outside and two guards posted outside the door. I hated to have her as a prisoner, but there was no telling what she would do right now. Each of the boys offered to stay with her, but she didn't want to even look at them, so they let her be. I'd also made sure the room was cleared of anything that could be used to harm or kill herself, knowing it would help me sleep better tonight I had done all I could for her.

The rest of us were split between two rooms with beds enough for each of us if we doubled up. May and Becka decided it was best to stay in my room so if anything did happen, they were close. The guys all argued one of them should be in the room too, but May put an end to that with a firm look. Instead, one of them slept in front of my door while the others tumbled into their beds just as drained as I was after the day's events. All this trouble and I wasn't even truly crowned their queen yet. What does that mean for the coming days ahead? Guess I was just going to have to trust my guardians and take it as it comes.

Eighteen

Death Comes for Us All

Even with all that had happened the night before, sleeping in a warm place with a soft bed and a roof over my head, I didn't stand a chance. My head hit the pillow, and I was out only to be woken up by what seemed like moments later by Becka.

"Cassarah, it's time to get up. I'm sorry we can't let you sleep longer, but it's time to deal with the clan leaders," she whispered.

Cracking open an eye, I looked at her somber face. I'd almost forgotten I'd sentenced three out of the five men who've led our people to death. Slowly, I sat up and looked out the window to find that it was gray and a light rain was falling. It seemed fitting for a morning such as this. Becka pulled me to my feet, and I saw the dress that was laid out for me to wear. Since the day I rescued Vasin, I hadn't worn a dress, and I'd not missed them one bit, but now that I would be acting officially as queen, I wouldn't be able to escape them forever. The dress was simple yet elegant in all black with silver accents, properly somber for the occasion. Becka and I fell into our old habits as she readied me for the day, making it oddly comforting knowing what was to come.

When I was dressed and ready to go, she slipped on a black cloak with the symbol of the dragon wrapped around the sword with a crown over the dragon's head embroidered on the back. "The viceroys brought it by this morning... seems they've been preparing for your arrival since Zan told them about you."

The stitching was stunning, and the detail on the dragon was unbelievable. I would need to find out who made this and thank them personally. They would be a good person to know if I needed any other work like this done. Unable to avoid what must happen next, I squared my shoulders and stepped out of my room and into the house's common space. There, I found the rest of my guardians all dressed in matching tunics that were also black with the same symbol on the back, only theirs didn't have the crown. Gavin and Phillip were also there waiting, but they wore deep purple, almost black tunics, the customary color of mourning in Norden. Both looked haggard like they hadn't slept well, and my heart broke for them.

As I stepped forward toward Gavin, Lawrence walked into the house but paused as he saw us all standing there. "My apologies, Your Majesty. I should have knocked and requested entry. Should I come back a bit later?"

Shaking my head, I turned to face him. "No, delaying this longer won't make it any easier."

Lawrence didn't say anything. He simply nodded and gestured for me to follow him out the door. Outside, Inali stood, saddled and waiting for me with two men shielding the saddle from the rain so I didn't have to sit on a wet seat. Cole stepped ahead of me and kneeled in the wet gravel, lending me his knee to step up onto. I raised a brow at him, surprised that he would offer such an obvious cheat to get into the saddle. How many days had they all tortured me with having to get on my horse with no stirrups? Deciding not to argue, I pulled the hood of my cloak up and crossed the ground to where he kneeled, grabbed Inali's mane, and pushed off Cole's leg. Doing this move in a dress, even one made for riding, wasn't easy, explaining why Cole had done what he did. Looking down at him, I smiled. "Thank you."

"Of course, Your Majesty. I'm always here when you need me," Cole answered in a low voice meant only for us. He reached up and took my hand, pressing a kiss to the back of it.

I couldn't tell you why this one small act seemed so intimate to me, but it made my heart flutter all the same. My guardians all mounted up and surrounded me as we moved forward along with more guards from the Sheca military, leading us to the spot they used for situations like this. The group was somber, no one speaking, and the only sound was that of hooves on the gravel of the road that soon turned into mud as we veered off the main stretch to one that took us farther back into the mountains. We stopped at a wooden stage that had a tarp pulled over the top of it to shield those under it from the rain. Many of the village people along with those I'd brought here yesterday were already gathered. They turned to watch us as we arrived, being led right to the stage, where another guard helped me off my horse.

Half the guards dismounted and stood before the stage while others stayed mounted and found places on the outer edge of the crowd. Dayson and Jade joined me on the stage, flanking me with every step I took as I joined the viceroys and Sal where they waited for me.

"Alsten filled us in on the events of last night," Mathew shared once I joined them. "I'm so sorry this happened and that our men were mixed into it."

"Thank you, but we cannot control the actions of others, or so my guardians keep telling me," I said with a sigh, letting my shoulders sink ever so slightly.

Eleazar nodded. "They are wise to share such wisdom. Days like this are hard for all involved, but you are doing the right thing for your people even though it doesn't seem that way. No one wants to take life unnecessarily, and those who do shouldn't be put in power. Seeing how this affects you tells me all I need to know about you as our queen, and I have much respect for you because of it. We have been without a true leader for so long that it will be a bumpy road to start, but once they see you have their best in mind, they will come around."

"That is my hope, but I'm not sure what they will think when they see what is happening here today," I murmured.

A hand rested on my lower back, making me turn to Dayson. "I need you to hear me loud and clear, Cassarah. I. Do. Not. Blame. You. My father is his own man. While I think there might be more to this situation, he still chose to act against you, our queen, and the person I am charged to protect. The vow I gave you as I became your guardian was not one I took lightly... none of us did. We promised to put your life ahead of ours, even if it means against our flesh and blood. You are the future of our people, and that is to be protected at all costs."

Tears started to well up, and all I wanted to do right now was hug him, but I knew I couldn't with so many eyes watching. Seeing my need, he raised a hand to cup my cheek and wipe away the tear that slipped out. I held his hand there for a moment, taking strength from it as Jade stepped up beside me and squeezed my other hand.

"Acton and I haven't been family in a long time, and there was nothing that could be done to save our relationship. I'm sad he has brought himself to this end, but as Dayson said, these are their choices and the consequences they must deal with for their actions. You gave them so many chances to change, and they didn't. You have to set the standard for when your mercy runs out, and this is what happens. Your heart is pure, but I refuse ever to let someone taint it with their actions. What happens here today will prove you are a woman of your word and *will* follow through on what you say, good or bad."

Their reassurance went a long way to making this entire event more barrable. What I had feared most about this was hurting them, these amazing men who have been by my side through all these recent ups and downs. I wanted to be there for them, but I didn't know how to help when I was the one causing them pain. As Dayson stepped away, I heard footsteps coming up the stairs to the stage, revealing the three clan leaders in question. Izel stood near the stairs and glanced over at me to avoid looking at his father. Through that look, I could feel him using his Birthright to give me strength and believe in myself, making me want to cry again. How could these men be so wonderful in the face of losing their fathers and brothers?

"Queen Cassarah, would you like one of us to make the announcement and sentencing?" Lawrence asked, pulling my attention back to them.

I took a moment to think that over. I could take the easy way out and let them deal with the crowd, but I knew the right move was to give the news myself. "Thank you, but no. I believe it is best that I handle this matter personally. This is the first instance of this happening, and I need to know the people understand I am the one who made this call."

The four older men in their color-coded robes bowed to me, placing their hands over their hearts as they did. "God's strength to our queen," they murmured before stepping to the far side of the stage, leaving it open for me and the three men who were about to meet their fate.

Walking to the front of the platform, I pulled down my hood so everyone could see my face, having no doubt who it was that was speaking. "My people, I come to you as your queen on this fateful day to announce the crimes done by these men and the punishment they will receive for it. These men, once leaders to those of us who lived outside of Sheca's protective walls, fell prey to greed and reluctance to see things change. Last night, they sought to bond with dragons in hopes of gaining their powers to give them the edge they needed to remove me from the throne. Those of you who are from Sheca understand the grave error they have made. For those of you who just arrived, know that it is akin to slavery where the only choice of freedom from it is death—slowly and painfully. Their other crime is that of treason to the Crown, working to undermine and kill me. I've discovered there is more treachery against the mercenary people as a whole, all done to keep them in power. For these crimes and others, they are sentenced to death."

As I was going to step back, Paxton came up the steps, hauling another person who was bound up onto the stage. "My Queen, we almost forgot this man in the mix of things."

There stood Porvan, Paxton's father, bedraggled from his journey and captivity in the fortress. I knew they had brought him along in the very back of the group under watch and forced him to travel on foot. Knowing now he'd been working with Payson to help the Lost King, he deserved no less of a punishment than his fellow clan leaders. Could this be the part I was missing? Had they hoped that by removing me, they could bring back Porvan to work with the Lost King to get them out of this mess? It was the only thing that made any sense, and for him, of all people, to know of the dragons' secret was dangerous on so many levels. It had to be finished here and now to protect everyone involved so we could start fresh. I nodded to the guards with the other prisoners, and they grabbed Porvan, shoving him down to kneel with the others. The look that passed between them told me everything I needed to know about what pushed them to this point. Porvan was a leech, and I should have already done this, but I didn't want to start my rule that way. It seems the universe had other plans for me.

Unsure of where to stand, I moved off to the side but still in full view of the crowd so they didn't think I was brushing off this matter. What shocked me the most was when they grabbed Garold and kicked him to his knees at the chopping block, and Dayson walked up with an axe. Surely, he wasn't going to kill his own father? It would seem that was exactly what his intention was as he raised the axe high above his head and brought it down with finality. No matter how much I stared at Dayson, he refused to look at me, only stepped back and handed the axe off to Jade as Acton was sprawled out on the chopping block next.

"Ah, so we come full circle. You finally get to kill off the rest of your family. Only this time, you don't get paid for it unless getting between the queen's legs is payment enough for you," Acton taunted. It appeared he wasn't finished, but Jade was as he put his whole body into the downward swing. As the head rolled away, he spat on it with disgust.

Izel stepped onto the stage, took the axe from Jade, and walked up to his father, fighting the guard's hold, even though his hands and feet were bound. "Son, don't do this. I know what you're trying to prove, but she isn't worth it. You don't know what it truly means for her to be the Dragon Queen. She will destroy the world, not save it."

"If you believe that of Cassarah, then you know nothing. I will not stand to have you slander her in such a way. Goodbye, Father," Izel said as he too dealt the final blow. A sob from the crowd was heard, and I held myself back from looking, knowing that Izel had a mother and a younger brother out there.

Finally, Porvan was positioned. Paxton snatched the axe from Izel's hands and marched up to his father. "Well, would you look at this? How the roles have been reversed. I tried to stop you all those years ago, and it almost killed me. I let you win then, never coming back to finish the job. Well, I'm back now, and you are getting the death you deserve... that of a common criminal." Before his father could say anything in response, Paxton swung so hard the blade got stuck in the chopping block. He muttered a few curse words and stormed off into the crowd who parted for him, not wanting to be touched by someone who just killed their own father.

Feeling that something else needed to be said, I started back to the center, but Dayson grabbed my arm and shook his head as Jade took center stage.

"Let it be known that we, the Dragon Queen's guardians, will do whatever it takes to protect our queen, proven here today as each of us has taken the duty of killing our fathers. Queen Cassarah is a woman of grace and mercy, but know that her mercy has its limits. When it comes to an end, expect to find us coming for you. Be the people who deserve a queen such as ours. Give her a chance to show you what she wants to see our people become. Long live the Dragon Queen!" Jade belted out at the end.

"*Long live the Dragon Queen!*" the crowd answered, their voices echoing off the mountains around us.

Nineteen

The Things We Do for Love

After the punishment was doled out, we returned to the house we had slept in and found the kitchen table covered in food. An older woman stood in the kitchen, removing a pot of steaming hot liquid that smelled amazing.

"Oh, you're back. Wonderful, just in time while the food is hot." She greeted us with a smile. "My name is Marta, and this is my home. I'm very pleased to be hosting you until you can move to the castle."

It hadn't dawned on me that this home had to be someone's and wasn't just left empty here for us to use. Many of our people had similar situations with others taking them in if they had room while the rest had to camp out until more permanent lodging could be made.

"Thank you so much for giving us a place to stay. It was heavenly to sleep in a warm bed after our travels," I shared as I sat at the table. "Everything looks wonderful. I hope we didn't make too much trouble for you having to feed us all."

"Nonsense, it is my honor to serve the queen and her men," Marta answered, brushing off my concern. "No, please sit, eat... I just finished making some kavat which should help you warm up after being out in the damp."

Marta filled the mug and gave it to me, but before I could take it from her, Izel intercepted it, took a sip before waiting a moment, then handed it to me. I gave him a questioning look, but he just smiled, made a plate, sampled everything, and then set it in front of me.

"Izel, did you just check my food for poison?" I demanded with a frown.

"Yes," he stated. "After all that has happened, I wouldn't put it past an angry family member or someone else in the clans to retaliate against the death of the clan leaders."

My anger flared at this, and I slammed the mug on the table. "Don't *ever* do that again! What would have happened if it were poisoned, and you died? What good would that have done anyone?"

"Better me than you," Izel answered as he made up a plate for himself and sat like he hadn't just risked his life for mine.

I knew it was their job to keep me safe, but I never intended for them to go out of their way to risk their lives by doing such foolish things like testing my food or killing their family members. "That is where we differ in our thought process, my dear guardian." I scanned the table with narrowed eyes at all the men seated at the table. "Don't think you're off the hook for the stunt you pulled back there. Whose idea was it for you to do the job? I'm sure there is someone here who has been given the title of executioner."

"As it so happens, there wasn't one since they haven't had to behead someone in almost two hundred years. Most crimes don't warrant death, and the criminals tend to be locked away for life or banished from the land. I hear a few were eaten by dragons, but that was because the offense was made against them, so they decided on the punishment," Paxton volunteered.

Letting out a huff of air, I shook my head. "I should have guessed it was your idea, seeing as you brought your father along."

"It was a joint effort between Jade and me," Paxton corrected. "But the others saw the reasoning behind it and agreed."

Becka placed a hand on my arm from where she sat next to me. "Why don't we talk about this later once we've eaten and had a chance to process everything that's happened this morning?"

Begrudgingly, I agreed and started on my breakfast which was the best I've eaten since the last time I was in Sheca. Fresh eggs, pork, and warm bread were such a treat and something I hadn't had since leaving my home. The mercenaries of the Raven Rose weren't farmers in the way that the people of Sheca were. They provided for us, but it was more in grains, using the livestock for milk and their coats to barter and sell. My hope was after this meal, I could change, head up to the castle, and start to explore what lies behind those doors, but that hope was dashed when a knock came at the door. A man entered, holding a message for me that Jade took from the man and looked over before he handed it to me. Just when I didn't think these men could get any more overprotective, they started to pull stunts like this. It made me miss the days of strategy and never leaving the mountain fortress.

The letter was a request from the viceroys to meet them after I was done with our meal to go over coronation preparations. It would seem that a queen's life wasn't her own, and as much as I wanted to explore the castle, I needed to secure my station officially as queen. Once this was done, I would be moved into the castle, and I could explore it to my heart's content when I wasn't needed to plan a battle or deal with other things that queens deal with. Those who believe that having a crown lets you do whatever you want is a lie. It means you are the last one to do as you wish.

"Please let them know I will be over shortly," I told the messenger. He bowed and backed out the door without saying a single word.

"What did the letter say?" Cole asked.

I glanced at him over the paper I still held and raised a brow. "I'm sorry, was this note written to you?"

Cole scowled. "Mouse, now is not the time to get sassy about things. We need to know what's going on to keep you safe."

"I'll tell you when I'm ready, but for now, I'm enjoying this lovely meal Marta prepared for us," I answered with a smirk.

Cole looked as if he was about ready to leap from his chair and snatch the letter from me when Abbott grabbed his shoulder and shook his head. "Let it go. She said she'll tell us."

This seemed to settle him for now, but he kept shooting daggers at me, letting me know I was going to pay for my stubbornness one way or another. I loved that these men took their role so seriously, but every now and then, I just wanted to let go and be us—the us who drank and played games together—and not the queen and her guards who needed to watch her every move. If we were ever going to have a life together, we needed to work on when to be in our roles and when to be ourselves.

We ate until we were stuffed and couldn't take another bite because everything was just so good. Marta was thrilled at our reaction to her cooking, but when we tried to help clean up, she shooed us out the door. "There is no way I will ever let the Dragon Queen and her guardians clean up after me. The village would shame me if they ever found out. Now go, you have much more important things to do."

As we stood on the porch of the house, Cole crossed his arms and gave me a look. "Would the Dragon Queen like to share with us where we are off to now?"

"If you must know, we are going to meet with the viceroys to go over coronation preparations at the village hall where they reside and hold council," I answered.

"There, now was that so hard?" Cole grumbled. "I'm not trying to be an asshole, Cassarah, but things are dangerous right now. We don't know who else might have been involved with the plan to overthrow you."

"I am extremely aware of the situation, Cole," I said as I headed down the steps and into the muddy road, making my way to the middle of the village. "What I don't understand is why you all are so worked up about it. I've been in danger since the day you came to find me at my parents' home. What has changed that now has you all so hyper-vigilant?"

"Naytan," Zan spoke up this time. "None of us expected anyone from Sheca to be assisting in the plot to remove you from being queen. Now that we know he had enough followers to make a move like he did, it makes us worry there are more hidden in plain sight. I've known these people all my life, and outside of Naytan and the few people who were with him last night, I wouldn't have guessed anyone was angry enough to do this. Now every person I look at, I wonder if they will attack you or are secretly planning your death."

Hearing him put it that way made me pause, face them, and look at them—really look at them. What I saw was fear. They were genuinely scared something would happen to me. Had I gotten so used to the fact my life was in danger all the time that I didn't see the toll it was taking on them as they tried to keep me alive? I'd been worrying about how they would feel if I picked them as a consort, but I hadn't taken the time to understand that what worried them more was the unknown dangers lurking around every corner. Even Becka and May, who I knew loved me like a sister, seemed to be worn a little thin.

"Let's deal with this and find some time for us all to talk tonight. Just us, all right?" I offered, knowing I couldn't ignore dealing with the coronation. They all agreed, and we headed off on a somewhat lighter note. I slowed to walk beside Gavin and caught his hand, intertwining our fingers. "You don't need to come with us to do this if you need some time to yourself or want to be with Phillip and your mother."

"No, it's better to keep busy. Mother doesn't want to see me. When I tried last night, she started to throw things at me, cursing me for ever being born. I think it's better right now to let her be," he answered, squeezing my hand. "Although I have to be honest, I didn't know my mother loved my father as much as she did. It always seemed like she was covering for him, ruling because she had to and not because she wanted to."

"I never understood why my father loved my mother so much. She was always so cruel to him, never having a nice word to say, but I could see in his eyes how much he loved her. I think that's what love is, though… being able to see the person behind all the mess and who they truly are. They always say that love is blind, but what if it's not that they are blind to their flaws but accept them as part of who they are? Imagine a love like that. It would be rather amazing, don't you think?" I mused.

Gavin chuckled, making me glance at him in confusion. "Love, you just described how you care for each of us. You don't see our flaws the same way others do because you look past them to who we are despite our shortcomings."

His words caught me off guard and left me unsure how to respond. "I do?"

"The fact you have no idea makes it even more amazing. Like I know you would pardon my mother despite all that has happened because you don't want to hurt me or Phillip. Know that I will never ask that of you, and you shouldn't unless Mother has proven without a doubt that she is a true supporter. Yet the fact that you've already considered it makes me humbled and fall even more in love with you than I already have."

I stopped so suddenly that Paxton crashed into me and grabbed my waist to keep me from falling into the mud. "Whoa there, spitfire, that would have been a messy fall."

"Sorry, I just stumbled, is all," I mumbled as I pulled myself back together, slipping out of his hold. I glanced at Gavin but knew that if I dwelled on what he just said, I wouldn't be able to focus on anything else.

He had told me previously that he had feelings for me and didn't want to leave my side, but I didn't take a declaration of love so casually. How could he possibly love me after all that's happened and now the death of his father? I wouldn't blame him if he wanted to be as far away from me as possible. Not having the time to deal with that as I walked up the steps to the main hall where the viceroys were, I set that worry aside and readied myself to become the Dragon Queen.

Twenty

Coronation Preparation

"Your Majesty, you've arrived just in time!" Mathew announced, making his way over to me. "I have Talia here to take your measurements for the ceremonial dress that is to be made."

Clearly, they were not wasting any time to get the ball rolling on these events. It was as if the execution had never happened. Mathew took my hand and led me into a small sitting room with a stool set up for me to stand on.

"We will leave you to get things settled while I chat with your guardians and consort," Mathew said with a bob of his head and swept out of the room.

The woman named Talia was shy and looked slightly older than me but not by much. "You'll have to forgive them. They have been waiting a long time for this moment."

"I hope to have their energy when I reach their age." I giggled, trying to ease the awkward atmosphere. "Do you need to remove my dress, or is leaving it on all right?"

"If you are comfortable taking it off, it will give me a chance to get all the measurements I need and record them so I can make you whatever is needed in the future. I am the best our village has to offer by way of a seamstress," Talia explained.

"Are you the one who did the stitching on my cloak? It is absolutely stunning. I've never seen finer work in all my life."

"Yes, Your Majesty, that is my work," she answered with a slight blush on her cheeks.

"Then I will slip out of this dress so that I selfishly might be able to get many things your talented hands have created," I shared with a smile and turned my back to her so she could help me with the ties.

Soon, I was in my shift, standing on a stool as Talia worked quickly and silently, moving with the precision of years of practice. There was something so simple about this interaction that was soothing after the craziness that had been happening around me. The fire in the sitting room filled the space with warmth so I didn't feel the chill while standing in my undergarments, and the soft sound of her taking notes and muttering to herself was welcome. Then all too soon, the moment ended, and Talia was helping me put the dress back on. Taking a deep breath, I opened the door and found Paxton waiting, guarding it while Eleazar was lecturing the others.

"You didn't need guardian lessons?" I asked, pausing next to him.

"They promised to fill me in later, but none of them would pay attention unless someone was here. I've seen my fair share of ceremonies while wandering through the kingdoms that I can catch on faster than most of them," he shared with a shrug.

"One of these days, I would love to hear about what it is that you did while you were presumed dead," I commented as I headed into the building's main space.

"Now, when the queen heads to take her purification bath, only the women can escort her past the archway. The purpose of this is to wash off the old life before being crowned and then staying *pure* until the ceremony is over. Do I make myself clear?" Eleazar demanded.

The guys glared at him, daring to suggest they would ever sully me in any way. "I don't think that will be a problem... my honor is still intact."

The viceroys turned to look at me when I spoke. "Of course, forgive me if you thought we were to assume otherwise, but the world has changed around us so much that we didn't want to be unclear of expectations," Lawrence explained. "These rituals are meaningful to us all, and we don't want to dishonor the gods by not following them as they should be."

"Of course, and I wish to honor them and our people by following them," I assured as I sat with the others. "Now maybe we can go over these expectations together?"

Lawrence turned to the others, and they seemed to speak to each other without using words, but when they agreed, they all nodded and turned back to us. "Let us start at the beginning, shall we?" Mathew suggested. "The event will take place a week from today. That will give us time to examine the castle and make the preparations needed. Talia is skilled, but getting a dress done sooner than that would take magic that none of us have discovered yet."

"Sounds fair to me, plus it will give us time to adjust to things here as well. I would love to be able to spend time in the castle as well, learning what we can that might be hidden away," I said, smiling over at Sal, who nodded excitedly in agreement.

"There will be a lot of work on your part that needs to go into this, Your Majesty," Eleazar warned. "Once we get through this, then you will have more time to call your own."

"All right, where do we start to get this whole thing moving?" Cole interjected.

Eleazar gave him a disapproving look but ignored the snark. "It would be best if you go up to the castle, check things out, and make sure it's only the drawbridge that needs immediate attention. Then with Talia working on the dress, it leaves us to prepare you for the vows you make to your people, the dragons, and the gods. They will need to be memorized, and unfortunately, the people who wrote them were long-winded, but the bright side is you already know how to read the language, making it easier."

"Who knew learning a dead language would come in handy?" I mused out loud, thinking back to the game of strategy my father and I used to play. "When does the cleansing bath take place?"

"That won't be until the day before the coronation," Lawrence answered, waving that information off. "Before we get to that, you'll need to visit the Dragon Lands and greet the dragons who gather there along with your partner, Vasin. They will need to know who to reach out to if they have concerns or there is trouble on their borders. When that has been accomplished, meet with General Alsten to set expectations while your guardians work with the command leaders to set up security for the day of the coronation. Then there is the banquet after the coronation to start preparing for, along with the need to pick staff to work in the castle once you reside there full time."

Hearing all of this caused my brain to start overheating like a pot boiling over. I'd been thinking that a week would be plenty of time to figure all of this out, but as they listed everything that needed to be done, I realized I was starting from scratch. There was nothing in place, and I would need to build the environment I wanted to live in for the foreseeable future. The castle would have nothing left in it, or at least I assumed, seeing as it's been four hundred years, whether it had magical protection or not. Food would need to be stocked, jobs assigned, and so many other things I'm sure I wouldn't think of until I discovered we didn't have it.

Helena... I needed Helena. She would know how to help me. Being the steward's wife and having to help deal with all the clans' needs, she would be a person I could trust to help me deal with all of this. I turned to Cole, grabbing his arm as if he was the last link to my sanity. "Do you know where your grandparents were put up?"

"Yes…" Cole hedged.

"Great, now I need you to get Helena and bring her here *now*," I ordered, needing him not to argue with me. He must have seen something in my face because he quickly kissed my forehead and left.

"Love, are you all right?" Gavin asked, reaching out to place a hand on my knee.

I opened my mouth to answer, but I wasn't sure what to say. It would be a lie if I told him everything was fine, but I didn't want him to worry or make it sound like I couldn't handle all this. Finally, I settled on just being honest. "There's just a lot more than I expected to deal with. I've been so focused on getting us here and safe that I hadn't taken the time to worry about what happened next. I don't know the first thing about running the inner workings of a castle or bringing on all new staff from a group of people I don't know. My hope is that Helena will be able to help me sort this all out so I can worry about other things no one else can help me with."

"Wisely said, Your Majesty," Mathew said as he handed me a cup of hot tea. "This is a personal blend I make that seems to help me when I feel overwhelmed. Shall we wait for Helena to join us before we continue, or would you rather us keep going?"

"There's more?" I cried, my shoulders slumping as I fell back against the chair I was sitting in. "Fine, tell me what else I need to do."

There was an awkward pause as if they weren't sure if they *should* continue, but Lawrence took me at my word. "The day of the coronation, you will need to get ready here since part of the ritual will be having you ride up to the castle and be announced. Once you enter the throne room, you will make your way to the front where the throne is, and we will be waiting for you. This is where you will give one of the vows, but we will help prompt you in a call-and-response-type situation. Then you will be given the key to the castle, and you'll turn to the left and give your vow to the dragons, face center and give your vow to the people, then turn to the right and give your vow to Sheca as a whole and the gods who protect it."

"Speaking of the gods…" Izel cut in. "I can't say I am familiar with what you are talking about. We never had a deity we paid homage to back in Norden."

"Hmm." Eleazar mused, rubbing a hand over his beard. "It appears we might need to make some adjustments on that bit since those who came from Norden won't know what we are talking about. Now that the castle is open, the Holy Place will be available to us, and we can bring back our worship to its rightful place. We can teach them of our gods they have forgotten but who have never abandoned them. Let us dwell on that for a day or two, but if you would like books or information on the gods, we can supply that."

Izel motioned his thanks and for Lawrence to continue. He cleared his throat as he tried to remember where we left off.

"I believe I was facing to the right, giving my vow to Sheca and the gods," I offered, hoping it would help.

"Ah, yes. Once you have completed all of that, you will take your seat on the throne, and we will place the crown on your head. The magic within the castle and what lives inside you will meld, giving you full control over everything within the castle walls. This is how the previous king was able to lock the place up as he did for his return. Without the key and your magic, nothing would have gotten through that barrier," Lawrence stated. "It might be best to have you enter the castle's keep first just in case any other backup protections are set in place."

"Smart idea," I agreed. "If it were me, I would put up extra blockades in areas where something important resides."

The older men all muttered their agreement, fell silent once again, and looked over the men sitting before them until Mathew turned to me. "Then there is the matter of announcing your consort or consorts as it were..."

"Explain to us what needs to be done or is expected from this part of the coronation," I suggested, knowing this would be easier if I understood what was involved in the event. If I could have avoided the whole thing being a public display, I would have without a second thought.

"There will be a simple ceremony tying you together in the eyes of the gods and our people. It will be expected that from this point, you will consummate the union in an effort to produce an heir for the future of your reign. That, of course, will happen later. It will just need to be witnessed by someone who can be trusted and isn't attached to you, such as a guardian or family member," Mathew instructed, wringing his hand the whole time, uncomfortable with the topic. "If you take more than one, the act will only have to be confirmed with one of them, and from that point on, you will be left to do as you please for the rest of your rule. It is an old tradition, but it is one that the people feel gives them the most comfort knowing you will provide for the future."

"I see. Does this need to be decided now, or do we have time to talk among ourselves in the coming week?" I inquired.

"We will just need to know a day or two before so that we might know how to plan our remarks for officiating the union."

"Then that is when you will have your answer. I don't feel comfortable giving that information before we have talked," I said simply.

Thankfully, Cole and Helena arrived, and we put a pin in that topic for now. Just as I'd hoped, Helena was who I needed to help me with the staff and banquet details. Working out what we could took up the rest of the morning, and I couldn't have been more relieved to have some of my list checked off. The plan was to break for lunch and then head up to the castle now that the weather had cleared and the sun was peeking out of the clouds, giving us plenty of light to work from as we opened the castle.

TWENTY-ONE

THE DRAGON QUEEN IS CROWNED

Now that we finished what we needed to with the viceroys and Helena, I decided it was time to travel back to the castle. I wanted nothing more than to hide away in the uncharted halls of the past and learn what mysteries it held. It didn't take us long to saddle the horses and ride up the road. The guys felt it was safe enough to let the horses cross the drawbridge if we did it one at a time so there wasn't too much weight. It took a little bit to find the stables once we all crossed, but when we found the smithy, I knew it had to be close. It was a long, narrow barn with stalls on either side facing each other with a dirt aisle down the middle. Everything was in perfect shape, not seeming to have aged a day, so we unsaddled the horses and set them up in the stalls. They were empty with no bedding, but it would work until we headed back for the night. Once we had the bridge fixed and it could handle wagons crossing it, straw would be delivered and the stalls set up.

Standing in the middle of the courtyard, I looked up at the sky with the sun beaming down on me, warming my face. I took in a deep breath of the crisp, clean air filling my lungs, invigorating me.

"You look like you already belong here," Abbott commented.

I tilted my head to look at him better. "Is it odd to say that I do feel like this place has been waiting for me? Right now, all I want to do is dive into its history, ignoring all the other responsibilities pressing in around me."

"No, I wouldn't say it's odd. The fact you are such a bookworm is what's odd," Cole interjected, coming to join us. "Who knew a noble woman could be so enamored with the past and learning things like you are? I always thought they would be more concerned about their dresses or dancing shit like that."

"It's the one thing my father did right," I murmured, shaking myself out of my daydreams and walking up to the castle doors, unlocking them, and shoving one side open enough to enter. "Best we light the lanterns while we can still see what we are doing."

Izel came up and handed me one already lit as if he knew I would ask for it. "Figured it would be best for you to have your own so you can investigate things as you please."

Leaning forward, I kissed Izel lightly on the lips. "Thank you."

"Well, shit! If I knew doing something so simple would get me a kiss, I would've been the first to do that," Paxton grumbled.

"Bold of you to assume you would get a kiss from our queen, being so new and shoving your foot in your mouth every chance you get," Jade shot back. "Do us all a favor and think before you speak."

Paxton looked ready to pounce on Jade, but he glanced at me and shoved past him, muttering to himself. That was an improvement—a small one but enough to show me he was trying to make an effort not to fight with the others. I followed after him into the darkness of the castle nave with its vast arched ceilings that our feeble lantern light wasn't strong enough to penetrate the darkness. On either side of the nave, you could step up to benches for people waiting their turn for an audience with the queen. Glass windows at least twelve feet tall stood every few feet, shuttered, leaving us in a soft darkness. I approached one and unlatched the first section of the shutters, but to get to the upper two, I would need a ladder.

"Here, let me help with that," Dayson said behind me before he swooped in, scooping me up to sit on his broad shoulders. I tried to hold in the yelp of surprise, but it echoed around the empty space, making the others chuckle. "Can you reach the latch?"

"I can get the middle one but not the top one. Who has a sword?" I called out to the others, having an idea.

"Yeah, I don't think any of us are going to hand over a sword for you to wave about in the dark, mouse," Cole objected.

Scowling at him, I set my hands on my hips. "Really, is your faith in Abbott's training so little that you don't trust me to hold a sword?"

Hearing this, Abbott turned to face his friend with a questioning brow, waiting for his response. Cole tried to speak a few times but gave up and tossed his hands in the air. "Fine, fine. I'll give the crazy lady sitting on the shoulders of an idiot a sword. Watch out Dayson, she might accidentally stab you in the process of opening the shutter. Don't blame me if it happens, I was just trying to look out for everyone."

Even though I tried to keep a straight face, I couldn't do it, and I burst out laughing and almost fell off Dayson's shoulders in the process. "Whoa, watch out, Cassy-bear... wouldn't want Cole thinking he was right about this situation, now would we?"

"No, that would be a travesty to inflate his ego even more than it already is," I answered, trying to pull myself together. "Okay, I'm good. I'll take the sword now."

Cole stepped up and held out the hilt of his sword but paused just before I could grab it. "You sure about this, big guy?"

"Give her the damn sword already," Dayson growled out.

Shrugging his shoulders, Cole handed over the weapon, and with Dayson's help, I was able to get the last latch free without any incidents. Izel and Abbott pulled open the shutters, and the room became much brighter. We would need to open a few more to negate the use of the lanterns, but it helped.

"Well, since you're up there, want to open more of them? We're gonna need to get to them all eventually, so why not start on this side?" Dayson suggested as he moved to the next window.

After a few, we figured out a perfect system and opened all the shutters on one side of the room, flooding the place with light. We would eventually do the same with the other side, but for now, this was more than enough to see by and take in the splendor of the stonework in the space. I returned the sword to Cole before Dayson set me down so I could wander the room. We were close to another set of tall wooden double doors I guessed would be the throne room. As I got close to the doors, I noticed that dragons were carved into the wood as if they were facing each other, a clawed hand resting where the door rings were, making it seem like you needed to get past the dragon to get to the throne.

I gasped as I entered, awestruck by what lay before me. The ceiling was made of glass so the room was bright, showing off the polished marble floor with gold veins running through it. The room was about half the size of the nave we just walked through but just as impressive with its high ceilings. At the far end of the room was a massive black stone dragon with jeweled eyes that glimmered in the sunlight, its tail wrapping around the throne as if protecting it from those who would dare take it from them. Before I knew it, I was walking up the steps to the simple stone chair with black velvet cushions that seemed lush to the touch. When I reached the top step, I felt something shift in the air, and the stone dragon came to life, lifting its head and inspecting me as it sat on its haunches. Its emerald eyes bore into my soul as its wings flared out, trying to intimidate me.

"Who dares approach the Forgotten Throne?"

"I, Cassarah of the Raven Rose clan, Dragon Queen of the Mercenaries," I announced to the dragon. "I have come with our people who have been gone and return to our home in our time of need. It is time for the people and dragons of Sheca to rise once again and take their place in the world."

The dragon blinked once, the only sign that he understood what I'd just said. *"Prove you are the Dragon Queen, the heir to the Dragon Castle and the Forgotten Throne. Take your place on the throne, and it shall decide if you are worthy, Cassarah of Raven Rose."*

"Cassarah, don't you dare do what the creepy stone dragon is saying," Jade barked out.

I whirled around, seeing them fanned out at the base of the steps, watching what was happening.

"She needs to prove to the magic in the castle that she is who she says she is. No harm will come to her. This is her rightful place... trust in our queen," Zan countered.

"Oh sure, of course, you believe that you come from this crazy place where magic is normal, and stone dragons coming to life isn't a sign you might be going crazy," Paxton muttered. "But sure, tell the woman we all have feelings for to sit on the throne and possibly get burned to a crisp."

"How little faith you have in your woman," May stated, crossing her arms. "Sit on the damn chair, Cassarah, and prove to them you're the warrior that you are so they stop treating you like a fucking flower."

Hearing May's words made me grin, but I knew she was right. As much as the guys cared, they did see me as something delicate and to be protected at all costs. This moment was the turning point—I knew it deep in my soul. The moment I sat on the throne, no matter what happened, I would be crowned the Dragon Queen, the dragons and the gods sealing my fate to these people for the rest of my life. With this choice, the coronation didn't need to happen, and I'd be lying to myself if I wasn't a little grateful for that.

I stepped forward before turning and slowly sat on the throne, resting my hands on the armrests, sitting tall, and squaring my shoulders. This is where I belonged, and nothing was going to change that, not even a stone dragon. I knew it just like I knew the men and women standing before me would stay by my side forever, no matter what came our way. In this moment of perfect clarity, I also knew each one of those men would hold a piece of my heart, and without them all, I wouldn't be whole nor would they. The gods brought us together because each of us held something the other lacked, but together we were complete, able to accomplish anything we set our minds to, like stopping the Lost King.

As all of these thoughts came rushing through my mind, I noticed I had closed my eyes at some point. When I opened them, I found myself in a swirl of blue light. My Birthright was like a tornado around me, and when I realized it, the magic burst from me and flowed through the castle, and I could feel it unlocking every door and bursting open every shutter like the castle was welcoming me back with open arms. I could also feel Vasin was nearby, perched at a roost made in one of the castle's towers created just for the ruling king or queen's dragon. Our bond hummed as our magic flowed through the rest of the castle and each other, creating the final piece to our already powerful connection.

"Cass, do you know what you've just done?" Vasin asked.

"Become queen?" I answered hesitantly. *"Because that's what I was trying to do."*

"You have done more than that. You've just freed the dragons from the deal they made with the first

KING OF THE MERCENARIES, ALLOWING THEM TO NO LONGER BE DRAWN TO THE MAGIC HELD BY ANY ANCESTORS THAT STILL HAVE IT. ANY BOND THAT IS MADE FROM THIS POINT ON WILL BE MADE OUT OF FREE WILL AND FREE WILL ALONE. YOU HAVE JUST CHANGED HISTORY, MY DEAR CASS!"

"How could I have done that? I just sat on the throne?"

"WHEN YOU REACHED OUT TO ME JUST NOW, YOU GAVE YOURSELF COMPLETELY OVER TO OUR BOND, WISHING FOR NOTHING IN RETURN EXCEPT MY FRIENDSHIP AND HAPPINESS. YOU DON'T WISH TO CONTROL ME OR TAKE ANYTHING FROM ME THAT I'M NOT WILLING TO GIVE, MAKING A NEW AGREE-MENT WITH THE RULING DRAGON AND THE RULING MERCE-NARY. ONCE A NEW OATH IS MADE, IT CANCELS OUT THE OLD ONE, FREEING ALL DRAGONS ALIVE AND TO COME FROM WHAT WAS DONE IN THE PAST."

I had no idea what to say to that, and before I got the chance to ask anything else, I was yanked back to the throne room at the pain of something being burned into my skin in the middle of my chest. I let out a scream that was echoed by others, but I couldn't focus on anything outside of what was happening to my body. Then it was over just as fast as it happened, causing me to slump forward in the throne, panting as I regained my senses. There was a strange weight on my head along with a dull ache in my chest, causing me to raise a hand, but it was met with cool metal instead of my hair. Confused, I lifted the metal off my head, held it in front of me, and found it was a crown. It wasn't gaudy or covered in jewels. It was a simple peaked circle with delicate metal stamping that made it look like dragon scales were pressed into the metal.

`"In the sight of dragons and gods, you have been chosen, Cassarah, Dragon Queen, ruler of the Dragon Castle, who sits on` *the Forgotten Throne. May your rule be long and prosperous.*" The stone dragon intoned as it returned to its original position like nothing had ever transpired.

"Ah, guys... did anyone else just get branded?" Paxton asked, pulling at the collar of his tunic.

There, right over his heart, was angry, raised pink skin in the shape of a heart with a crown around it. That had me looking at my chest, but mine was in the center just under my throat, and it was a crown that matched theirs and the crown I held in my hands. "Why is mine different?"

"Because you are queen, and we are your consorts," Zan said as he ran his fingers lightly over the raw skin. "You claimed us all..."

I shifted my gaze over to May and Becka, whose eyes were wide, watching us. Becka tossed up her hands and shook her head. "Cassarah, you know I love you but not like that. May and I didn't get another mark. I think Zan is right about the consort theory. It's the only thing that makes sense."

Slowly, I pushed myself up out of the throne, my whole body aching from the amount of power that just coursed through me, making me a little unsteady. Walking down a few steps, I stopped when I was at eye level with all the men I'd just marked. The certainty I'd had in the midst of all that had just happened was now gone, and I felt vulnerable as I looked each of them in the eyes. "Are you all accepting of that mark?"

Jade was the first to act, stepping up and grabbing my hips to twirl me around before setting me down and kissing me soundly on the mouth. "My little bird, there is nothing I want more than to be by your side and in your bed for the rest of my life."

Twenty-Two

What Secrets Does the Castle Hold?

"Not so fast, Grim Reaper," Dayson announced as he pulled me out of Jade's arms. "You're not the only one who has been waiting for this moment, so share the love, *brother*."

Soon, I was passed from one man to another, each showering me in kisses and hugs until it came to Zan and Paxton. Both of them obviously bore my claim to them as more than just my guardian, but we hadn't really had a chance to know each other in that way. Zan held out a hand in my direction with a soft smile as his smoky, unseeing eyes bore into my soul. He might not be able to see me in the traditional sense of the word, but with Ezzu's help and something else that was just him, I knew he saw me better than any of the others. I placed my hand in his and let him pull me to his chest, where he wrapped his arms around me and rested his head on the top of mine.

"I know we are new to each other and things might take some time, but you are more than worth the wait, and I will enjoy discovering who you are, Cassarah," he murmured into my hair, then pulled back far enough to kiss me on the forehead and the tip of my nose.

His words made me melt in his arms along with his kisses, feeling the sincerity in them, and setting me at ease that he wasn't unhappy being claimed by me. Zan released me as I turned to face Paxton who stood there looking extremely unsure of himself.

"Cassarah... look, I know I'm an asshole and always seem to say the wrong thing around you or pick a fight with the others, but I would like the chance to see what might happen between us. Clearly, the gods seem to think we might be good for each other, and I'm inclined to trust them on this matter. I've never met a woman I respected more than I do you, even in the short time I've watched you and how you carry yourself through all this shit going on. If there is a woman who could make something useful out of a man like me, it would be you, and I'd really love to see what we can do together."

Paxton's words were so honest and probably the first time I'd seen him truly take something seriously. His gaze never wavered from mine as he spoke, trying to show me as much as tell me how he felt. I held out both hands to him which he took, hope lighting up his face. "As I sat on the throne and magic was flying around me, I reached perfect clarity. At that moment, I understood that each of you hold something I need, and in that same regard, I have something you need. I've been sheltered and controlled in how I act or express my emotions. On the other hand, you let them fly freely, never second-guessing yourself as you speak your mind. Sometimes, it needs to be toned down just as I need to show more and take risks. I think we can both learn from each other, and if something more blossoms from it, I don't think I would mind at all," I shared, giving him a wide smile.

In his excitement, he let out a *whoop* of joy, pulling me in for a bone-crushing hug before he tossed me up and caught me, only to cup my face and press his lips to mine. A little startled, I froze, but then it just felt right, so I returned his kiss but still kept it chaste. "Spitfire, you and I are going to make one hell of a team... I just know it!" Paxton announced as he grinned, looking down at me. "Now what do you say we find out what other trouble we can get into around this castle?" Intertwining his fingers with mine, he tugged me to follow as he took off across the throne room back out to the nave, now bright with all the shutters open.

Off to the left was another set of double doors which revealed a set of stairs leading up to the second level of the castle. Once on the second floor, we walked down a long hall with paintings of the previous kings and their dragons along with other artwork depicting the battle that caused the first king to discover Sheca. Another painting showed the first king, his family, and other various moments in history with brass plates on the bottom of the frames stating who or what the painting was. There were several rooms off the hall on either side that we peeked in on, but most of them were sitting rooms, a game room, and the ballroom at the end of the hall. The polished hardwood floor shone in the light, but what took my breath away was the mural on the ceiling of dragons flying and people in beautiful clothes dancing.

"I think I could lay on the floor and stare at that ceiling for hours and still not see everything," I whispered, not wanting to disturb the peacefulness of the room.

A body pressed up against my back, wrapping its arms around my waist. "I think that every time I look at you, love," Gavin said in a hushed voice, his lips brushing the shell of my ear, making me shiver. "Just when I think I have you figured out, you show us something new we hadn't noticed before. Something tells me life with you will never be boring."

I twisted in his arms to face him and brushed some of his curls out of his face before I could think better of it. This seemed to please him immensely, and he caught my hand to press a kiss to my palm, slowly holding my gaze. For an act that was so innocent and simple, it made my body flair with heat and need like some wanton woman. "Now I just think you're spinning tales to butter me up, Gavin. There isn't all that much to figure out about me. I'm a fairly simple person."

"Now that is where you are wrong, little mouse," Cole countered, boxing me in from behind so I was trapped between them. "The prince is right... you are like a puzzle. Just when we think we have it all figured out, we find another piece we need to fit in somewhere. You are like a drug to us, Cassarah. We want to have all of you, but that isn't something you hand out freely. It has to be earned, and the high we get... it's addicting."

"I wasn't there the night of the ball for those accepted into court, never getting the chance to see you all dressed up. I would very much like to witness this with my own eyes after getting a taste of it for dinner the other night in the castle," Gavin shared, brushing the back of his finger along my cheek. "I think the sight of you would make this mural pale in comparison."

"Just think, now that we bear her mark, we get to monopolize her time at these events, keeping her all to ourselves," Cole added. "I quite like having that sort of place in your life," he admitted, brushing my hair to the side to kiss the back of my neck, causing me to inhale sharply at the touch.

The sound of someone clearing their throat had us all looking off to the side where Abbott stood with Izel. "As much as I hate to break up this moment for you three, we still have plenty more of the castle to go through."

"You're absolutely right," I blurted, thankful for Abbott tossing me a lifeline to keep from getting swept away in these emotions. "We still haven't found the living quarters yet. If we want to move in here sooner rather than later, that should be our main focus today."

Cole gave Abbott a dirty look and muttered something under his breath about being a cockblock. Ignoring his frustrations, I joined

Izel as we headed back into the hall to look for stairs to the castle's next level. They were hidden off a short side hall I assumed would typically be guarded so not just anyone could wander up into the rest of the castle. This floor was absolutely for the people who lived here, with a dining room that had a vaulted ceiling and a railing for the fourth floor to look down into the room which I guessed was where the bedrooms were. This level also had a beautiful library filled with books and scrolls I had to be pulled away from by the guys.

"Little warrior, there will be plenty of time to come and hide away here, but we need to get a feel for the whole castle first," Izel pointed out.

I pouted but followed them out of the room into the connecting one that was an office. A large wooden desk sat as the focal point of the whole room with more books on the shelves behind it, but they seemed to be records and journals more than books for leisure. I trailed a finger over the volumes. They didn't feel aged at all, and the paper still left on the desk wasn't yellowed or dried out from the years it's been there, making me truly believe this place was just as they left it. Would there be clothes in the rooms or personal things they couldn't take with them on the journey into Norden? It seems there would only be one way to find out.

Past the living section on this floor, we discovered some bedrooms that had more of a guest feel about them with each room a replica of the other with a slightly different color scheme but no real personality intertwined. As we made it to the fourth floor, the rooms took on a completely different feel with far more character, and you knew that people lived in this space, making it their own. The king's suite took up the whole left side of the hall with a sitting room, study, dressing room, and then the bedroom and bath. Everything was in cream colors with blacks, grays, and gold intermixed, giving it dimension. I loved everything about it and was pleased to find it so much to my liking that I wouldn't have to change much. The others spread out, checking the rooms and arguing over who would get what space, making me smile as I listened to them.

I ventured deeper into the bedroom, amazed at the massive bed with its canopy only covering the head area more for decoration than utility. What drew me, though, was the plush window seat that overlooked the village below and gave you an amazing view of the mountains that protected us. Unable to fight back my curiosity any longer, I moved to the closet, pulled open the dresser doors, and found there were, indeed, clothes left behind. It was a mixture of men's and women's, mostly night clothes and undergarments made from silky fabric. Stepping farther into the dark room since there were no windows, I found trunks stacked along one wall. I opened them only to have dresses surge out, spilling onto the floor. It appeared they left everything they didn't need behind—shoes, jewelry, and everything else a person could possess. This revelation had me moving to the study and the writing desk, sitting in the chair, and pulling open drawers.

One of them was locked, but on a hunch, I took the key from around my neck and used it to open the drawer. Inside, I found a worn journal and a note tucked into an envelope with my name written on it. Carefully, I pulled both items out and set them on the desk, unsure if I wanted to see what was written in the letter. How could someone from four hundred years ago possibly know *I* would be the one to be here at this moment and discover this letter? Taking a deep breath, I broke the seal on the letter, pulled out the paper inside, and unfolded it.

If my vision is of what will come, the Dragon Queen will be reading this letter once the castle has been reopened. In the event the Dragon Queen isn't reading this, then all hope is lost, and the world as we know it will be destroyed by our own pride and shortsightedness, but I refuse to believe so little of our people.

Cassarah,

I know this will be hard to wrap your head around, but I was given a vision when I bonded with my black dragon, Dotho, and his venom ran through my veins. King Yash thought he was doing the right thing for us when he told the other kingdoms about the magic dragons can bestow on us. It brought us mercenaries respect and helped create the foundation of our people and kingdom as we were starting out. Time has passed, and the effect of this choice is taking its toll on the dragons. They are dying out and refusing to breed in an effort to stop the cycle. In my vision, I saw what must be done to save dragons from becoming extinct, but it means giving up so much. It will cause division, and many of the people I take with me will struggle. Their lives will never be easy, but it is the price we must pay in atonement for what we've done to them.

Those I left behind were not the weakest of us but the strongest of heart and will be good stewards of our home while we had to leave it. With their care, Sheca will become a thriving people, and they will keep the dragons from dying out while we take the long road to break the original oath. I wish I could say I was strong enough to do it myself, but the moment I was offered the power, I took it, and with the knowledge at my fingertips, I knew I could rule the world if I wanted to. My penance for this choice is that I have to leave with the others, securing the castle until you come along.

Cassarah, you will be the best of us with your pure heart. You will be able to do what none of us have—walk away from the power given to you by your black dragon. In the time our people need a wise and compassionate leader, you will rise above all other leaders we've had before. Many will try to stop you, but trust your heart, your guardians, and above all, your dragon for they will never steer you wrong. Embrace the humbleness and tender heart that others will scorn you for, as this will lead you in the right direction when facing someone as cold and broken as the Lost King. Do not underestimate him, Cassarah. He has no soul and will stop at nothing to get what he wants. Even then, he will want more to try to fill that void within himself.

You have opened up the castle and all that it has to offer. Learn all you can about the past for both our people and the dragons because in that lies the truth you will need to defeat the Lost King. You will be protected in Sheca to learn what you must and train our people into what they should have been all along—those who fight for others who cannot defend themselves. It was what our people were founded on, but we kings lost sight of that and hid ourselves away when we needed to be fighting.

The gods' blessing on you, Cassarah,
King Cardon

Twenty-Three
Time to Explore

I don't know how long I sat there reading and rereading what was written, trying to make sense of it all. A king from four hundred years ago wrote me a letter, and things he had written about were already coming true or had happened. Could it be possible that a dragon's venom was that powerful to allow him to see all that was to come? Did he see how everything was going to end? Setting down the letter, I opened the journal, and it was filled with entries of King Cardon's life from the point he had bonded with his dragon to the night before they were going to leave. It was written in the same language we use now, but the letter was written in the old tongue. Could it have been a precaution to ensure that if the wrong person saw it, they couldn't read it? Why did I feel like the more I learned, the more questions I had instead of answers?

"Cassarah?" My head snapped up at Becka's voice. "You all right? I've been calling for you."

"Sorry, I just got distracted when I found some notes and other things left behind in the king's desk. There is even a closet full of clothes for both men and women as well. Did you guys discover anything in the other rooms?" I wasn't sure I was ready to tell them all about this letter or what it might mean.

"Come look for yourself. It's a little creepy," Becka said as she waved for me to follow.

Frowning, I stood, wondering what could be so creepy. Surely, there wasn't anyone left in the place that had become petrified after so many years. Becka led me to a room that seemed to have been used by a woman with all the soft pinks and the vast amounts of lace adorning everything. There on the dressing table was a note she had clearly opened and laid out to read. If her letter was anything like mine, I wasn't sure I wanted to read it, but my curiosity got the better of me, and I picked it up.

To the future person who will reside in these rooms,

My name is Daina, and I am the eldest daughter of King Cardon, the third king of the mercenaries. We are leaving tomorrow, and I've been instructed to leave a note for whoever might take over this room when the Dragon Queen comes. Father only allowed us to take what we would need or couldn't replace since our new lives in Norden would be much simpler than what I've grown up knowing. They tell us the spell they will put over the castle makes it so that nothing will age, and it will be just as we left it. I hope this is true because I just had a few new dresses made I will never get to wear. I hope they fit you so they get to be used. Know that I loved and treasured everything in this room, and I hope it serves you as well as it did me growing up.

PS—If you need a little spice in your life, I've hidden my favorite sordid romances under the mattress. They helped me through many tough times being unable to go to parties since I wasn't in very good health last year.

Glancing up from the letter, I found Becka standing there with three books in her hands, grinning. "Did you think I wouldn't go look after she told me where to find them?"

Laughing, I took the book she offered and shook my head at the title, *Under the Moonlight: Poems and Sonnets to Stir the Heart.*

"Goodness, these are quite descriptive, aren't they?" I shared, blushing at some of the things I was reading.

"Seems like you should keep them so you know what to expect when you take the next step with your men," Becka teased.

I gaped at her, snapping the book shut. "Becka!"

"Oh please, everyone can see that they are stepping up their game to be the first one you take to bed. What man wouldn't want to have that feather in their cap? Soak it all in while it lasts... on second thought, you do have eight of them, so maybe not," Becka mused out loud, tapping a finger on her chin. "Do you think more than one of them would want to *play* at a time? Would you let them if they wanted to?"

"I haven't the slightest clue what you're talking about, and I'm not sure I want to know just yet." I huffed, tossing the book back to her.

"Now I wouldn't be so hasty, Cassarah," May interjected as she entered through a side door connected to the room she'd been looking at. "I can speak from experience that having more than one lover in bed with you at a time is absolutely something you want to know *all* about. Nothing beats a man thrusting into you from both sides."

They burst out laughing as they took in my stunned expression as detailed visuals flooded my mind of what that could even look like. "Wait, are you saying you let them enter in the back as well as the front? What purpose would that serve? Children can only be produced from the vagina."

"Clearly, we have our work cut out for us if you think that sex is just for producing a child. When you find the right partner or partners, in your case, sex is something that can take your physical relationship to a whole new mind-blowing level of passion. I have zero feelings toward any of your men, but I would bet my life on the fact they will make you see stars if given the chance. Know that I am always around if you have questions or want help figuring out how to do something. There isn't much I haven't tried," May informed me, adding a saucy wink.

"May, I want to be just like you when I grow up." Becka sighed.

"Ah, ladies, there you are…" Gavin started to say until he caught sight of me with my cheeks blazing with my embarrassment. "Should I come back?"

Darting forward, I grabbed his arm and pulled him out of the room. "No need. They just finished telling me what they needed to."

I could hear the echoes of their laughter as I continued to lead Gavin away from them and the topic we'd just been discussing. "Love, where are we going?" Gavin asked after a minute.

Stopping quickly, realizing I didn't know, he bumped into me, and we both stumbled. We ended up in a heap on the floor with me sprawled out on top of him, his face in the middle of my chest. It took him a moment to figure out where he was, and I didn't know what to do, so my hands just seemed to flutter at my sides.

"You know there are plenty of bedrooms to use if you guys want to get frisky, right?" Paxton asked as he peered down at us.

"Help me up, will you," Gavin asked, resting one hand on the floor and holding the other up to Paxton.

He just grinned at the hand for a moment. "Sorry, man, I'm not really into guys like that, but you might want to ask one of the others if you're having a hard time getting it up."

"That's not what I meant at all, Pax, and you know it," Gavin muttered as he awkwardly rolled off me to lay on his back beside me.

"You know, for a prince, you're not very smooth with the ladies, are you? I would have thought with a title and all, you'd been slipping them into your rooms since the day you sprung your first salute. At this point, the Grim Reaper is beating us all, and I can't say I'm thrilled with that outcome," Paxton rambled as he dropped to sit on the floor between us. "You guys seen the indoor garden they have up here? Talk about cool things you don't really need but are impressive. I think I picked out my room too. The king's brother used it, and he had a thing for hidden compartments. In his letter, he told me that he hid a bunch of cool stuff in the room, but I would have to find them using only two simple clues."

As Paxton rattled on about things, I sat up and shifted so I leaned against the wall trying to get my heart rate under control. The feel of Gavin's body and knowing that I caused the hard length I felt in his pants made my blood heat and rush through me. A tension in my body that I hadn't felt before until these men started to be more forward in their attention started to ache deep in my stomach. Having just been talking about things with May and Becka didn't help matters, either.

"What do you think, spitfire?" Paxton asked, snapping my attention back to them as they both sat there waiting for my answer.

"I think that you taking that room is fine. You'll have to let me know what you find," I answered, hoping that was what he'd been asking.

Paxton smiled at me and rested his head on his knee. "While I'm glad you're interested in finding that out as much as I am, that isn't what I wanted to know…"

"Don't be an ass and just ask her again. Clearly, she got bored with you rambling about your room since that's when she checked out," Jade pointed out from where he leaned against the wall near me, watching our interaction.

"When did you show up?" I demanded, a little worried that someone could sneak up on me so easily.

"A little after Paxton, but unlike him, I didn't need to inject myself into the moment to steal your attention away from Gavin," he answered, offering me a hand which I took and let him pull me to my feet. "He was asking if you wanted to stay the night here since it has everything we need, or if you wish to return to Marta's home. The sun is setting so if we are going to head back, now would be best."

I mulled over the options, but even though we could sleep here, we didn't have everything we needed. "Let's head back for tonight, then we can work with the villagers to gather what we need. The stables need to be set up along with other supplies, such as food and firewood to heat the rooms. Living in a stone palace will be much colder than the wooden ones you've been living in. Plus, I think it would be wise to let the viceroys know what happened here and see if we might be able to diminish the number of things we need to do for the coronation."

"Do you think they will really let you skip things?" Paxton asked, hopping to his feet.

"Seeing as I already have this on my head, I don't think they can argue with the fact that I'm their queen," I said, pointing to the crown on my head.

"True, and we all bear your mark now, so maybe they will let you do things at your own pace instead of the traditional way," Gavin suggested. "It was one of the things I was really dreading about my wedding. Who wants someone in the room with them to check and see if you were able to do what was needed to make a baby?"

"I was going to talk with them about that, anyway. There is no way I could even entertain the idea of having a child right now. It would put me in a position where I couldn't help our people or fight in the battles that are to come."

"Do you want them... kids, I mean?" Jade asked, his light green eyes watching me with curiosity.

"I wasn't sure, but I think with the right people in my life and knowing I made the world a safer place once the Lost King is gone, will make me change my mind," I answered softly, reaching out to take his hand. "There are eight men who would make sure any child I had would be the safest child in all the kingdoms."

"Damn right, we would," Jade said under his breath. "Come on. Let's find the others so we can make our way back."

We returned to the village, and once we shared a small portion of what we found in the castle, the viceroys suggested we have dinner with them and Alsten. This way, we could start dealing with matters of security and getting workers out there to help us turn the castle into a livable place once again.

"So you say that everything is just as it was?" Alsten questioned, sipping his glass of wine. "How can that possibly be? I've never heard of magic stopping time like that in only one place or for that long."

"There is so much to go through that King Cardon left behind, I'm sure I'll find some answers to a lot of our questions. Really, this makes things so much easier for us, though. It's just a matter of restocking the castle than starting from scratch. If we had to build all new furniture and things like that, it would be crazy," I pointed out.

"You make a good point, but you mentioned when you first came back that you had bigger news to tell us," Lawrence inquired.

As we traveled back down, I'd packed away the crown, not wanting to announce what happened before I talked it over with the viceroys, who, I might add, inducted Sal into their ranks. He now worked and lived with them in their quest to preserve and uphold traditions. I pulled the bag from the back of the chair and unwrapped the crown, holding it out for them to see.

"It would seem that in order to complete the release of the spell on the castle, it needed to crown me queen of its own accord. I have been blessed by the gods and the dragons as the new queen of the mercenaries. They also took care of marking me and my consorts as the power settled throughout the kingdom," I explained, pulling at the collar of the shirt I was now wearing. The guys showed theirs as well, proving that they matched with mine.

The viceroys stared at us with open wonder.

"Well, that certainly makes things far more interesting," Mathew said, grinning at us.

TWENTY-FOUR

THINGS TO DO AND PLANS TO MAKE

"Does this mean we still have to go through the entire coronation process?" I asked, praying they would tell me I didn't have to do it at all.

Mathew looked at the others, and once again, they did that silent communication thing, and Lawrence cleared his throat. "While much of it will be for formalities' sake, I do believe it's what's best for our people to have the coronation ceremony. We can forgo such things as the cleansing, memorization of the vows, and the observance of your consummations with your consorts. Although we do ask that you spend the night with at least one of them for appearance's sake. We hold strongly to our traditions no matter how antiquated they might feel."

"I can accept that," I offered. "Even though we have the blessings of the dragons, I would still like to journey out to meet them since our oath with them has changed. Vasin has shared that they will be eager to talk with him about what happened, and I agree it would be best. As for the guards, Alsten, when would be the best time to meet them and allow them to give their fealty to their new queen?"

"Allow me to organize things with them and recall the soldiers I have in other lands keeping track of the Lost King's movements. While we wait, it might be best to devise a plan for those guarding the castle and you. I know many would prefer not to have to leave the safety of our valley as well as some who have been hoping to see some of the outside world. As I've mentioned before, it's only been a short while that we've been expanding our reach," Alsten explained.

"Works well for me. I plan to travel out to the Dragon Lands with my men so that they also might be known to them," I reasoned. "My wish is that we can build a new friendship with the dragons that is not based on our need to bond with them. I do hope that keeps happening since I know the joy it can bring to have a companion like Vasin in my life, and I know others do as well. We just need to ensure that what I've freed them from won't be able to happen again. The loss of both human and dragon life is too great a cost."

"It's absolutely incredible you were able to break the old oath and replace it with a new one," Eleazar shared, shaking his head. "You've been here a mere two days, not even, and you've changed our world more than we ever dreamed."

Sal grunted his agreement and slammed his wine chalice down. "I always knew great things would come from our wee Cassy. She just needed to learn how to stick up for herself. The knowledge she has trapped in her pretty head was getting stifled with the scared little waif she was when I first met her."

My brows shot up at this newfound information. "So all the impossible tasks you gave me and the hours spent pouring over old scrolls you couldn't read was to build me a stronger backbone?"

"Of course. Did you really think I wouldn't prepare you for the world you were about to take over? I've seen the dismal state these so-called mercenaries had turned themselves into, scrimping and scraping for whatever work they could find. Once, we had been a people to be feared and respected, but without a true leader, they let fear rule. Now that you are here and have the power to lead us, I know things will change quite quickly, I would think," Sal stated.

Cole let out a chuckle. "Would you look at that... old Sal does have a heart."

"Watch it, boy. You might be a consort to the queen, but it doesn't mean I still can't make your life hell," Sal barked back. "You could have been just like your father, but you chose to be the opposite which I will never understand. The mind you have isn't something we see often."

This surprised me. I knew Cole was smarter than he ever showed or people gave him credit for, but for Sal to call him out like that meant I've only seen a glimpse of the true story.

"Those days have passed, and I'm happy with the life I chose. It landed me here, didn't it? If you'll recall, I was sent on the mission to sneak her out of her home because I was the best," Cole countered, giving me a wink. "I'd say that worked out well for me."

Mathew cleared his throat, drawing attention in his direction. "I would very much like to take a look at the library you have in the castle. Would it be safe enough for me to do so tomorrow?"

"I don't see why not. But do keep in mind that even though it has some comforts, it doesn't hold any warmth, food, or supplies," I warned.

"You know the one place we didn't see was the kitchen. Do you think they are in a separate building?" Abbott questioned. "We didn't spend much time with the outbuildings except for the sta-bles."

"Ah!" Eleazar cried as he stood and hurried out of the room.

"Don't mind him. Sometimes spicy food doesn't sit well," Mathew shared conspiratorially.

"I heard that!" Eleazar yelled from wherever he'd run off to.

The older men snickered while we waited to see what got Eleazar so excited. Shortly, he returned with a large roll of paper. "Ann, come help me clear this table. We have important things to look over."

Ann appeared out of the door attached to the kitchen with a scowl on her face. "You could ask nicely. The things I do for the three of you would astound the people of this village," she muttered while picking up plates.

Eleazar wasn't patient enough for her to clear the rest, so he shoved them aside and took a napkin, wiping off the table to make sure it was clean and dry. Finally, he spread out whatever he'd been holding and stepped back with a pleased smile. Curious, I got up, walked around the table to stand next to him, and found he had a drawn sketch of the castle and the grounds.

"How is this possible? I didn't think anyone could get in," I gasped, flipping through the large sheets to see every story about the castle was documented.

"That is true, but when some of the castle staff were left behind to look after things, they helped create these drawings. We viceroys, of course, kept them a secret, not wanting just anyone to know what the castle might hold. I think we've only brought these out once since we took our positions, and that was only when the previous men showed us we had them," he informed me.

I shifted the pages until it was the one that showed the layout of the outbuildings. We already knew about the stables and smithy next to it, but we hadn't seen the soldiers' barracks were also in that area. "Abbott, the kitchen isn't detached, but it's under the throne room, and it looks like there are hidden stairs that lead to the upper dining room as well as to the second floor where the ballroom is. The work that went into this castle is brilliant, but I shouldn't expect anything less from our people. They seem to have a knack for staying hidden."

The others got up and crowded around me as they looked over everything, pointing out what we'd seen and discovering more we hadn't found in our venture today. This castle was complex and had many secret passages, but what I found interesting was the fourth level. It had a honeycomb setup with one room in the middle, and the others branched off it, connecting them all like one large space full of rooms and sitting rooms alike. There was even another dining room if whoever wanted to stay in the space didn't want to venture down to the other.

"What do you suppose this floor was created for? It's an odd setup for a living space, almost as if the people wanted to make sure they all shared the same space but still have the illusion of personal space," I mused out loud as I scrutinized it even more.

"That, Your Majesty, was created in mind for the Dragon Queen and her consorts so they might all live together in harmony. King Cardon spent many years redoing that whole level of the castle. Right after his coronation, he moved his room down to the third level where it used to be for guests alone and started restructuring the entire fourth level into this. No one understood why he would do such a thing when he chose one wife for himself and kept his family close. It never would have worked for him to live in an environment such as this, so he finally started to talk about the Dragon Queen prophecy," Eleazar explained.

My brain took a moment to understand what he was telling me. "King Cardon made those rooms for *me*?"

"Well, us technically, if I understand the man right," Paxton corrected. "We know he had a vision. Who knew... maybe he saw all of us too. I mean there are just the right number of rooms. Look, there are even two on the outer edge that are more separate for the girls that exit out into the main hallway. They are still there for you as guardians but are set apart from where we'll be *intermingling*."

"I need to sit down."

Someone wrapped an arm around my waist and pulled me tight against their chest, holding me up instead. "I think we should call it a night. Who knows what dealing with that much power did to drain her," Jade instructed the others. "If we are going to see the dragons tomorrow, we'll need our rest."

Before anyone else could comment, I was swept up into his arms and carried out of the room and toward the door. "Jade, I can walk," I argued.

"I have no doubt about that, but I still want to carry you all the same," he answered, cradling me tighter. "Never thought I would wish for you to hurt your leg again so I can hold you like this more often."

"Don't even joke about that. It took long enough for me to be able to walk on it, and it still aches after a long day. The last thing I need right now is not to be able to walk." I huffed but allowed myself to tuck my head against his neck.

There was something about Jade that always made me feel safe. I knew he'd killed people as a job and that I shouldn't feel this way about him, but I couldn't help what I felt. He was my dark knight who always had my back, appearing when I needed him most. Just as the spirit dragon had said back at the castle, these men completed me in a way no other could. We reached Marta's house all too soon, and he set me back down on my own two feet, but I wasn't ready to let go of him just yet, so I intertwined our fingers as we entered the house.

"Oh, you're back. I wasn't sure if you would be," Marta said as she rose from her chair by the fire. "Can I get you anything, Your Majesty?"

"No, we just came from dinner with the viceroys," I assured her. "Please, there is no need to wait on us. You've done so much for us already, giving us a place to stay and wonderful food to eat."

"It's a pleasure. This house has been so quiet since my son married, and they built their own house. I told them they could live with me, but they wanted something of their own to build their new lives in." She sighed, returning to her seat. "Oh, don't let me keep you as I blather on about the good old days. It's just been so lively having you lot around."

Looking at her, I had an idea but no clue if this was the right call to make. "Marta... how would you feel about coming to live at the castle and being our head cook? We would obviously find more people to help you, but I've never had better food in my whole life than what you've given us the past two days. It won't be right away, so if you need time or you're not interested, just say the word."

She blinked at me a few times in surprise, which I wasn't all that shocked about since I just blurted it all out. "That is a wondrous offer, Your Majesty. Can I take a day or two to think it over? I'm just not sure I would be cut out for that kind of thing."

"Of course, take the time you need. Helena is helping me with staffing the castle, so if you have any questions or have people in mind you want to work with if you decide to take the job, you can talk to her," I said, bumbling over my words.

"Thank you, Your Majesty. I will reach out to her if I think I need to, and again I'm so extremely flattered you would ask," Marta answered with a soft smile.

I bobbed my head, offered a quick goodnight, and headed back to the room I'd slept in the night before. Flopping on the bed, I covered my face and groaned in embarrassment.

"Finally, our queen has a weakness," Cole announced as he followed me. "She can take down clan leaders, save crown princes, tell off a murderous Lord, but don't ask her to hire a cook."

"My mother would be horrified if she saw that," I muttered.

The mattress beside me sank, and my hands were pulled away to reveal Cole looking down at me. "Ah, little mouse, if this is the only thing you struggle with in life, then I think you're doing just fine. Marta is a fine choice for a cook, and I think you made the right call.

Just give her time to think it over. Serving the queen is high praise. I think you just caught her off guard."

"After this, I'm going to let Helena do the job offers, and if I like someone, I'll just tell her to do the deed," I stated.

Cole leaned down and kissed the tip of my nose. "You know you're awfully cute when you're flustered like this. Your cheeks get all pink, and you wrinkle your nose just like the little mouse you are."

"Don't you think it's time to change the nickname? I mean, I am the Dragon Queen, after all. Your little mouse has gone and changed into a lion."

A look passed over Cole's face I couldn't quite read, but he just dipped his head lower and sealed his lips to mine. My whole body went lax at the attention, and I wrapped a hand around the back of his neck to hold him there. All too soon, he pulled away and smiled. "You will always be my little mouse I stole in the dead of night. Pleasant dreams, My Queen. We have another busy day tomorrow." With that, he slipped out of the room.

Twenty-Five

An Alliance with Dragons

T he following day was clear, and the sun shone brightly as we flew. Vasin knew the best place to meet with the dragons, but it would be deeper into the Dragon Lands than we'd ever been before.

"Cass, you trust me to always keep you safe. Why are you questioning my choice to take us into the Dragon Lands?"

"It's not you I don't trust but the other dragons. Last time, we were just on the border, and they attacked us. What will they do when we are farther into their kingdom?"

"Things have changed since yesterday. All the dragons know what you did. That new oath was felt across all the kingdoms and even some you don't know about. What you and I did affects all dragons living and yet to be born. This is a cause for celebration, not anger. Besides, it's time I took up my mantle as you have taken yours."

"You mean as leader of the dragons?"

"Now that they don't need to be in hiding, there is much we dragons will have to face as our world has

OPENED UP TO US ONCE AGAIN. RULES WILL NEED TO BE ESTAB-LISHED SO WE DON'T FALL INTO A TRAP LIKE IN THE PAST."

"*Do you think any dragon will want to interact with us humans after what we've done?*"

"*NOW THAT FREE WILL IS BROUGHT BACK TO THE SITUA-TION, I THINK THERE WILL BE MORE DRAGONS BONDING WITH PEOPLE. THIS TIME, THE DIFFERENCE WILL BE THEY CAN BE APART FROM EACH OTHER, AND IF ONE DIES, THE OTHER WON'T SUFFER. THERE WILL BE FAR MORE FREEDOM AND CHOICE IN THE PARTNERSHIP THAN PREVIOUSLY.*"

"*Has it changed how things are between us?*"

"*NO, WHAT IS DONE IS DONE, BUT IT WILL END WITH OUR GENERATION. I'M NOT WORRIED, THOUGH. YOU AND I WILL HAVE A LONG LIFE TOGETHER AND GET TO SEE THE FRUIT OF OUR WORK FOR A FEW GENERATIONS.*"

I smiled at that, running a hand along Vasin's neck as we flew over the vast Dragon Lands that changed from barren deserts to lush green fields with rivers flowing through them. Vasin had told me it's been hundreds of years since humans ventured this deep into the lands and knew this thriving land existed, but it did my heart good to know the dragons hadn't been suffering in their self-exile. I could only dream of what our world would be like to have dragons once again flying freely where they chose and becoming a common sight in our skies.

As we reached a large oasis, Vasin began to circle, letting out a roar that seemed to carry through the air for miles. Birds burst from the trees and brush around the water, filling the sky with activity as a few dragons snapped them up for a snack as they landed. For this trip, I asked our clan dragon riders to come with us, trusting them more to go on this specific venture than those of Sheca. We'd been through battle and come out the other side unscathed, and it gave me confidence to have them at my back. I could also communicate with these dragons while I was still having a hard time doing so with those from Sheca. Once we all landed and dismounted, they approached Vasin and me, freeing their partners to roam about as we prepared for Vasin's call to be answered. Along with his physical call, he'd also reached out mentally, summoning those in the area to him.

It didn't take long before they arrived in droves, almost to the point of blocking out the sun with their massive wings. Dragons of all sizes and colors came as called, making me wish I could capture this moment forever in my mind. I had never seen something so magnificent in my life as this, and I was excited I got to share it with the important people in my life. Paxton let out a shrill whistle and waved at them excitedly, while Cole almost fell as he stumbled back from a purple dragon who swooped low and flapped its wings, stuffing up the wind and letting out a bugle of joy.

"This is craziness!" Dayson called out as he laughed, turning in a circle to see it all.

Ezzu leaped off Zan's shoulder and joined the throng of dragons, only to return with a group of other small dragons playing in the air currents. Closing my eyes, I tossed back my head and opened my arms wide as I felt the joy flowing off these dragons. It was almost too much to handle, but then Vasin rested his head against my back to keep me upright, helping me stand tall in the torrent of emotion. One dragon let out a roar, and the others followed suit as they landed, belting out their triumph at the oath being broken and a new, more promising one put in its place.

"WE DID THIS, CASS. YOU AND I CHANGED THE FATE OF ALL DRAGONS. BREATHE IN THIS MOMENT BECAUSE YOU DESERVE EVERY BIT OF IT."

Tears of joy rolled down my face as I heard his words, causing me to turn and wrap my arms around his snout, hugging his large head as tightly as I could. "Never has a human been blessed with a better pair-bond as I have. Without you in my corner, this never would have happened. We deserve this moment because, as you said, without you, this never would have happened," I whispered, feeling the words needed to be said out loud.

"*They wish to speak with you by having me translate for them.*"

Nodding, I stepped back, wiped away the remaining tears from my face, and took a steadying breath. Ready to face a horde of dragons, I turned and gasped as the open grassy area surrounding the oasis was filled with dragons all turned to face me. Then as if someone gave a signal, they all bowed their heads to Vasin and me, letting out a low croon that seemed to ripple through the masses. Once the sound died down, they raised their heads to the sky, and those that could, shot fire into it, engulfing us in its warmth and light. Just when I feared we might set the environment around us on fire, they ceased, settling down into an easy, relaxed stance.

"*We welcome the Dragon Queen to our lands and show our respect and gratitude for freeing us. The dragons across the world owe you a debt that cannot be repaid in one human lifetime.*" Their voices echoed through my mind as Vasin opened up communication between us.

"*There is no debt to be repaid,*" I assured them. "*I did what was needed to make amends for the prison we put you in when you trusted the first of us. A pact of friendship between humans and dragons should never come with chains that bind you together into acts you are unwilling to do. True friendship needs to be given on both sides. You blessed us with magic and your bravery, but we did nothing in return to deserve it. I hope this new oath will bring forth many bonds of true friendship and create a wonderful partnership for the rest of your lives if you choose to make that type of connection.*"

"Your gentle and true heart speaks honestly, and even though you say there is no debt, know that we will gladly assist you in this battle with the Lost King. He threatens our world as much as he does yours. We see the evil in his spirit and wish to bring it to an end. He was once bonded to a dragon, but when his dragon wouldn't do as he demanded, he killed his pair-bond. We don't know how he survived the ordeal, but we would like the chance to avenge our fallen comrade."

"I would be honored to have you fight by our side if that is what you wish to do. As I am bonded to Vasin, your leader, we will do all we can to get you the revenge you justly deserve in this matter," I announced, placing a hand over my heart and bowing back to them. *"I pray this will be the beginning of a symbiotic relationship between our people. If a need ever arises for your kind, know we will be at your service in any way we can."*

"Would you allow some of our flight to join you and your men? There are those among us that wish to be a part of this alongside your guardians."

I couldn't keep the smile off my face at this request, knowing that all of my guardians who didn't have dragons would absolutely welcome them. *"They would gladly accept a friendship with those who would like to return with us."*

"Until we speak again, be well, Queen Cassarah, friend and champion of dragons." With another deafening roar, they took flight, leaving behind seven dragons to come back with us.

Grinning, I stepped forward to greet the dragons. "Welcome, new friends. Please allow me a moment to explain to the others what is going on, and then I'll leave you to pick your partner for your time with us."

"What's going on, Cassarah?" Izel asked as he came to stand beside me.

Spinning on my heel, I face my guardians with a beaming smile. "These wonderful dragons would like to return with us to Sheca and work alongside us as we plan our attack against the Lost King. It would seem he once had a dragon he was bonded to that he killed and somehow managed to survive the event where no one has before him."

"Wait, are you saying these dragons want to partner with us individually? As in bond with us like you and the others have with your dragons?" Cole questioned as he kept glancing over at the dragons behind me.

"It will be slightly different now with the new oath in place. They will pair off with you, yes, but it will be up to both of you if the bond is put into place. Even with the bond given, it will still give you and your dragon full autonomy from each other, meaning they can come and go as they please. If the venom is given, the magic will be given as well but without the fear of killing each other if something should happen to one of you," I explained, double-checking with Vasin to make sure I was explaining this right.

"Okay, so what do we do now?" Abbott asked, looking a little worried.

Taking his hand in mine, I led him forward to the row of dragons. "You will get to experience a slightly different version of a dragon hatching. The seven of you who don't have dragons line up and allow them a chance to get a feel for you. I knew the moment Vasin's gaze landed on me we were meant for each other, and some knew even before they were hatched that they were a good match. Trust what your heart tells you because they don't pick based on your appearance or mental prowess, they look at your soul."

They did as I asked, lining up with some space between them, and as I retreated to Vasin and my other bonded guardians, we watched. Cole was the first to be picked, but I should have guessed at how the purple dragon acted toward him earlier. He stepped up to my best friend and shoved him with his large, scaled head, knocking him to the ground and snuffled him all over, making happy chirping noises. I tried not to laugh as Cole attempted to get up, but his dragon wasn't having any of it, gripped him by the back of the shirt, and dragged him out of the line.

"You have to be kidding me. This is the dragon that matches my soul!" Cole grumbled as he wriggled, trying to free himself.

A sleek blue dragon covered in scars approached Izel who reached out to him with a hand. The dragon pressed his forehead into the touch, causing Izel to smile in carefree way I'd never seen before. Clearly, the dragon had been through a lot, and I couldn't think of a better person to help him with those mental wounds than Izel. May was picked by a red dragon spouting fire out its nose, daring the woman to shy away from its advances, but May stared the dragon down without batting an eyelash. It let out a puff of smoke that enveloped them, and when it cleared, May was already on the dragon's back as it leaped into the sky. Becka was possessively wrapped up in a green dragon's tail as it hissed at the brown dragon standing behind Dayson. The two dragons growled at each other, but Dayson set a hand on his dragon's chest, pulling its attention back to him. He murmured something to his new companion, and they ventured off toward the water together, leaving Becka laughing as her dragon licked her face. This left another purple dragon and a golden female to pick between Abbott and Gavin.

The purple dragon moved forward, but the golden flung out her wings, blocking the other dragon with a warning hiss and lash of the tail. She moved forward as if she was a court lady on her way to claim her betrothed, and I couldn't say I was surprised when she curled up around Abbott, letting out a heavy sigh. The purple dragon flapped his wings, propelled himself toward Gavin, and skidded to a stop before the prince. They looked at each other for a good long while before Gavin took the final step and reached out to the dragon who bowed his head to accept the touch. With that final move, all my guardians were blessed with their very own dragons which made things much simpler in the long run.

Ninnat, Tahir, and Ifra mingled among the new dragons, greeting each other and welcoming them into our family. We stayed at the oasis for a while, letting the new riders get to know their dragon companions, but all too soon, we had to depart and return to reality. Everyone was all smiles as we climbed on our dragons and took off, falling into formation with Vasin and I leading and the two golden females flanking us while the others followed in a staggered formation.

Twenty-Six

Late Night in the Castle

Once we returned from the Dragon Lands with our new companions, it was full steam ahead on the coronation and setting up the castle for us to live in. When I thought my life had been busy before, it was nothing compared to this. Some days, I felt like I never had a moment to think before another person asked me a question or needed my approval. Seeing as there was more that needed to be done to get ready for the coronation, even with all that was accomplished when I opened up the castle, I pushed it back another week. I would fall into bed each night at Marta's house, praying I would be left to sleep until the morning.

My guardians were kept busy as well, many of them switching off to deal with things they needed to do. They had determined I would always have at least three of them around, if not more, to keep an eye on things. When I went to the barracks, all of them showed up, feeling on edge, knowing it was the largest group of people who could hurt me. I was pleased to discover that those who didn't agree with me becoming queen had partnered with Naytan and had already been dealt with. Many soldiers were eager to meet me and swear their fealty to the Dragon Queen. Through my studies with the viceroys, I learned that my guardians, consorts or not, were above General Alsten, and when they gave an order, it was as if I gave it myself. This helped as I left them to deal with how to station things at the castle and work with Alsten on a rotation of men leaving the valley to keep an eye on what was going on with the Lost King.

"Your Majesty, you really should take a break for food... you've been working for hours," Ann commented as she set a plate of food down for me on the desk I was using. "It's not good for the mind to work that hard by candlelight."

This made me smile as I thought of the early days of training when Sal gave me mountains of work to do. "I'm sure you're right, Ann. I have a terrible habit of getting lost in my work." When she pulled the lid off the plate, the aroma of fresh bread and cooked meat made my mouth water. *How long has it been since I've eaten?*

"At this rate, Talia is going to have to adjust your dress with how much weight you are losing," Ann tutted, pouring me a glass of water.

"I doubt that between what you and Marta have been feeding me," I answered with a smile. "Thank you for looking after me while I'm here. I know it can't be easy with the trouble those men who pretend to be old get into."

"It is a pleasure to have someone who doesn't need constant looking after spending time around here. Although, I think Sal is also helping keep them grounded as they pour over the books and scrolls he brought with him," Ann said with a sigh. "Eat your meal. When I come back, I expect it all to be gone," she warned, giving me a pointed look.

"I promise," I answered, shifting the books I was looking through to the side so I could pull the tray over.

On the days I was here pouring through books I took out of the castle library, I was left pretty much alone with one of my guardians roaming around the place while more were close by but didn't need to be in the same building. I didn't really move from the desk Mathew had given up to let me use while they worked in another room they were setting up for the history of the mercenary clans. To my surprise, Gavin would join them, learning alongside them about the people who had adopted him while I was trying to catch up on the past. King Cardon had said everything I needed to know would be in these books. I was beginning to think it was a lost cause, having been buried away in the vast library. As I munched away at my meal, it made me wonder if he'd kept what I needed to know in his office, that he was being literal in the fact that that room held what I needed to know.

Shooting to my feet, I dashed out the door, finding Jade pacing on the patio. "Little bird, what's wrong?"

"Nothing's wrong. I think I just figured something out, though," I explained with a grin. "Care to join me on a late-night adventure to the castle?"

"I'm not sure that's a wise idea. They were working on the bridge today," Jade cautioned.

My grin widened into a smile. "Good thing we don't need to use it. Vasin found a roost that connects right to the king's bedroom, and that is where I need to go." He narrowed his eyes at me as if weighing the risk of us going without any of the others. "It will be fine. No one stays at the castle this late, and we'll be on the third floor, or are you telling me the mercenary assassin isn't up for the challenge."

Jade stepped into my personal space, coming nose to nose with me, his light green eyes flashing with the challenge. "Don't start something you can't finish, little bird."

His breath was warm on my face, and I wanted nothing more than to close that last bit of space between us and let him show me just what I was starting. Instead, I grabbed his hand and dragged him down the steps to the road that led up to the castle.

"Vasin, any chance you're around to give us a lift to the castle?"

"I'M NEVER FAR FROM YOU, CASS, EVEN WITH ALL THAT IS GOING ON. WHAT IS IT YOU ARE SEEKING AT THE CASTLE THIS LATE?" Vasin asked as I felt him head in this direction.

"King Cardon said that all the information I would need would be in the history found in the castle. I've been pouring through the books in the library, but I think it's what I'm supposed to be looking at is in his rooms, not the library. It would be easier for him to keep things hidden away there than in the public space anyone in the castle had access to."

"THAT IS A GOOD THEORY," he agreed as he landed before us. *"COME, WE SHALL DISCOVER WHAT THE PAST HAS TO HOLD FOR YOU."*

Jade scooped me up and settled me on Vasin's back before he climbed up behind me, making sure to at least secure one of the straps around my waist. I knew he still wasn't over the time he caught me as I was free-falling through the sky when I fell off Vasin. Allowing him to keep me safe made me feel treasured, even if I did want to smack him every so often. Soon, we were gliding through the air, circling the tower that had an opening and platform just for this purpose. Stairs led down from the tower into the closet of all places in the king's personal chambers. We lit a lantern I'd left in the room when I'd been back here last, knowing it would be useful.

"What is it exactly we are looking for?" Jade inquired as I started pulling all the journals, scrolls, and any other tidbits of information I could find on the shelves.

I paused and set the lantern on a side table as I met his gaze. "When we first came to the castle and I searched through this room, I found a letter addressed to me."

"Many of us did. It seems the king expected the castle to be occupied again at some point."

"No, Jade, this was different. He used my *name*, not the title of Dragon Queen but by my given name." I walked to the desk, pulled it out from the journal I'd slipped it into, and handed it to him. "He knew a lot more about me and even you, my guardians. It's how he knew to build the fourth floor the way he did. Kind Cardon *knew* we, as in you and I, would be here at some point."

"How can this be? He writes to you as if he knows you. If he's seen the outcome of our people, why doesn't he tell you how to fix it?" Jade questioned as he gazed down at the letter. "He speaks of things as if they have already happened for him."

Reaching out, I took the letter from him and took his hands in mine. "Have I ever told you about the dreams I had of Queen Miranda?"

"Queen Miranda?"

"I forget you didn't know her as that... the Raven Queen," I corrected. "When Vasin and I first came to the Raven Rose clan, I harmonized with him. This is where he allows me into his mind, and we essentially become one being. In doing that, I have access to his vast knowledge he shares with all the dragons that are living. It's where they store every memory that every dragon has ever had since King Yash bonded with his dragon. The rule of that place is that only the dragon can control the information, but I didn't listen, and I almost got lost in his mind. Cole was able to ground me and help bring me back to my own body, but from that point, I was able to have these visions about a woman and her men. Turns out it was the Raven Queen, and I got to watch her life as a child until the day she died. They were so real, I could feel her emotions as her dragon and the men she loved with all her heart died. It was as if my heart was carved from my chest, and my soul shattered along with her. If his visions of us were anything like that, then yes, they were real to him. It would seem like it already happened, and he just had to stand by and watch, able to do nothing." I paused and took a deep, shaky breath as I tried to calm myself. "This is why I believe this letter and what it says. If there is a way for us to beat the Lost King and his army, it will be found somewhere in this castle."

Jade searched my face when I finished speaking as if needing to understand something I wasn't telling him with my words. "Is this why you hold us at a distance because you know what it will be like to lose us? You think that waiting to let us into your heart until after you've dealt with the Lost King will protect us both from that pain, don't you…"

Tears filled my eyes as his words hit my heart like a dagger. He was right. All of them have worked their way deep into my heart, but I refused to acknowledge it for fear I would lose them before I got enough time with them. The pain that ripped through Miranda when she watched her men die to save her wasn't something I was willing to risk. They all loved me enough to wait because I asked without question, but now that Jade knew, he was never going to let that stand. He was always the one pushing me, challenging my feelings for him and the others. My dark knight wasn't scared to make me mad when he knew I was wrong, and just the look in his eyes right now told me I was absolutely going to lose this fight.

Pulling me to his chest, he wrapped a hand around the back of my neck, keeping still as he kissed me. Our kiss was desperate as I wrapped my arms around him, fisting his shirt in case he dared to move away from me. Now that he'd exposed my fear and forced me to face it, I couldn't run from my feelings anymore. His other hand slid down my hip until he scooped my ass up and set me on the desk so I was more level with him as he pushed my legs apart to fit up against me. I felt his fingers slide into my hair, cupping the back of my head as he deepened our kiss, our tongues tasting each other in the most intimate way I'd ever experienced. He growled against my lips as if he wasn't getting what he needed from me, but I didn't know how to help, never having been in this position before.

When he pulled back from me, I cried out, fearful he would stop. Instead, he gripped my face with both hands, his eyes wild with passion as he looked at me. "Cassarah, I love you with every fiber of my being, and I can't stand not being able to show you just what that looks like. I know you're scared, but I refuse to let that bastard king win by controlling this part of our life together. Whether it's one day, one week, or one month, I want to be able to love you for however long we have and not regret missing out on this. Do you trust me?"

"Yes," I breathed out, my lips brushing his. "With everything that I am, I trust you, Jade."

"Then trust me enough to love you," he begged.

"Show me... show me what that looks like, my dark knight," I said as my hands slipped under his shirt to lay flat against his skin. "Show me how to love like you do."

Twenty-Seven

Finally Love Has Come

Jade slammed his lips to mine as he picked me up, causing me to wrap my legs around his hips as he walked into the bedroom. He gently laid me out on the bed, letting his hands run from my face down to my hips as if memorizing the feel of my body. He took the bottom of my shirt and started to lift it, kissing along my bare skin as it was exposed, letting his tongue glide, tasting me. A sigh slipped from my lips at the feel of his mouth on my body—it was almost like a fire was starting to burn just under the skin, fueled by every touch he made. My head fell back as he reached my breasts, his fingers skimming over the fabric wrapped tight to my chest. I was a little worried he would have trouble getting that off me, but I should have known better.

I gasped at the cool touch of one of his daggers gliding along my flesh as he deftly cut away the obstructing fabric, freeing me to his gaze. Making quick work of my shirt, I tossed it to the side, knowing it was just getting in the way. Looking up at Jade, he just sat there hovering over me, his eyes drinking in the sight of my bare skin like he was looking at a work of art.

"Absolutely stunning," he murmured as he leaned in, kissed my lips lightly, shifted to my jaw, and worked down my neck as his fingers fluttered over my breast.

When he rolled my nipple between his fingers, I moaned, the feeling of it almost too much for my brain to handle. "What are you doing to me?" I panted.

"Loving you until your brain can't fight it any longer, and you open up to us like a flower to the sun. Little bird, I will set your body free until you are floating among the clouds," Jade whispered along my skin, his gaze holding mine as his mouth closed over the other bud.

I tossed my head back, unable to focus on anything but the pleasure exploding through my body, and we'd only just begun. Eventually, Jade moved lower, reaching my pants which he slowly undid and slid off my legs, leaving me completely bare to him. "I want to feel you too," I requested, lifting a hand to tug on his shirt. "Be naked with me."

Jade grinned at that and quickly whipped off his shirt, giving me the gift of staring at his chest that rippled with lean muscle under his mahogany skin. As quickly as he could, he stepped back off the bed to shuck off his pants before returning to crawl over me, kissing up my legs as he spread them wide. Soon, he kneeled in the open space, leaving my center in full view, but I wasn't ashamed or fearful of what might happen next. Without fail, Jade will always have my well-being in mind first and foremost. To my surprise, he laid his body on mine and rolled us to the side, letting my leg hike up over his hip, and he just trailed his fingers along my body, kissing me in an intoxicating manner. We were so lost in each other I didn't feel his fingers slip between us and stroke over my core, making me moan into his mouth as he circled my nub. After reading one of the books Becka found in her room in the castle, I might have experimented with some they kept talking about in how to pleasure yourself. What Jade was doing was far more electric than I was able to do for myself.

"Are you ready to fly, little bird?" Jade asked as he rolled me onto my back again.

Biting my lip, I nodded, unsure of what he would do next, but I couldn't wait to find out. My body hummed with energy that didn't seem to have an outlet, but my guess was that Jade knew just what I needed. Moving down my body, he slid his hand under my ass and lifted me slightly as he kissed my center, laving it with his tongue, causing me to cry out in pleasure. "Oh God, whatever you're doing, don't ever stop!"

He chuckled, causing vibrations that only added to the whole experience, making me thrash as he held me tightly. Just when I felt like I was going to lose my mind, I felt his teeth brush against the nub of pleasure, as the book called it. A feeling that seemed to match free-falling in the sky overcame me suddenly, and I moaned as my body tightened and my legs slammed shut but were stopped by Jade's head. No matter how I begged, Jade didn't give up what he was doing to me until I lay there spent with sweat glistening on my skin and my chest heaving. Now I knew what women talked about when they said there was so much more to sex than what we learn. From the talks that May and Becka had with me, I knew what Jade did wasn't sex but felt just as good, and it was the best way to experience pleasure without risking a child. Thankfully, I'd started taking the elixir Alto made me to prevent that from happening—for now.

Jade came to lay beside me as my body calmed down enough for me to remember my name. "That was amazing," I whispered, turning my head to look at him, brushing my fingers along the side of his face. "Can I explore you next?"

Jade turned his head, kissing my palm. "Only a fool would deny his queen her request," he teased. "Do with me what you will. I am at your mercy."

Rolling so I was lying alongside him, I let my finger trace his muscles as I've longed to do since he took his shirt off. Curious if his nipples affected him the same way, I circled them, letting my fingernail scrape over the top of them. This pulled a groan from him, making me far too pleased with myself. What other sounds could I elicit from this man? Venturing lower, I was met with thick hair where his manhood met his body, but when I let my finger slide down his shaft, it was as smooth and soft as silk. It bobbed at my touch seconds before Jade hissed, making me pull back my hand and look up at him.

"Trust me... you aren't hurting me at all. I've been waiting so long for this moment, I'm not sure how long I will last under your undivided attention."

Smiling at this, I rolled on top of him and let my head rest over his heart, letting it give me the courage to show him I did love him and wanted everything he was offering me. Sitting up, I lifted myself off his body and straightened his cock for me to settle on. His hands rose to grip my hips, drawing my attention back to his face.

"If you're not ready for this, I am complete with what we've already done, little bird. To see you shatter under my touch will live in my dreams forever until you want to make this choice," Jade shared, his eyes full of love.

"I'm done hiding my true feelings for you and the others, Jade. I love you to the very depths of my soul, and I couldn't think of a more perfect moment to wipe away any doubt you might have about my feelings," I answered as I lowered myself onto him. I reached out and placed my hands on his chest as I breathed through the sharpness of him pushing past my barrier, taking ownership of this moment for myself and the men I love. They were mine, and I was theirs, and damn those who would see this as improper since they weren't us.

The feeling of being full was new and strange but not unwelcome. Jade hugged me, kissing my forehead as he let me adjust to him being inside me, drinking in this moment of becoming one. Tucking a finger under my chin, he lifted my face to his and kissed me, letting his other hand comb through my hair as he started to move. Everything about this moment was perfect and beautiful as if I'd been waiting all my life for Jade and my other guardians to help me trust my heart.

As my body relaxed, he sped up, and the sound of our pleasure filled the room, but there reached a point when I needed more. Pulling out of his hold, I sat up, rolled my hips against his thrusts, ground my center against his pelvis, and got that added stimulation I sought. Jade didn't miss a beat and moved with me as I sped up, feeling that pressure building up in me once again, making me chase after it. I whimpered as I crested and exploded with joy that prickled along my skin in the best way possible. Jade slammed into me, holding me still as he thrust wildly, grunting as he burst within me, making my pleasure echo through my body once again.

Depleted, I flopped against Jade's chest, panting and grinning like a fool. "That needs to happen again... when I feel my legs again. Why on earth do they make it sound like this is awful for women?"

"Because, little bird, it only feels like this when you give your heart to it. This experience wouldn't happen with just anyone, but I agree we will absolutely be doing this again, and again, and again for as long as you'll let me."

"We have to go back, don't we, since we didn't tell the others we were coming up here?" I sighed into Jade's neck.

"I think we can stay a little longer and get one more round in before I have to share you with the others again," Jade answered, kissing the top of my head. "I'll just need a quick nap first."

After the nap, Jade woke me up with his head between my legs. This time when he thrust into me, he was on top, staring down at me like I was his world. Every time we tried to get up and leave to head back, we kept getting distracted and ended up spending the night in our little love nest until the morning light woke us up. Vasin dropped us off in the open field closest to Marta's house, and we walked back still in our lover's glow. That is until we stepped through the door and saw the others waiting for us.

"What the fuck, Cassarah?" Cole barked the moment he saw me and rushed over. "Do you know how worried we've been? Where the hell did you two go last night that you couldn't bother to inform the rest of us?"

"Don't you dare talk to her like that," Jade growled, shoving Cole away from me. "You might be her consort, but she is still our queen and will be treated that way. Cassarah was with me up in the castle. We went looking for something in the king's study and ended up spending the night there."

"You should have at least left a note with the viceroys that you left. I didn't know if she'd been kidnapped or was lying hurt somewhere. It's my job to keep her safe, and if I don't know where she is, how can I do that?" Cole shot back. "Put yourself in my shoes, *Reaper.* What would you do if she went off with just me, and you didn't know what happened or when she would be back? Do you really feel like only having one of us is enough to keep her safe?"

Hearing the fear in Cole's voice had me moving around Jade and wrapping my arms around Cole. "I'm sorry. You're absolutely right, and I should have left a note. When I asked Jade to take me up there, I didn't think we'd end up being there all night."

Cole hugged me so tightly I was having trouble breathing. When he loosened his hold, he gripped my chin and turned my face up to his, slamming his mouth to mine. He kissed me like I'd been gone for months, not hours, and even though I'd just spent the night with Jade, my body yearned for Cole. Now that I had let myself accept how I felt about these men, I could understand how easy it is to love more than one at the same time. Each gave me something the other couldn't, making every connection unique.

When Cole broke our kiss, he rested his head against mine, holding me. "Don't do that to me again, little mouse. I'm not sure my heart can take it."

"I'm sorry I worried you," I whispered just for him to hear.

"You know some of us were worried about her as well," Dayson interjected when it didn't seem like Cole would ever let me go. "You need to work on the whole sharing thing there, brother."

Cole let out an irritated huff but released me to face the others in the room. All of them looked upset on various levels, but none seemed quite as angry as Cole had been. Still, I had been selfish in what I'd done by not letting any of them know we'd be gone all night. Part of being a good leader was learning from your mistakes, and this had been a misstep on my part. "I owe you all an apology. Cole's right, and I should have left a note or told anyone else back at the village hall where I was going. Then when I didn't come back, at least you would have known where to start looking. I will do my best to ensure it doesn't happen again."

Abbott stepped forward and grasped my hands. "We are learning how best to look out for you as well, and I think the shock of not knowing how to find you if we lost you hit us all hard. Being in the village makes us feel safe, and we've let down our guard when your protection needs to be at the top of our list all the time, not just when we feel danger is possible. These people are growing to love and respect you, but there will come a time when you have to make a call they won't agree with, and it will make them lash out. As your guardians, we need to be aware that this can happen at any time without warning. So if you need a break or time to yourself, you just need to let us know so we can make that happen and ensure your safety."

Hearing Abbott talk, I realized I had needed a break, a night to just be Cassarah, a woman in love, and not the Dragon Queen. "We'll figure this out together. We are all going to make mistakes... it's learning from them that's important."

"Wise words, little warrior. Now come, eat breakfast with us, and fill us in on what you were looking for," Izel instructed, pulling out a seat for me.

At this moment, I knew we could make this work—all of us together. Now we just had to survive the battle that was looming in on us.

Twenty-Eight
The Plot Thickens

"So the king knew the Dragon Queen would be you?" Zan questioned once I'd filled them in on the letter and my dreams. "Do you think he experienced what you did with the Raven Queen or just had one long vision?"

"That is what I was trying to look for in the study, but we didn't get far," I explained, hoping they wouldn't ask me why we didn't get more information. Each of them seemed to mull this information over, far too distracted to question the rest of what I said.

"All right, so we all go back with you and sort through what he had left in his study. With all of us helping, it will happen much faster, and then we can come up with a plan of action," Paxton offered.

I was surprised at Paxton's idea. He'd been one who was all action and didn't waste time on the details. For him to spearhead the idea of spending the day looking through old books and scrolls was not like him. "It would make things go faster. Have we gotten any reports on the Lost King's movements?"

"There hasn't been much movement. It seems he is making Norden his base, gathering all his troops in one place. There are more of them than we first expected. Even with the dragons, this is going to be a battle that will be told for generations to come," Izel shared.

Knowing that battle loomed in the distance was one thing, but realizing I was going to be the one to find a way to stop it was something I still couldn't wrap my head around. The coronation was in two days, and after that, it would be full speed into battle plans. We'd already been having the soldier training double-time and having everyone else brush up on their skills since they didn't practice as much as the soldiers did. Even in the midst of celebration, we kept the upcoming battle in our minds, never forgetting that danger was lurking out there that could get us killed.

"Shall we head up there now? I think it might be best before anyone else comes to claim me," I suggested, standing from the table.

"No time like the present," Gavin agreed as we gathered plates to bring into the kitchen.

Marta made it clear we weren't allowed to assist in any other way, or we would be slapped on the hand, queen or no queen. It seems all of us mercenary women had a stubborn streak to us, but since she agreed to be our cook, I relented.

"If we pack up things, we should be fine to spend the night at the castle. I heard they got all the basic supplies dropped in by dragon instead of worrying about wagons," Dayson said with an excited-looking grin. "It's about time we all got settled in our real home before we have to leave it again for a short while."

Matching his grin, I hugged him, thrilled with the plan. "Sounds amazing to me, and we haven't spent much time on the fourth floor other than walking through the rooms."

"You didn't stay there last night?" Becka asked, a twinkle in her eye.

"No, we ended up in the king's bedroom since it was so close to the study," I answered, then caught on to what she was hinting at. Clearly, she knew that it wasn't just time alone that led to Jade and I staying there for the night. I planned to talk to them all once we got the information we needed and settled in for the night. I didn't mind

May and Becka being around, but when it came to our intimate lives, it should just be us talking.

"Can we take our dragons?" Gavin asked. He'd built quite the bond with his purple dragon he named Gatir.

"Since they are still working on the bridge, I think it's best," Izel reasoned. "I'm sure they will be done later since there is much to bring in and prepare for the coronation, but they've been managing with dragons dropping people off."

Some doubled up with others, but those who newly acquired their dragons had difficulty not spending time with them, which I understood. If I had the option of that when I first bonded with Vasin, I would have, but I pushed thoughts of my mother away before it could cloud this moment with people I cared about.

As if I never left, I found myself back in the king's study sorting through books again, still not finding what King Cardon had left for me to learn. I picked up an old scroll brittle with age and written in the old language. It was an account during the days of the first king where he had to deal with a man who'd gone crazy out of the blue. He'd been one of the higher-ups in the military because his magic was strongest in his ability to control people's bodies. Later, it was discovered his son had been gifted with the same magic, only instead of it being in control of bodies, it was their mind. He could implant a thought that would change the way a person acted. This reminded me of Izel's gift, but his was emotion-based but not to the point of changing your own mental awareness. This sounded more like what the Lost King could do. It seems he used his gift on his father, and over time, his father's brain deteriorated to the point of madness. It was believed the mind fought to take back control and instead lost itself to the magic that was used. The dragon the boy had was also affected and soon died, taking the young boy with him, both lost to insanity of the mind.

"Pax," I called out to where he was sprawled out on the floor, napping.

"Huh, what?" he answered, jolting awake as if he were trying to disprove he was sleeping. Rubbing his eyes, he wandered over to me and wrapped his arms around my waist, leaning his chin on my shoulder to look at the scroll. "Ah, I hope you're not looking for someone who can read that because I'm going to be zero help."

Chuckling, I set the scroll down and turned to face him. "I need you to tell me everything you know or remember about Henry as a boy. You said your father got reports and was asked to deal with a few things throughout the years."

"What are you looking for specifically?" Paxton asked, his brows knitted together. "There are a lot of things I remember about that time, but I don't see how any of it would be useful to you."

"The dragons told me he was bonded to one and somehow the dragon died, but he is still living... how does that happen? In this scroll, I read about a boy who seemed to have a similar power to Henry, and his dragon died because the boy used his powers on that dragon. Shortly after, the boy died along with his father, all of them out of their mind. While I was kidnapped, I heard my captors talking about how people under the Lost King's influence went mad and turned into puppets who couldn't even speak," I explained. "So we need to figure out why Henry is still alive if his dragon isn't."

"Are they sure his dragon is dead?" Paxton countered.

I opened my mouth to answer but paused. Instead, I closed my eyes and reached out to Vasin. *"Why do the dragons think Henry's dragon is dead?"*

*"W*E CAN NO LONGER CONNECT WITH *X*OTHA, AND THAT ONLY HAPPENS WHEN A DRAGON HAS PASSED ON. *O*THERWISE, WE CAN ALWAYS FEEL EACH OTHER'S PRESENCE CONNECTED TO OUR SHARED MEMORY, WHICH FADES WHEN THE DRAGON DOES."

"What type of dragon was Xotha?"

"A BLUE DRAGON... BY OUR MEMORIES, HE WAS SMALL BUT VICIOUS. *I'*M NOT SURPRISED THEY WERE DRAWN TO EACH OTHER."

"Do you know how they met or when they bonded?"

*"I*T WAS WHEN THE BOY WAS SMALL, HE SLIPPED OUT OF THE HOUSE AND WANDERED INTO THE FIELDS, AND *X*OTHA WAS DRAWN TO HIS MAGIC. *I*T WAS ONE THAT CONNECTED TO HIM ON A LEVEL NO ONE ELSE HAD BEFORE. *X*OTHA DIDN'T WASTE ANY TIME AND BIT THE BOY, FLOODING HIS LITTLE BODY WITH VENOM. *I*T'S REALLY A MIRACLE THAT *H*ENRY SURVIVED. *I*T EXPLAINS WHY HIS POWER IS SO STRONG, THOUGH, AND AT SUCH A YOUNG AGE."

Snapping my eyes back open, I met Paxton's bright blue curious eyes. "What did Vasin have to say?"

"I don't think his dragon is dead," I announced. Everyone paused what they were doing to look at me with questions written all over their faces.

Pulling out of Paxton's hold, I started to pace up and down the room. "Hear me out. Vasin said that Henry bonded with his dragon as a child, and his whole body was flooded with venom, making him as strong as he is today. I was reading another account of a child who also had a gift similar to Henry, and he used it on his dragon. What if it didn't work because *that* little boy wasn't strong enough to make it work on a mind as vast as a dragon's?"

"Are you suggesting that the Lost King has somehow managed to use his gift on his dragon, having total control over it?" Zan clarified.

Chewing on my lip, I paused to look at them. "It makes sense, doesn't it? He wants power over everything, and the dragons said they believed he was killed because he wouldn't follow orders. What if instead of killing his dragon, Henry manipulated its mind?"

"That would turn the dragon insane just as a human would. In everything that I've been learning about relationships between dragons, there is no way one could survive being cut off from the collective minds of the others," Gavin argued.

"I'm not arguing that. I think it's one reason we haven't seen his dragon around. Vasin said that his dragon, Xotha, was vicious by nature. Now add that he made his dragon go insane. It would be a loose end with deadly repercussions if it was killed," I stated, pausing to see if they were catching up to where my mind was already at.

"Holy shit," Cole blurted out. "If we find his dragon and kill it, we kill him. We could stop this whole war from happening if we can take out that one piece. Then his whole plan would crumble."

"I think he did it to try and gain the knowledge that the dragons have hidden in their minds. If their bond was so strong and started at an early age, it's possible they could communicate with each other like Vasin and I can. The bond's strength, trust, and venom is what makes that possible, and a child's trust to its dragon protector would be immense."

Now Abbott was on his feet, rolling open a map on the desk. "So where would you hide a dragon that was out of its mind and could destroy everything on site?"

"Errit," Jade and Paxton said together.

"You two seem pretty certain about that. Why?" Izel inquired.

"If you ever want to keep something a secret, you lose it in the wastelands of Errit," Paxton explained. "There is nothing out there, and you must have the right set of skills to survive."

"There are many plateaus, ravines, and caves where you could hide things. It's the best place to put smuggled goods. No one's ever found my hideaway, and that's where I made it," Jade said. "Tahir and I hid out there for a few months after Acton framed me for killing my parents. I was sent on a job to kill an official and his wife who were going to leak the location of one of the clans to the king and queen. I was the only one who could get in close enough to get the guy since he was already in Royal City. What Acton didn't tell me was that my father was the man who was going to sell us out. The room was dark, and I don't make a habit of looking my targets in the eye. It wasn't until I'd already done the deed and heard my name on my mother's dying breath. Of course, I returned to the clan, confronting Acton about it, but he claimed he had no idea what I was talking about. Acton always hated our father, who beat on him when he didn't come out as the best for his training year. Then our father married my mother once he found out she was pregnant and had me who he doted on. Acton's first move as clan leader was to call a meeting of the clan leaders and put me on trial. Somehow, Acton framed things to look like I'd known what I was getting into and took the job so I could have the leader's position and would kill him too, if given the chance. I was banished from the clan lands for a year as punishment, and I was just on my way back when I rescued Cassarah."

Jade rubbed the back of his neck as we stared at him in shock. "All that to say is I hid out in Errit for most of that time working as an assassin since people there will pay a pretty penny to make their problems disappear. After a year exploring the place and hunting down my targets in the canyons, I still didn't find everything there was to see. It would be perfect to lose a dragon there."

"I have to agree with the man. It's where people go to lose things," Paxton added.

"Fine, so we have a place to start looking, but as Jade made clear, it might be impossible to find if you don't know where to look," Abbott pointed out.

"Then we give them a reason to use his dragon," I determined. "If you were the Lost King, what would you want to stop from happening at all costs?" I could feel their eyes on me as I moved to the window that overlooked the village. "Send an invitation to my coronation to the King and Queen of Creisal."

Twenty-Nine
Great Risks, Great Rewards

"**A**re you out of your damn mind!" Cole snapped.

"You realize by doing that you are broadcasting that we exist to the whole world, right?" May added, folding her arms over her chest, telling me she was very upset with me.

"How exactly do you think that's going to go over when she finds out we are holding her sister captive and killed the king?" Paxton questioned.

Gavin lifted his fingers to his lips and let out a shrill whistle, shutting up everyone. "Now that I have your attention, I think that Cassarah is making the right move. If I extend the invitation, letting her know I am consort to the Dragon Queen and she is invited to the coronation, she can't refuse. It's like saying she won't come to my wedding, and that would reflect poorly on her which she will never allow. Since Mother sent out a message to her already for them to talk regarding the Lost King and telling her about our alliance, she won't be any the wiser about what has transpired here. Mother is under careful watch and hasn't been allowed any visitors but my brother and I. If the Lost King thinks we are building an alliance with Creisal before he can make a move, it will give us the numbers to stand a fighting chance if we can't find his dragon and destroy it."

"And the prince thinks his brother has all the brains," Becka teased, clapping him on the back. "Okay, so we send this letter, the king and queen accept, then what? Are they going to stay in the castle with us? Do we have the staff to handle whoever they might bring because if I know noble people, they don't go anywhere without people to attend to them."

Moving to the desk, I pulled out a sheet of paper, quill, ink, and blotter before taking my seat. "We will be on the fourth floor, allowing these rooms to be used by the Creisal royalty and their attendants. We just have to move everything out of the rooms and put it in storage until we can go through it in detail later. The staff is already preparing to host the whole village, so I think adding more people won't be an issue at this point."

"Yeah, says the woman who clearly has no idea how much work that really will be," Becka mutters, running her hands through her hair. I gave her a disapproving look which made her groan. "Fine! I'll see what we can do to get this dealt with as soon as possible, but what do you plan to do with things here?"

"This study, while connected to the king's bedroom, can be locked and spelled to keep them out. It still allows them the sitting room, dressing room, and bedroom, plenty of space to have them stay for a few days," I answered as I transcribed the one and only invitation that would be going out. "Gavin, would you be able to leave right away to deliver this?"

"Absolutely, but only if Pax comes with me. I've never flown on my own that far, and he knows the lay of the land, having been there far more recently than I have," Gavin said, turning to the man in question.

Paxton made a big show of being put out but relented like we all knew he would. "What the hell better to be doing this than dusting the furniture for visiting royalty."

Rummaging through the desk, I found what I needed for a wax seal and press with the Sheca royal symbol on it. Finished, I stood and walked over to Gavin, tucking the letter into his tunic where I knew it would be safe before pulling him into a kiss. I let my fingers comb through his hair as his lips moved against mine, and his fingers dug into my hips, trying to hold himself back from taking this further. Breaking the kiss, I looked up into his eyes. "Be safe, my prince. Have Ninnat or Gatir reach out to Vasin if there is any trouble."

"Don't worry, love, we'll be just fine," Gavin answered, kissing my forehead.

Pulling out of his hold, I went to Paxton, who watched me with uncertainty. We've become much better friends since we first met, but I think he'll always be one who can get a rise out of me, no matter what. I liked that about him, though. It brought out the fiery side of me I didn't know I possessed. "Make sure you come back to me in one piece. That's a direct order from your queen."

He grinned at my sassy words and reached out to snatch me close before dipping me back and kissing the hell out of me. It wasn't long before I could feel the heat of it searing through my body as it made my toes curl. Righting me, he winked. "As the queen commands, I, her humble servant, shall do."

"Don't make me do this without you watching my back," I whispered as I clutched his shirt, letting him see how much he was starting to mean to me.

"I promise on my life I will return, and together we will make that bastard king wish he'd never come for us," Paxton vowed in the most serious tone I'd ever heard him use. Cupping my cheek, he kissed me again—this one full of promise and feeling before he let me go and headed for the stairs to the tower.

Watching them leave, I started to move forward, but strong arms wrapped around me, trapping me against his chest. "Tell me they'll be all right, Day."

"There is one thing I can promise you, Cassy-bear, and that is those men will do whatever it takes to get back here to you. That's what men in love do. They defy all the odds against them to make it back to the woman who holds their heart and soul," Dayson murmured as he rested his head on mine.

The shadow of their dragons taking flight passed over the windows, alerting us to their departure. It shouldn't take them more than half a day to get there, and it was the middle of the afternoon. Chances were his aunt would want them to stay the night and leave in the morning, making their return late morning. What could go wrong?

The rest of that day was spent cleaning out the king's room, starting with the closet since it held all the chests of clothing. I asked that it be sent to Talia so if she could use anything in them to repurpose and make clothes for others to do so. I'm sure they were a little out of style after four hundred years, but the material was still good. By the time we were done removing everything and cleaning the basics, I wanted nothing more than a hot bath and someone to rub my shoulders. Becka, bless her, made us a simple dinner with Abbott's help since I was useless in the kitchen.

Instead of making a formal matter out of it, we ate right there at the butcher block in the kitchen, dreading the thought of having to make it up to the fourth floor. "Would it be wrong of me to have Vasin fly me up to the third floor so I don't have to do the stairs?"

"Looks like someone is out of shape, having enjoyed the relaxed life of studying and being carried around," Becka teased.

I scowled at her, but she was right. I hadn't been training like I should have with everything going on. "At this point, I would do the obstacle course twice with a bag of rocks before having to scrub another floor."

"Never thought I would see the day someone would volunteer for that kind of punishment." Abbott laughed.

Cole heaved himself out of his chair and walked over to me, sprawled out in mine, reaching out a hand. "Come on, little mouse. Let's get you upstairs before you become one with the chair."

"Only if you let me have a piggyback ride," I said with a pout on my lips, to which he just bent over and kissed me.

"Fine, now get up before I change my mind," Cole whispered in my ear, letting his teeth scrape the outer shell.

Stunned, it took my brain a moment to catch up to what he said and get moving so he couldn't back out on his offer. Squatting down with his back turned in front of me, I wrapped my arms around his neck, and as he stood, my legs positioned themselves around his waist. He then wrapped both arms behind me, cupping my ass in the charade of not letting me slip.

"Damn, Cole, you are one well-trained puppy," May sassed with a hoot of laughter. The others joined in teasing him as we walked away and began the journey to the fourth floor.

Cole didn't say much, and neither did I. I just enjoyed his closeness and the steady beat of his heart. Once we got to the third floor, I spoke. "You can let me down now. I'm sure I can make it up one flight of stairs on my own."

"You, my little mouse, are going to stay right where you are," Cole ordered, squeezing my ass.

"Why do I get the feeling you're expecting favors for carrying me up to my chambers?" I answered in mock surprise. "Don't you know that I'm a noble lady?"

Cole chuckled, looking at me out of the corner of his eye. "You are no noble, and I'm not a gentleman. What do you say we take the risk?"

Laughter burst out of me as he quoted what he said to me the night we first met, and I threatened to kill him for seeing me in my nightgown. "You were absolutely right. I'm not a noble lady... being a mercenary has been far more exciting."

As we reached the fourth floor, he headed down the hall to the right instead of walking into the central community space. There had been so many other things to deal with I hadn't explored the rest of what this level had to offer so when Cole brought me to an open bathing room, I was shocked. Two large stone pools of steaming water greeted us with the welcoming aroma of lavender and mint. Cole set me down next to a stone bench with woven baskets on it to place our things in.

"I thought this might be a welcome treat after the hard work you've been doing the past two weeks," he explained as he rested his hands on my shoulders.

"How is this possible?"

"With a little help from a dragon or two and natural spring water flowing from where the castle is built into. There are massive ovens below the pools that we stock with wood and let the dragons set it ablaze, leaving us with enough coals to keep these pools warm for a long time. I learned the hard way not to get in without checking the temperature... thought I was going to be boiled alive."

"Is it safe now?" I questioned as I walked over, dipping my hand into the steamy water. It was definitely hot, sending shivers of delight up my body, but it wasn't boiling.

Cole's hands slid up my stomach to the tie for the leather vest I was wearing, pulled the string, then began to undo the rest, slipping it off my shoulders. "I think we should find out together," he murmured, brushing aside my hair to kiss along my neck.

A soft sigh left my lips as I bent my head to give him better access. "That sounds like an amazing idea."

At my agreement, Cole gathered the bottom of my shirt and pulled it over my head, leaving me in my pants and cloth bindings. He untucked the end of the binding and slowly turned me in his arms, unraveling me to reveal his prize. I could feel his gaze washing over my body as the cloth fell away, leaving me bare to him, giving me the courage to meet his eyes.

"Never hide from me, Cassarah," he whispered, brushing a thumb along my cheek. "I know it took me longer than it should've when we first met to see the beautiful soul you have and the courage that radiates off you. We both know I'm not the world's easiest person to get along with, but if you'll allow me, I would like to be by your side for as long as you will have me."

"Cole, there is no way I could do this without you by my side. I love you," I shared and cupped his face between my hands. "I've loved you for a long time. I just wasn't willing to admit that to myself yet because I was scared, but I'm not anymore. This world is full of uncertain events, and I refuse to let another day pass where I don't tell you that I love you."

"Cassarah," Cole whispered before he wrapped me in his arms, kissing me like I was the air he needed to live. His large hands spanned across my back, digging in like I might disappear if he didn't hold on tight enough.

I tugged at his shirt, needing to feel him against me to know this was real, and we were finally admitting the truth to each other. Cole ripped off his shirt and kicked off his pants quickly before tugging mine down. I yelped as he picked me up and carried me into the pool, where he settled us in the warmth of the water, causing me to moan at how wonderful it felt.

"Oh, just you wait, little mouse. I'll give you something to moan about," Cole whispered in my ear as he shifted so I was on the stone seat and he was kneeling before me. Spreading my legs, he looked up at me, his eyes full of heat and love as his fingers slid up my thighs to where they joined the rest of my body. "I don't need specifics, but have you already done this with one of the others? Just need to be sure I don't hurt you."

"Yes, last night," I answered truthfully. Honestly, I'd expected to be sore today from all that Jade and I did, but it wasn't too bad, or maybe it was just that the rest of my body was achy as well.

This made Cole pause. "Was that your first time? If it was, this might be too soon. I don't want to make you more uncomfortable."

He started to pull away, but I caught him, guiding him back to me. "Trust me when I say you are *not* making me uncomfortable. I want this as long as you are okay with it."

His brows shot up at that. "You think I'm pulling away because you were with Jade last night?" I nodded, not willing to risk saying the wrong thing. "No, little mouse, we men have already had conversations with each other about the best way to manage sharing you. We needed to come together and set things among us as men so that we would never make you feel guilty when this happened. My caution has nothing to do with him, only that I want to make sure if you're uncomfortable, adding more friction isn't the best solution." His thumbs rubbed along the inside of my thighs, making my body tingle. "There are other things we can do, though."

Scooping up my ass, he lifted it so I was now floating on my back in the warm water as he sank lower so his face was level with my body. The first flick of his tongue had me crying out as my needy body was finally getting the attention it so badly desired. Never in my life did I think I would have a man feasting on me the way Cole was drawing moans of pleasure that echoed off the stone room along with the water as it sloshed against the sides as I thrashed under his attention. Just when I didn't think there was more he could do to drive me wild, he slipped a finger into me and started to caress my inner walls. If I'd been sore, there wasn't a chance in hell I was feeling it now as he added another finger to the mix, drawing out sounds I never thought I would make. My climax crashed into me like I'd jumped off a waterfall and plunged into the cold water below, constricting my body around his fingers, refusing to let him leave me as I survived these waves of pleasure.

Slowly, my body relaxed, and Cole had to catch me as I started to sink, unable to do anything to support my body. Cradled in his arms like a child, we sat there as I let the glow of what he did to my body linger before he started to wash me. Taking a soft cloth, he lathered it up from a bar of soap and began his work, running it all over my body, soothing sore muscles. When he was done, I returned the favor and used the slick of the soap to help ease his hard cock, not wanting him to be left out of experiencing the pleasure he'd given me. Finished in the bath, Cole wrapped us in towels and carried me to my bedchamber, where we slept tangled up in each other for the night.

Thirty

The Queen of Creisal

"Your Majesty, I understand you are anxious after your men, but I need you to stand still, or I might sew you to this dress accidentally," Talia chided.

I let out a heavy sigh and stopped my fidgeting. "I'm sorry, Talia. It's past noon, and they should have been back by now."

"Have faith in your men. They would have sent word back if there was a problem," she said as she walked around me, looking critically at the dress.

"You're right. Paxton might be impulsive and rash, but Gavin will keep his head, smoothing out any issues that might have happened. Plus, if the queen did decide to come with, it being such short notice, it wouldn't be that easy to prepare overnight," I reasoned.

"See, nothing to worry about. Now to more important matters... are you ready to see the dress?" Talia asked, giving me a bright smile.

Through all of our fittings, I was never allowed to see the dress on or what the whole thing looked like put together. She would only bring the parts that needed to be adjusted. Today was the first time all of it had been put on my body at one time. "Yes, please. I can't say that I miss wearing gowns, but this isn't just a gown."

"No, this is far more than your average pretty piece of fabric," Talia agreed as she pulled the sheets off the wall of mirrors in the dressing room.

I gasped as I caught my first glimpse of what she'd created. Everything was black and dark pewter that seemed to shimmer in the sunlight like dragon scales. The corset's under-color was pewter with black edging and designed with scattered leather scales that had been cut out and sewn on. A full skirt flowed from the bottom of the corset to the floor and rippled out into a long train behind me with more scales and crystals sewn into a stunning pattern that seemed to move like a living thing. Fitted leather sleeves went up my arms and were held in place by a beaded collar around my throat with a black lace train flowing from the back of it. Both the train and the skirt I was wearing could be removed once the formal part of the coronation was complete, leaving me in soft black leather pants with a scale pattern etched into them to match the sleeves. This is the kind of dress I imagined a warrior queen would wear, ready to jump into battle at any moment if the need arose.

"Talia," I whispered in awe of what she'd created. "Never in my life did I think I would have the honor of wearing such a dress."

"The honor is mine, Your Majesty. This has been a dream of mine to create one day, and you are the perfect person to wear it."

A knock came at the dressing room door, and May stuck her head in then caught sight of me and entered the room. "There's no way to doubt you're a queen, looking like that. You're gonna make Queen Catharine jealous when she sees you."

I whirled to face her. "They're back?"

"Almost. Paxton flew ahead and gave us the alert that Gavin was coming with the Creisal royalty and their entourage," May explained. "Might be best for you to change into something a little simpler to greet them when they arrive."

"Is the drawbridge finished?" I asked as Talia helped me remove everything.

"Was done first thing this morning, and before you ask, Helena and Marta have been working all morning preparing for them to arrive. Seems they had little doubt that your invitation would be ignored. Cassarah, breathe... everything is going according to plan, and the people you put in place are doing their jobs so you can do yours," May pointed out, giving me a knowing look through the mirror.

"Can you send Pax in?"

"Paxton!" May bellowed, startling me. Talia accidentally stabbed me with a pin.

"Your Majesty, I'm so sorry," Talia blurted as she saw a pinprick of blood well up.

I grabbed her hand, forcing her to look at me. "It's all right. These things happen. Let's just get the things with pins off first, hmm?"

She swiftly removed the rest of the gown, leaving me in just the corset and pants as Paxton entered. "You hollered for me, oh scary one?"

May just sniffed at him and left the room, giving me a nod before she left, letting me know she would be right outside. Paxton's face broke into a smile as he whistled his approval of my attire. "Spitfire, if I weren't already at your mercy, I would beg to be right here on my knees."

Talia gasped at his crude words, but I just rolled my eyes. "Really, Pax, that's all you've got? No," I said, holding out my hand to stop him from saying whatever was going to come next. "Tell me what happened in Creisal."

"We made it there in good time, and Queen Catharine was happy to see the little prince right away, wanting news about what happened in Royal City. Gavin played nice with his aunt, telling her all she wanted to know but not spilling too much important information. The prince has skill, I'll give him that… silver tongue for sure, setting everyone at ease within seconds," Paxton shared as he sat on the chaise lounge, kicking his feet up. "They fed us a lovely dinner which I almost didn't get to enjoy since she thought I was Gavin's manservant, but we got that cleared up pretty quickly. Then after dinner and drinks, the king and queen agreed to join us, happy to attend your coronation. It's not every day that a mysterious woman gets crowned queen to rule over an even more mysterious group of people like those only whispered about here in Sheca."

I could tell by his tone and how flippant he was that something happened, but he wasn't willing to tell me with Talia in the room. Catching her eye, I nodded toward the door with a smile to which she bobbed a curtsy and slipped out of the room, leaving us alone. Taking a seat at the end of the chaise, I looked Pax in the eye as I spoke. "Now tell me what really happened and why you're so pissed off."

"Nothing happened per se, but if you thought Queen Mary had her nose up in the air, then you better get ready for her sister. I don't know what it is about them that makes them think they don't shit in a bucket like the rest of us… you know what I'm saying?"

I couldn't help but grin at his example. "Hmm, I figured it would have at least been a porcelain jar instead of a standard bucket like the rest of us simple folk."

"Cute, spitfire, real cute," Paxton grumbled as he sat up and pulled his legs off the couch. "When Queen Catharine finds out about her sister and what happened to her brother-in-law, shit is going to hit the ceiling. I wouldn't be surprised if, instead of an ally, you end up with another person conspiring to kill you in your sleep. We can't let them stay here with you. I don't trust her to be anywhere within ten feet of you if I'm being honest."

Placing my hand over his, I intertwined our fingers as I leaned my head on his shoulder. "I love that you want to keep me safe no matter what it takes, but this is part of being queen. My life will always be in danger, and even after the Lost King is killed, there will be someone new to take his place. There isn't a way to rid the world of evil people, but we can make sure they know if they come after us, we will end them. Right now, Queen Catharine hasn't done anything to us, but I promise you I won't let her disrespect you, our people, or me in my home on our land. If she can't play nice, then I will gladly send her home tied to a dragon if I have to."

Leaning into me, Paxton slipped an arm over my shoulders, hugging me to his side as he kissed the top of my head. "You have no clue how incredible of a woman you are, do you?"

"I am who I am and who I was always meant to be. As for incredible, that only happened because of you guys being in my life, pushing me to be more than I could have ever dreamed for myself," I answered, snuggling into his hold. "Can I trust you not to stab her or her people until I tell you it's all right?"

He let out an exaggerated sigh. "I suppose so."

"When will Gavin and the others be back?"

"Left to let you know what was going on and to send back some dragons so we could get them here on time. That's the one downfall of our location... there isn't really a road to travel in and out of here," he pointed out.

"Are we sure that's a downfall? If the rest of the world is what I remember it to be, then I think I'm okay being hard to get to," I mused out loud as I looked up at Paxton.

He grinned and pressed a kiss to my lips. "There truly couldn't be a more perfect woman than you. As much as I hate to leave you, I need to lead the dragons to the rondeau with our guests. We thought getting them as close to the border as we could would be faster so the flight time was less."

"Go on, get out of here so we can show this snooty royal what a real queen should act like," I said as I stood and pulled him up with me. "I've got to get things ready here, and you can't keep stalling. Coronation is only a day away."

"As my queen commands," Paxton answered with a dramatic bow.

"Oh, and send Talia back in, please," I called after him, which he acknowledged with a wave.

It was dinner time when Gavin returned with his aunt and uncle, but we were ready for them with all the pomp and circumstance they would be used to. From what Paxton told me, I felt it was best to set the tone and greet them in the throne room rather than escorting them to a private sitting room. Seated on the throne under my guardians' watchful eyes dressed to impress, I sipped on the glass of wine I held, needing to give myself something to do as I waited, trying to appear calm. I wasn't nervous—I just despised having to deal with all the unnecessary theatrics, but it was what was expected of me. Once tomorrow was over and there was no doubt in anyone's mind that I was queen, then I would start changing things.

"Your Majesty, may I present King Thomas and Queen Catharine of Creisal, accompanied by their children, Prince Charles and Princess Amelia," the herald called as the massive doors to the throne room opened, revealing the king and queen.

Since Sheca didn't have a class system, those who wished to see the greeting were welcome to attend. People gawked and talked among themselves as King Thomas escorted his wife down the aisle to the throne, their children behind them. Catharine looked incredibly similar to her sister, making it impossible for people not to know they were related. King Thomas was a slight man but made up for his stature with a confident air about him, making me notice for the first time that King Edward hadn't had that—Queen Mary did.

Setting my glass aside, I stood and descended the stairs to meet them at the bottom, putting me on equal footing as we greeted each other. "Welcome to my humble kingdom. It is an honor to have you accept my invitation on such short notice."

"I must admit I wasn't sure what the right choice was in this matter, but our dear nephew is quite persuasive," Queen Catharine said, her face softening as she glanced at Gavin who had come to stand behind me. "It surprised us that he would give up his throne to become your consort, but I suppose love makes us do foolish things," she tacked on, pursing her lips.

Lifting a hand, I waited for Gavin to place his in mine before I drew him to be at my side and gazed up at him. "Love makes honest people out of us, and I am the one who is blessed to have such a man by my side. It means a lot to us, having your support. Many would be blinded by the fact that our arrangement isn't normal by society's standards."

"You mean the fact that you have *seven* lovers." She sniffed. "Lovers come and go, but consorts are chosen under the eyes of the gods and hold a special place in court."

"That's exactly right. I'm delighted to see you still honor the gods after many have forsaken them. In fact, all seven of my consorts have been blessed and marked by the gods themselves, although they are good lovers too..." I shared with a smirk. "Come, you must be famished after your travels. Dinner is prepared and ready for us. If you'll follow me." Turning, I tucked Gavin's arm through mine, and as we passed Abbott, I did the same with him as well. I needed to prove my point that all my men were on equal footing in their station and my feelings for them, no matter what remarks a bitchy queen had to say.

Dinner was certainly going to be an adventure, that's for sure.

THIRTY-ONE
IT WON'T END HERE

As we took our seats in the dining room on the third floor, I could already tell that something was upsetting the visiting queen, and part of me wanted to ignore it altogether but knew it would only make matters worse. Surprisingly, I didn't have to address anything since it didn't take her long to blurt out her concern.

"Where is my sister and King Edward?" Queen Catharine demanded. "I thought surely they would be present at this dinner since you are allies and we're family."

I glanced over at Phillip and Gavin, knowing this was going to be hardest on them. Before I could say anything, Phillip rose from his seat and took his aunt head-on. "Due to some unfortunate events, Mother is being held under house arrest after Father tried to kill Queen Cassarah upon our arrival to Sheca. As I am Crown Prince, I am the one who is acting in Mother's stead and continue to keep our alliance with Queen Cassarah."

"What?" King Thomas snapped, slamming his fist on the table. "I will not stand for this! We must see Mary at once. I refuse to sit at a table with the woman who killed my brother-in-law."

"Uncle, did you not hear what I said?" Phillip questioned, his brow creased. "Queen Cassarah did nothing to warrant being attacked by my father. Sadly, he went too long without his medication, and Mother wasn't able to manage him as she typically does, leading to an irrational choice to attack Sheca's queen. Her guards acted in her defense, leading to his death. She did nothing wrong. Calm yourself and think before you make an enemy of both Sheca and Norden because I am prepared to back up my alliance with Queen Cassarah in this matter."

"You would do this to your family?" Queen Catharine cried.

"Family? You haven't left Creisal since I was born. The last time we saw each other, you swore to my mother you would never avenge her if her *mad* king managed to kill her in her sleep. Why are you upset about this situation? It was justified in every way, so stop pretending to be the doting aunt when you were never part of our lives unless it was to ridicule our mother or look down on us from your lofty seat." Phillip all but snarled out his words.

This was a side to Gavin's little brother I'd never seen before, and in a way, it made me incredibly proud of him. He always seemed more mild-mannered, and as I learned firsthand, they smell blood in the water waiting to attack, yet here he was putting his own blood in their place.

Neither of them had a response to what Phillip had just said, so I nodded to the scared servers waiting at the door to go ahead and place the food on the table. I didn't think we would get another lull in conversation, so best to do what we can. I know I needed some food in my stomach. Feeling it might be safer, I decided to engage with the prince and princess instead of their parents—the younger generation might feel differently about things.

"Have any of you flown on the back of a dragon before?" I asked.

Princess Amelia's face lit up at the question. "Mother never allowed us to before, but that was the most exhilarating thing of my whole life."

"I remember the first time I flew Vasin. It was late at night when the sun was gone, and it was terrifying but also wondrous," I shared as a plate was set in front of me.

Having someone taste my food was an argument I had all day with the guys, but they won out when they used logic. Using a taster whenever it wasn't just us kept me and the person doing the job of tasting safer than if I only used them on coronation day. Our guests needed to think this was normal so they wouldn't think to try poisoning my food themselves.

"Dragons are ruthless and vile creatures. I'm glad we no longer have an agreement with them in our kingdom," Queen Catharine stated. "Seems you have quite the infestation of them here, but who could expect much from *mercenaries.*"

Now it was my turn to take the bitch down a peg. Slowly, I rose to my feet, drawing everyone's attention and causing May to step closer to me since she and Becka were the only guardians not seated at the table. I met their gaze, letting them know I wasn't going to do anything too rash. I called my Birthright to me, and my bow materialized in my hand with the quiver on my back, which I pulled an arrow from and knocked it on the string.

"Now, I believe I might have misheard you, but did you just say that dragons were an infestation upon our lands?" I asked as I caressed a finger down the shaft of the arrow, not bothering to give them my attention. "See, here in Sheca, we have an incredibly close relationship with our dragons. Some might say it's a connection unlike any other when you bond with a dragon. They see into a person's soul, and if you are found worthy, they will consider a bond with you." My eyes flicked up to meet her face. "Are you saying that the other half of my soul is a blight on this kingdom and myself?"

The look of panic that crossed the queen's face as she realized the massive mistake she just made in saying what she did warmed my heart. As if on cue, Vasin flew past the wall of windows in the room and let out a burst of flame for added effect. I tried to keep the look of surprise and joy off my face as I realized that Vasin had gained his fire far sooner than expected.

"It seems I do not understand the relationships between dragons and their pair-bonds. It has been many generations since we've had dragons bless us with their presence in our kingdom," King Thomas said, trying to placate me.

Releasing my hold on my bow, I pulled my magic back into me as I took my seat, a smile beaming. "It just so happens that I've made a new pact with the dragons, and I believe they will start gracing our skies like they have in the past once again. They will be free to connect with those they wish, regardless of their status or connection to the Crown. We just have to deal with the matter of the Lost King first."

King Thomas latched onto that rope like a lifeline. "Yes, it's devastating what happened in Royal City. You were there, weren't you, along with your guardians."

"She's the reason we made it out of the castle at all," Gavin interjected. "She and the dragon riders she brought with her made sure we got out of the castle and to safety. When Cassarah gives you her allegiance, she will uphold it no matter the cost to herself."

"Don't let the sweet words of a man in love fool you, though. Queen Cassarah isn't one to be trifled with. Along with our father, four of her clan leaders acted against her, and she sentenced them to death the following morning without trial," Phillip added, nodding to me in respect.

"How is it that your mother still lives?" Queen Catharine inquired.

"She didn't act against me... her husband did, and I don't believe in punishing those who were drawn into a situation. Right now, she wishes to kill me, but she is also grieving the loss of her husband. This makes her unable to think clearly, so Phillip is acting in her stead. I'm sure you knew that the offer to attend my coronation was more than just good manners. We need to work together If we hope to keep what's left of our continent out of the Lost King's clutches. Once he is established in Norden, he'll be coming for us both. You have the numbers when it comes to the military, while I have the dragons and a very skilled group of people who can get in anywhere. It makes sense to me to build an alliance but seeing how our conversation has gone, I'm not sure I'd be willing to uphold an alliance with people such as yourself," I spoke bluntly.

This seemed to shock the king as he spluttered his wine. "You would toss away an alliance with us because you don't like us?"

"Was an alliance even on the table? I got the clear impression that you despise me, my consorts, our dragons, and the fact we are mercenaries. Tell me, would that make you want to accept an alliance with someone who's tossed everything you are in your face as an insult?" I demanded.

He seemed to look at me—*really* look at me—like it was at this moment he saw me as a queen. "No, I would have kicked them out on their asses or killed them for such slights as you've just listed."

"Yet here you sit alive and well, being fed with a warm, comfortable bed waiting for you," I taunted.

"Why? Even if you are desperate for our help, which I don't think you are, why suffer this humiliation?" King Thomas asked, truly stumped.

I cocked my head to the side, unsure if I wanted to tell him the truth but decided it was time to reveal the type of queen I was. "I needed you as bait. You see, the Lost King has a dragon that's gone mad because of the magic that's been used on it, but I have a feeling he doesn't have much control of it, so he locks it away. Killing that dragon kills the king, and the whole thing ends before it can even start. Problem solved."

"You... you mean... bringing us here..." Queen Catharine started but was too terrified to finish.

"Bringing you here would make the Lost King think we were brokering an alliance, and doing that would make his job so much harder, seeing as we have the advantage of having the sea behind us blocking him from coming at us from all sides like he did in Norden. That, and as I pointed out to you, I have quite the military, and he knows we have far more dragons at our beck and call than anyone realizes, but that won't be enough to stop him if he takes you out first."

"Like we would fall that easily." King Thomas scoffed.

"You're here now, aren't you? Did you even bother to put your military on alert or draw them in closer to the cities that would be attacked first?" I countered, seeing his expression fall. "I didn't think so. You left your kingdom, and now it's ripe for the picking. You would only do that if you are stupid or confident you had backup such as a flight of dragons at your disposal, thus making the Lost King think we have an alliance, and we are celebrating it here and now."

"That, Your Majesty, is the biggest benefit you get from an alliance with Sheca, Queen Cassarah herself. A mind unlike any other you've ever witnessed before," Gavin responded, lifting my hand to his lips.

Smiling at him, I noticed something caught his attention as he looked past me out the windows to my left. Fear flooded his gaze, having me twist in my chair just in time to see a dragon outside the window—one that I'd never seen before. It was once blue, but its coloring seemed to have faded to an almost white color. Its eyes were completely black, void of any expression. Acid seeped out of its mouth as it all but grinned at us before letting out a roar, hurling flames at the glass windows. They held under the first hit, but I wasn't sure it would for a second.

"Everybody out!" I bellowed. "Get out of here now!"

"Vasin! Where are you?" I screamed in my head. *"Xotha is here, but I'm not sure he's alone, and there is something definitely wrong with him."*

"I'M COMING, CASS. I DON'T KNOW HOW HE SLIPPED THROUGH. WE'VE BEEN LOOKING FOR HIM, BUT WE CAN'T FEEL HIM LIKE WE CAN OTHER DRAGONS. IT'S LIKE HE'S A GHOST."

"Ghost or not, he's real and pissed."

The second attack came, and I grabbed Princess Amelia who was scared stiff and unable to move, and tossed her out of the way and toward the door. Glass shattered everywhere, and the room filled with flames. A hand reached out and grabbed me, dragging me under the stone table for protection behind the support that ran down the middle of the table.

"Don't worry, I've got you, Cassy-bear," Dayson assured me. "Wait 'til he takes his next breath and run for the door, you understand? I'll be right behind you."

The flames died out, Dayson scooped me up, and we made a dash for the door. Just as we were about to make it, a white dragon tail wrapped around us and yanked us back. Dayson's grip on me faltered as he slammed into the table, slipping from the dragon's hold. I fought with everything I had to get this damn dragon to let me go, furious I didn't have any weapons until I remembered I was always armed. Using my Birthright, I manifested an arrow and stabbed it into the flesh of the dragon, making Xotha scream at the pain. Still, he didn't let me go, and I was almost at the edge of the window, and past that was a drop that no one would survive. This couldn't be it. I refused to die this way. I was the one who was going to rid the world of the Lost King with my men at my side no matter what.

I drew on my magic again, wrapped it around my body like a shield, and thrust out with it, hoping it would loosen the hold around my waist. It seemed I used too much power, and it went off like an explosion, freeing me from the dragon but also knocking me off my feet and out the window. Flipping head over heels, I reached out to grab anything I could to stop my downward descent until I could be rescued. I sobbed as my hand caught hold of a rock jutting out of the cliff, bringing me to an abrupt halt that hurt just as much as I imagined landing on the ground would. There I was, dangling from a cliffside in the darkness of the night alone.

The screech of a dragon sounded above me, and I dared to look up, seeing Xotha diving right at me, his jaw gaping at the promise of snapping it closed around my body. Just when I thought all hope was lost, Vasin slammed into the dragon, smashing them into the ravine wall opposite me. Their battle was brutal, claws and teeth latching on to anything they could manage, making me fear Vasin might not survive this encounter. I thought a crazed dragon might be easier to deal with, but when it doesn't give a fuck about pain or anything but the one task it was given, it was even more dangerous. Xotha broke free and surged at me again, but Vasin latched onto his wing, pulling him to the left and slamming him into the rock wall again. The damage was already done, though. I'd tried to get out of the way, causing my fingers to slip until the stone crumbled under the last finger, tossing me back into a free fall.

As I looked up, watching Vasin do everything he could to save me, Xotha got in his way each time, keeping my black dragon from saving me. As if to protect me, my eyes fell shut of their own accord, and I was transported back to a time when I experienced something like this before. It was my first dream of Miranda, the day she lost everything and died protecting her people, the moment I felt what it was like to truly love someone enough to give your life for them.

Now, like her, I had people I loved that much, and even if it looked like there was no way out of this, I had to try. I had to get back to them. There's no way we were finished with this battle.

My eyes snapped open. I wasn't going to let this be the end of it all…

To be concluded in *The Final Battle*

About Author

Elizabeth Knight

Elizabeth is originally from Illinois but is now living in sunny Phoenix, Arizona. Though she is newer to publishing, Elizabeth has been writing for nine years. She started in YA Fiction but recently found herself loving the Reverse Harem genre. Like her favorite books, Elizabeth loves to write about strong women of all varieties. Not all strength is flashy or apparent at first glance—some lie just under the surface.

Don't Miss Out!

Be the first to know what is coming next by following Elizabeth's social media! You never know when or what will be coming next!

FWebsite: ElizabethKnightBooks.com

Facebook: Elizabeth Knight's Unicorn Queens

Instagram: elizabethknightauthor

TikTok: elizabethknightauthor

Newsletter: sign up here

ALSO BY

Mercenary Queen – Complete Series
Birthright
Dragon Queen
The Forgotten Throne
The Final Battle

Sunshine & Rainbows Omegaverse
Bailey-Rose Duet - Clouds & Daydreams + Petals & Promises

Knot All Omegaverse
Knot All Is Lost: Part 1 & Part 2 (Complete)
Knot All Is Ruined: Part 1 & Part 2 (Complete)

Caprioni Queen – Complete Series
Book 1 – Glitter & Guns
Book 2 – Blood & Heartache
Book 3 – Revenge & Truth
Book 4 – Love & Power

Omega Assassin - Complete series
Book 1 - Dual Nature
Book 2 - Hidden Nature

Book 3 - Perfect Nature

<u>Standalone Books</u>
Nicolette: Ladies of the MC
Lying Lainey: Underground Omega Syndicate

<u>Hidden Empire Series – Complete series</u>
Book 1 - Two Tricks
Book 2 - Three Tricks
Book 3 - Four Tricks
Book 4 - More Tricks
Book 5 - Our Tricks

<u>Hidden Empire Novel</u>
(SUGGESTED TO BE READ AFTER FOUR TRICKS)
Harper's Renegades

www.ingramcontent.com/pod-product-compliance
Lightning Source LLC
Chambersburg PA
CBHW070457300726
48975CB00007B/2214